Confessions *and* Catechisms *of the* Reformation

Edited by **Mark A. Noll**

APOLLOS

Apollos (an imprint of Inter-Varsity Press),
38 De Montfort Street, Leicester LE1 7GP, England

First British edition 1991

British Library Cataloguing in Publication Data
Confessions and catechisms of the Reformation.
    1. Protestant churches. Catechisms. Confessions of faith
    I. Noll, Mark A. *1946-*
    238

   ISBN 0-85111-421-0

To

Nat Hatch

Contents

Acknowledgments

The hard work of a number of dedicated people make this book possible. Cassandra Niemczyk scoured the library and diligently worked on the texts. Catherine Schumacher did a wonderful job getting the confessions onto a diskette, and Mary Noll pitched in with very valuable last-minute typing. Carol Kraft offered indispensable help with Zwingli's German. At Baker Book House, Allan Fisher has been not only a patient editor but a good friend for many years. I should note that some of the material in the general introduction, as well as the specific introductions to Luther's Small Catechism and the Thirty-Nine Articles, is adapted from articles I contributed to Baker's *Evangelical Dictionary of Theology* (1984).

The book is dedicated to Nat Hatch who, with great conviction, has repeatedly called upon modern Christians to take time to recover the past. It is my hope that this book can contribute in some small way to that most worthy goal.

MARK A. NOLL
July 1990

Introduction

This book presents ten important confessions from the era of the Reformation. Each was composed with great care, even those where the actual writing had to be done on the run. The authors of these confessions were attempting to capture something essential about Christianity, concerning either a limited range of debated issues or the entirety of belief itself. In their day the themes raised by these documents were of greatest public interest. For some of the authors they were literally matters of life and death.

Three of the confessions arose directly from the pioneering Protestantism of Martin Luther. Three express varieties of the "Reformed" faith associated with John Calvin, Ulrich Zwingli, John Knox, and the Protestantism of Switzerland, southwestern Germany, Scotland, France, and Holland. One is a statement of Anabaptist belief that spells out the special concerns of these "radical" Protestants. An additional confession is the doctrinal standard of the Reformation in England. And two represent official responses by the Roman Catholic Church to the boiling pot stirred up by the Protestants. At least six of the statements retain official status for different groups of modern Christians, although the exact nature of that status is often hotly debated. Together they are some of the most revealing literary products of a turning point in the history of Christianity.

The confessions in this book are meant for students—whether in college classes, in church study groups, or at home—who want to know what all the fuss was about in the sixteenth century. For most of these confessions there is an immense scholarly literature. Almost all of them have been the subject of minutely detailed analysis and most of long-lived controversy. The purpose of this book, however, is not to add to those scholarly debates but to introduce the vital documents themselves.

At the end of the twentieth century, concern for history is daily undercut by excitements of the moment or threatened by fears and aspirations for the future. Yet nothing could be more damaging to an understanding of the Christian faith than neglect of the past. Almost the same can be said for taking the measure of our civilization. The confessions in this book were addressed to the central questions of human existence: Who am I? Who is God? How does God tell humans about himself and about the world in which they live? What institutions has God given to humanity? How are those institutions—church, government, the family, the economy—supposed to function? These are the questions that the authors of the sixteenth-century confessions took up. Since they took them up in a white-hot atmosphere of ardent debate, and since some of those who addressed these issues possessed minds and hearts of extraordinary profundity, the answers they offered are as important for understanding the course of Western history since the sixteenth century as they are for probing the nature of the Christian faith.

The Reformation was a pivotal era. It led to a division in the church that was felt more deeply than the earlier split between Eastern Orthodoxy and Roman Catholicism. Now Christians alienated from each other faced off within Europe rather than from opposite ends of the Mediterranean. The rise of Protestantism and corresponding responses by Roman Catholics also accelerated many of the forces that have created modern Western life, including capitalism, representative government, a higher evaluation of the individual, and the rise of empirical science.

The importance of the Reformation era is the justification for presenting these confessional statements. At a time like the present when Europe is being reconfigured as it was also in the sixteenth century, there is greater rather than less relevance to these statements. Four hundred and fifty years ago they were the banners under which intrepid leaders broke up and then attempted to reassemble a rapidly changing world. In the same way, at a time of warmer ecumenical relations, especially between Catholics and Protestants, there is greater rather than less relevance to these documents. As Oliver O'Donovan, an Anglican ethicist, has recently put it, "our universal communion in the truth of the gospel will not come about by the denial of denominational traditions, but only by the critical appropriation and sharing of them" (*On the Thirty-Nine Articles* [Exeter: Paternoster, 1986], 10).

Few would now argue that any of these confessions should be completely and absolutely authoritative in the modern era, at least without some modification, adaptation, or reinterpretation to adjust the confessions to contemporary situations. At the same time, prospects for thoughtful Christian faith among both Catholics and Protestants, no less than prospects for a better understanding of Western civilization, are seriously damaged if in the confusions of our own day we refuse to listen to these voices from the past.

The following paragraphs sketch some of the historical conditions in which these confessions were written and offer preliminary reflection on their theological significance. They also mention some of the resources available for those who desire to study in greater depth the confessions and the worlds in which they emerged. This introduction, however, is not meant to instruct students on how to think about the confessions. The confessions are here to be pondered, dissected, compared, and contrasted for their own sake. All were written for popular audiences of one sort or another, so none requires unusual expertise to be interpreted. The Protestant and evangelical convictions of the editor no doubt skew the introductory material. But the intention has been to provide the clearest possible access to what are some of the most important statements of Christian conviction in Western history. All of them carry their own weight. Each can speak for itself.

The Historical Context
of the Sixteenth-Century Confessions

The term "confession" can be found in the New Testament (e.g., 1 Tim. 6:13). In the early church the word was used to describe the testimony of martyrs as they were about to meet their deaths. Its most common usage, however, designates the formal statements of Christian faith written especially by Protestants since the time of the Reformation. As such, "confessions" are closely related to several other kinds of brief, authoritative summations of belief. The term "creed" most frequently refers to statements from the early church that Christians in all times and places have affirmed—the Apostles' Creed, the Nicene Creed, the definition of Christ's two natures in one Person from Chalcedon, and (less frequently) the Athanasian Creed. Orthodox churches hold to the authority of seven ancient ecumenical creeds. The Roman Catholic Church continues to use the term "creed" for later doctrinal formulations (as "the Creed of the Council of Trent" of 1564), but their statements from Trent in the sixteenth century function much like Protestant confessions. "Catechisms" are structured statements of faith written in the form of questions and answers which in the Reformation era often served the same purposes as formal confessions.

In this book, the meaning of "confession" is stretched slightly to incorporate personal or group statements of faith that never became official doctrinal standards for churches or denominations. The more normal meaning refers to the formally recognized statements of a particular group's Christian convictions.

Conditions in the sixteenth century were ripe for the composition of confessions, both official and personal. The publications of Luther, Calvin, Zwingli, and other Protestant leaders were bringing momentous theological questions to the fore. When entire communities, or just their leaders, became Protestants, an immediate demand arose for uncomplicated yet authoritative statements of the new faith. Sometimes such statements precipitated the move to Protestantism. Leading Reformers—this time Catholic as well as Protestant—were deeply involved in the day-to-day life of the churches where they sensed the uneasiness of the people, whether at the abuses in the old church or at contemporary innovations. On all sides, spokesmen recognized the need for brief theological summaries that all could understand.

The nature of Protestantism and the character of the sixteenth century also stimulated the urge to write confessions. Protestant Reformers posed Scripture as the ultimate authority for all of life, even if this undercut received Roman Catholic tradition. They spoke of the priesthood of believers and the internal testimony of the Holy Spirit, in spite of the fact that these teachings called the pronouncements of Rome's infallible magisterium into question. The Reformers also challenged Roman Catholic influence in the state. They proposed a new reading of history to support their own push for reform. And they wanted to restore a New Testament purity of Christian , belief and practice. Yet every assault on an established belief and every challenge to a traditional practice called for a rationale, a concise statement of the reasons for change. Before long, Protestants also needed to say why they were proposing contrasting answers as they went about reforming the church.

It was not, however, merely in the religious sphere that change prepared the way for new confessions of faith. Europe in general was evolving rapidly. Virtually every support for traditional Roman Catholicism was coming under fire. If Protestants challenged Roman Catholic interference in government and involvement in the economy, so too did monarchs of the new nation-states question the church's traditional political role, and the burgeoning class of merchants challenged its accustomed authority in the world of trade. If Luther and Calvin called upon Rome to rethink its interpretation of Scripture, so too did leaders of the Renaissance challenge other intellectual traditions in art, political theory, literature, and history. If Protestants raised troubling questions in theology, so too had several generations of academicians raised troubling issues in philosophy. In short, the world of the sixteenth century needed new statements not just to reorient Christian belief, but to reposition Christianity itself within the forces of early modern Europe.

The great outpouring of confessions in the sixteenth and early seventeenth centuries performed a multitude of functions. Authoritative statements of Christian belief enshrined the new ideas of the theologians, but in forms that could also provide regular instruction for the common people. They raised banners around which local communities could rally and which could mark boundaries from opponents. They made possible a regathering of belief and practice for unity (at least on the local level), even as they established a norm to discipline the erring. For Roman Catholics, the confessionlike statements of Trent made it possible to discriminate between acceptable modifications in its ancient faith and unacceptable deviations from its traditional norms.

Very early in the Reformation, Protestants began to set down their visions of the faith. In little more than the first decade of reform in Zurich, Zwingli superintended the publication of four confessional documents: the Sixty-Seven Articles (1523) which brought his own canton to break with Rome; the Ten Theses of Berne (1528) which solidified reform in that city; a Confession of Faith for Charles V (1530) which informed the emperor about Protestant convictions; and an Exposition of the Faith to King Francis of France (1531) which asked the French sovereign for more even-handed treatment of Protestants. In Germany, meanwhile, there was a similar flurry of confessional activity. Luther's Ninety-Five Theses of 1517 were a personal statement, but they were soon followed by many more formal confessions. By the time Luther published his Small Catechism in 1529 and the Lutheran princes presented the Augsburg Confession to the emperor in 1530, the Lutherans had become old hands at formulating confessional documents.

The same pattern was repeated in other Protestant regions. Soon after the magistrates or the common people accepted Reformation teaching, a single individual or small group would be commissioned to write a definitive statement of faith. The process was the same for Basel, Geneva, and Zurich in Switzerland, for the French Protestants, for Lutheran communities in Germany and Scandinavia, for Scotland, Holland, Bohemia, Poland, and England. At the close of the Council of Trent (1545–1563), which defined orthodox Catholicism in lengthy canons and decrees, Rome also recapitulated its faith in a brief, authoritative statement.

The nature of Protestantism as a politically and religiously diverse movement prevented the formulation of a single Protestant confession. Yet in the Reformation's "second generation" considerable consolidation did occur. Lutherans wrote many confessions throughout the sixteenth century, but in 1580 they specified in their *Book of Concord* a definite list of authoritative confessions: the Apostles', Nicene, and Athanasian Creeds, the Smalcald Articles (1537), the Formula of Concord (1577), and especially Luther's Small and Large Catechisms (1529) and the Augsburg Confession (1530). Scandinavian Lutherans tended to consolidate even more thoroughly by neglecting the *Book of Concord* and rallying instead around just the Augsburg Confession (Scandinavians usually spoke of the *Confessio Augustana*).

In Reformed areas the same process was at work. The different Protestant cities of Switzerland wrote many catechisms and statements of belief, including several that attempted to mediate Protestant differences over the Lord's supper. Eventually, however, several of them settled on the Second Helvetic Confession (1566), originally composed for his own use by Heinrich Bullinger, Zwingli's successor in Zurich. Although the Heidelberg Catechism (1563) was written to pacify Protestant strife in just that one city, it became a rallying symbol for Reformed groups in Germany, Holland, and elsewhere. Similar consolidation occurred in the British Isles, where the Thirty-Nine Articles (Lat. 1563; Eng. 1571) were promulgated with the sanction of Elizabeth I as the official statement of the English Church. Those in England and Scotland who leaned more consistently toward Calvinism were relatively pleased with these articles, but they still proposed modifications or alternative symbols of their own. This process led to the Lambeth Articles (1595), the Irish Articles (1615), and eventually, after the outbreak of the English Civil War, to the Westminster Confession and Catechisms of the 1640s. Although Protestants would continue to write confessions, several of these earlier documents achieved a dominant position that has lasted into the present.

Given the diversity of Protestants, it is not surprising that proponents of the Reformation put confessions to use in diverse ways. Confessions certainly reflected the developmental stage of the group for which they were written. Luther's Small Catechism of 1529, a manual for private and family instruction, has more spontaneity of expression and concern for simplified essentials than the Augsburg Confession of 1530, composed for presentation to the emperor and to theologians, or the Formula of Concord of 1577, written to quiet a lengthy series of theological controversies among the Lutherans. Confessions also differ depending upon the purposes of the documents. The canons and decrees of Trent go on at great length because of the need to respond fully to Protestants. By contrast, the Profession of the Tridentine Faith is very short because it was designed to convey the gist of Trent's decisions to a far-flung and numerous audience. It also makes considerable difference whether confessions came into existence with the support of an entire community or as the outcry of a besieged minority. England's Parliament approved the various editions of the Thirty-Nine Articles and gave their author and revisers much time for their work. Quite predictably, the articles turn out to be a comprehensive and balanced statement. The Anabaptist Schleitheim Confession (1527), on the other hand, was written under great duress by Michael Sattler after only brief consultation with his colleagues. Not surprisingly, it turns out to neglect general areas of Christian agreement in order to emphasize the distinctive doctrines and practices of the Swiss Brethren. Although sometimes overlooked, such historical conditions explain a great deal about the particular character of the different confessions.

The Religious Significance
of the Sixteenth-Century Confessions

Any study of Reformed confessions inevitably raises religious or theological as well as historical questions. In the sixteenth century, it was possible to distinguish broadly between two sorts of statements: those which emphasized the drama of redemption and those which placed greater emphasis on truths of the faith. The first gave heightened attention to the Person of God and his loving mercy toward sinners, or at least moved these topics to the top of the agenda. They included, from the statements reproduced below, the Augsburg Confession, Luther's Small Catechism, the Heidelberg Catechism, and the Thirty-Nine Articles. The second began with questions of authority before going on to a discussion of God's activity. Among these were the Genevan Confession and the canons and decrees of Trent. Many of the two types of confessions were fully compatible with each other, and some, like Zwingli's Sixty-Seven Articles and the Profession of the Tridentine Faith, managed to push both redemption and authority to the fore. In structuring themselves along different lines, the documents testify to the way in which theological vision shapes confessional emphasis. They also hint at how Christians in later centuries would come to divide over exaggerated distinctions between religious authority and religious experience.

Even weightier religious matters, however, are at stake with the confessions of the sixteenth century. But these issues are at least somewhat different for Roman Catholics and Protestants. Protestant confessions serve as bridges between scriptural revelation and particular cultures. They apply Christian teaching to a particular problem or in a particular place. As such, many Protestant confessions have had their hour in the sun and passed quietly away. Others, because of affective power or balanced judiciousness, have endured. Some of these, however, have become so important to their communities that in practice it becomes nearly unthinkable to challenge them openly. In such instances, their Protestantism begins to wear thin. Yet the stated rule for Protestants remains, as the great student of the creeds Philip Schaff once put it, that "the authority of symbols, as of all human compositions, is relative and limited. It is not coordinate with, but always subordinate to, the Bible, as the only infallible rule of the Christian faith and practice" (*Creeds of Christendom*, 1:7). Many Protestant confessions acknowledge this fact directly by including a statement that even the best of human documents are liable to error.

The realization that confessions err, combined with Protestant allegiance to Scripture and insistence upon universal priesthood, has led many Protestants to disparage confessions entirely. A rallying cry for this point of view, which gained popularity in America during the early nineteenth century, was the slogan, "No creed but the Bible." More recently, Protestants on the liberal side of the theological spectrum have objected to the practical authority of confessions as infringements on intellectual integrity or personal religious rights.

Against these objections to confessions arising in Protestant bodies descended in one way or another from the confessional Protestantism of the sixteenth century, several arguments are possible. First is the historical observation that in point of fact all Protestant bodies have operated under the authority of either formal, written confessions or informal, unwritten standards that function like confessions. In the latter case a series of inarticulate guidelines, often regulating belief and practice to the minutest detail, shapes the thought and actions of the members of the communion as fully as confessions do their adherents.

Second is a practical consideration. Written confessional

documents do in fact encourage clarity of belief and openness in theological discussion. Unwritten standards, by contrast, are overly susceptible to the manipulation of power brokers or the vagaries of selective application.

A third defense, especially tailored for Protestant consciences, is scriptural. In many places the New Testament offers formalized summaries of belief which are taken for granted as aids to faith and practice (e.g., "what we preach," 1 Cor. 1:21; "the truth," 2 Thess. 2:13; "the gospel," 1 Cor. 15:1-8; "the word," Gal. 6:6; "the doctrine of Christ," 2 John 9-10; "the sure word," Titus 1:9; "the standard of teaching," Rom. 6:17; "the traditions," 1 Cor. 11:2; "tradition," 2 Thess. 3:6; and even that which we "confess," 1 Tim. 3:16). Defenders of Protestant confessionalism regard these biblical precedents as ample defense for the legitimacy of confessional guides.

Roman Catholics, on the other hand, have a different theological situation. Protestant confessionalists acknowledge the work of the Holy Spirit in the unfolding of doctrine throughout history and in the writing of confessions, but they regard that work always as an illumination or an extension of the absolute standards of Scripture. The churches have no independent capacity to compose confessions but are everywhere dependent upon the authoritative norm of Scripture. And they may certainly make mistakes. Roman Catholics, on the other hand, treat Scripture as a norm, but believe that the Holy Spirit can inspire the teaching magisterium of the church in such a way as to make its definitive pronouncements coordinate in authority with the Bible. While many later Protestants have claimed special illumination from the Holy Spirit, there is nothing in Protestant confessional statements quite like the claim found, for example, in Trent's decree on purgatory, that "the Catholic Church *instructed by the Holy Ghost*, has, following the sacred writings and ancient traditions of the fathers, taught in sacred councils and very recently in this ecumenical council that there is a purgatory" (emphasis added).

The problem such thinking raises for Catholics is the question of change over time. In other words, are the Spirit-inspired pronouncements of Catholic confessions set in concrete? Protestant confessionalists may *act* as if confessional statements were given directly by the Holy Spirit, but Catholic confessionalists actually *say* it. For a long time it was thought that the Catholic view did in fact entail a rigorously undeviating sense of doctrinal truth. And so it was that, under the authority of the canons and decrees of Trent, there seemed to be little flexibility in Catholic teaching, except as popes or councils, instructed by the Holy Spirit, recognized other doctrines as truth. (Examples would be the definition of papal infallibility by the First Vatican Council in 1870 and the dogma of the virgin Mary's assumption into heaven promulgated by Pope Pius XII in 1950.)

Another approach to Catholic confessions arose, however, in the nineteenth century. Exemplified best by John Henry Newman's *Essay on the Development of Christian Doctrine* (1845), this view perceived the church's teaching in organic rather than mechanical terms. In this conception, the Holy Spirit would never lead the church to contradict previous confessional teachings, but might show how truth itself could grow. Such growth, in turn, might lead to new perceptions of the truth that, while not contradicting earlier teaching, look somewhat different. Thinking like Newman's made for some of the Catholic flexibility toward the canons and decrees of Trent that was exhibited in the declarations of the Second Vatican Council (1962–1965).

In the sixteenth century, however, questions about the development of doctrine over time were not nearly so pressing as questions about the doctrines themselves. Contrasting stances on those doctrines are what the documents of this book illuminate most directly. Questions about how perceptions of divine truth change may have been implied in the rush to define Christian truth. Yet the vigor with which Protestants and Catholics, in contrasting ways, confessed their faith amid the crises of the Reformation era draws our attention back to the doctrines themselves. How truth may develop over time is our problem. If we are to benefit from what they said, we must harken as carefully as possible to what they held to be the truth.

The Texts

Since this book is intended as a smorgasbord for students rather than a gourmet banquet for scholars, notes and introductions have been kept to a minimum. Brief introductions set the documents in historical and theological perspective. Each

of these introductions indicates the book from which the confession was taken; those books invariably contain a wealth of
useful information on the statements. Each introduction also
mentions a few other English-language sources that expand
upon the circumstances of the particular document.

The sixteenth century was an age immersed in the Bible. All
ten of these confessions, accordingly, are saturated with the
words of Scripture. Most citations to the Bible, however, have
been omitted for interests of space except where they were
contained explicitly in the texts. An exception is made for the
canons and decrees of the Council of Trent, where scriptural
citations are included in order to indicate that seriousness
about the Bible in the sixteenth century was not restricted to
Protestants.

Readers committed to modern gender conventions will
immediately recognize, and hopefully understand, the linguis-
tic conventions of the sixteenth century that allowed for the
use of "man," "men," and "his" to speak for all human beings.

In the documents themselves, editorial insertions are
enclosed in brackets, while parenthetical material or scriptural
references from the originals appear in parentheses.

Principles of selection for choosing these ten documents,
instead of other worthy examples, were representativeness and
size. The main confessional standards of major traditions
(Augsburg for Lutherans, Heidelberg for the Reformed, Trent
for Catholics, the Thirty-Nine Articles for Anglicans) are presented in their entirety or (with Trent) in substantial extracts.
The Ninety-Five Theses and the Small Catechism are relatively
short documents that indicate the direction of Luther's very
significant convictions. Zwingli's Sixty-Seven Articles and the
Genevan Catechism did not have the lasting impact of Calvin's
catechisms in Geneva, the two Helvetic Confessions for
Switzerland more generally, or John Knox's Scots Confession
in north Britain. But they are succinct statements that at least
give a flavor of the diversity within early Reformed Protestantism. The Schleitheim Confession is one of the few formal
statements a group of Anabaptists was allowed to make in the
early years of their movement, and it provides an admirable
picture of main Anabaptist convictions. By limiting selection
to the first two generations of the Reformation, significant documents like the Belgic Confession, the Westminster Confession

and Catechisms, and other important statements had to be omitted. The compensation in limiting choices to the first sixty years, or two generations, of the Reformation is to make possible more comparisons of nearly contemporary statements.

Finally, it is a privilege to acknowledge the help of more sophisticated and comprehensive collections of creeds and confessions, and to suggest a few resources for the further study of the Reformation era and its statements of faith. A constant companion of mine for the last twenty years has been the extraordinarily useful compilation of John H. Leith, *Creeds of the Churches: A Reader in Christian Doctrine from the Bible to the Present*, which is now available in a third edition (1982) from Westminster/John Knox (Louisville). The only justification for publishing this collection of confessions and catechisms of the Reformation alongside *Creeds of the Churches* is that the latter volume ranges over the whole history of Christianity and so cannot serve as directly those who are interested specifically in the confessional statements of the Reformation. The greatest resource in English for anyone interested in creeds and confessions remains Philip Schaff, *The Creeds of Christendom, with a History and Critical Notes*, first published in 1877 and currently available in three volumes from Baker Book House Company. It has been a mainstay in preparing this book.

The following volumes are among the many good introductions to the study of the Reformation era. The Catholic perspective of O'Connell and Evennett balances the Protestant leanings of the others, although all of these books exhibit unusual charity and balance of viewpoint.

Bainton, Roland H. *The Reformation of the Sixteenth Century*. Boston: Beacon, 1952.

Chadwick, Owen. *The Reformation*. Rev. ed. Baltimore: Penguin, 1968.

Dickens, A. G., and John M. Tonkin, *The Reformation in Historical Thought*. Cambridge, Mass.: Harvard University Press, 1985.

Evennett, H. Outram. *The Spirit of the Counter-Reformation*. Edited by John Bossy. Notre Dame, Ind.: University of Notre Dame Press, 1970.

Grimm, Harold J. *The Reformation Era, 1500–1600.* 2d ed. New York: Macmillan, 1973.

Jones, R. Tudur. *The Great Reformation.* Downers Grove, Ill.: Inter-Varsity, 1985.

O'Connell, Marvin R. *The Counter Reformation, 1560–1610.* New York: Harper and Row, 1974.

Ozment, Steven. *The Age of Reform, 1250–1550.* New Haven: Yale University Press, 1980.

Ozment, Steven, ed. *Reformation Europe: A Guide to Research.* St. Louis: Center for Reformation Research, 1982.

Pelikan, Jaroslav. *The Christian Tradition, Vol. 4: Reformation of Church and Dogma (1300–1700).* Chicago: University of Chicago Press, 1984.

Spitz, Lewis W. *The Protestant Reformation.* New York: Harper and Row, 1985.

A number of reference works have also been helpful in preparing this book, including the following, which offer both reliable information and extensive bibliographies.

The Catholic Encyclopedia. New York: Robert Appleton, 1907–1914.

The Encyclopedia of the Lutheran Church. Minneapolis: Augsburg, 1965.

Evangelical Dictionary of Theology. Grand Rapids: Baker, 1984.

The Mennonite Encyclopedia. Scottdale, Pa.: Mennonite Publishing House, 1955.

New Catholic Encyclopedia. NewYork: McGraw-Hill, 1967–1979.

New Dictionary of Theology. Downers Grove, Ill.: Inter-Varsity, 1988.

Oxford Dictionary of the Christian Church. 2d ed. New York: Oxford University Press, 1974.

1

The Ninety-Five Theses of Martin Luther (1517)

Martin Luther (1483–1546) is known, quite rightly, as the first great teacher of the Protestant Reformation. His own painful journey from self-doubt to faith in a gracious God rapidly became an inspiration to other Protestants. While movements of reform in Switzerland, France, the Netherlands, Eastern Europe, and Britain soon diverged, sometimes substantially, from norms Luther established, his work remained an honored point of departure for these other Protestants. Luther's passion for the grace of God revealed to needy sinners in Christ, no less than his devotion to the Scriptures and his defense of the priesthood of all believers, opened the doors through which other Protestants followed.

Luther first gained widespread attention through posting his "Ninety-Five Theses." The actual content of these theses, however, can prove surprising on first reading. They do not mention justification by faith. They are, from a later Protestant perspective, excessively deferential to the pope. There is also no explicit defense of biblical authority over against the traditions of the church or the authority of the Catholic magisterium.

Reprinted from *Luther's Works*, volume 31, edited by Harold J. Grimm, coyright © 1971 Fortress Press, by permission of Augsburg Fortress.

While these Protestant emphases are all implicit, the explicit purpose of the Ninety-Five Theses is to examine only one particular problem.

That problem is indulgences. The issues at stake may now seem medieval, merely scholastic, or simply irrelevant. Yet by attacking accepted church practice at this point, Luther embarked upon a course that led naturally to the major teachings for which Protestantism is known.

By 1517 the use of indulgences had become a well established practice in the church. Their importance depended upon the Catholic teaching concerning penance which had evolved in the early church and the Middle Ages. By Luther's day, Roman Catholics believed that Christians required one of the church's seven sacraments—namely, penance—to be forgiven for the sins they committed after baptism. This sacrament consisted of several elements: "contrition" (or sorrow for sin), "confession" to a priest, the pronouncement of "absolution" (whereby the priest told the penitent that the sin was forgiven), and "satisfaction" (or a way of discharging in this life the penalty entailed by the sin). Satisfaction, or penitence, did not by itself bring forgiveness, for that was an act of God's grace. But it was necessary, both to make temporal amends for the sin and to strengthen the penitent against further temptation.

Indulgences had entered the picture by the eleventh or twelfth century as the church's way of remitting or discharging the satisfaction or temporal penalty required in penance. Indulgences depended upon the belief that Christ, the virgin Mary, and the saints had established a treasury of merit (that is, of goodness and good deeds above that required for salvation), which the church could use to remit the earthly penalty for sins. The first extensive indulgences had been granted for service in the Crusades. Later they were given for visits to holy places in Rome and then for other causes specified by the popes. Often there was a payment.

The particular indulgence that led to the Ninety-Five Theses had been granted by two popes, Julius II in 1510 and Leo X in 1513, to raise money for building Saint Peter's basilica in Rome. In 1515 Leo X authorized Albrecht, archbishop of Mainz and Magdeburg and bishop of Halberstadt, to sell this particular indulgence in his territories. Albrecht, in turn, named the Dominican monk, Johann Tetzel, to conduct the actual sale. Tetzel's formal statements about the indulgence made the proper distinction between eternal forgiveness by God and temporal satisfaction required by the church. But his eager salesmanship rendered that distinction largely irrelevant. To ordinary people it seemed as if Tetzel was saying simply that purchasing an indulgence could mean the forgiveness of one's own sins or, if done on behalf of the dead, could release souls from purgatory (this is the distortion that Luther attacks in thesis 27).

To Luther, the crass selling of forgiveness represented much that had become corrupt in the Catholic Church. Forgiveness was God's gift, not a human prerogative. It stemmed from divine grace, not from something that people did. It meant a change of heart, not an exchange of funds. It arose from Christ's sacrifice on the cross, not from the persuasion of a huckster.

In response to Tetzel's activity, Luther prepared his theses. He wrote them in Latin, hoping that they might stimulate academic debate. Although there is some controversy about what actually happened to the theses, the traditional story seems reliable, that Luther at noon on the Eve of All Saints' Day, October 31, 1517, nailed a broadside of the theses to the University of Wittenberg's bulletin board. The bulletin board was the door of the Castle Church. No one showed up to debate, but Luther himself sent copies of the Latin text to Archbishop Albrecht, as well as to his friends. More important, enterprising printers soon translated the theses into German, which created a sensation. The Reformation, to put it crudely, was on.

In the theses Luther takes pains to contrast genuine Christian sorrow for sin with the artificiality of insincere satisfactions. The theses which draw that contrast most directly—especially 1, 62, and 92–95—also move closest to the theme of justification by faith. Luther's belief in justification by faith informs this document, but it also seems to have been clarified in his mind by the ferocious debate that broke out after its publication.

The Ninety-Five Theses were a confession of only one person's faith. They have never served officially as a church's doctrinal standard. At the same time, they do represent an extraordinarily significant contribution to the process of clarifying

Christian faith that would lead to many formal confessions in the sixteenth century and beyond. Useful introductions and explanations of particular matters in the theses can be found in the works listed below. Here, it may be helpful to note that Saint Severinus and Saint Paschal (thesis 29) were medieval popes who purportedly sought to remain longer in purgatory so that they might have greater reward in heaven; and to observe that Luther's warnings about the corrupting temptation of fund raising (thesis 54) is as relevant in the age of electronic preachers as it was in the day of indulgence sellers.

Finally, as a modern footnote, after the Second Vatican Council, Pope Paul VI in 1967 declared that indulgences were only effective when the heart turned from sin and that the purpose of indulgences was more to encourage charity among the faithful than to discharge a mechanical satisfaction.

Text

Luther, Martin. "Ninety-Five Theses." In *Luther's Works, 31: Career of the Reformer I*, ed. Harold J. Grimm, 25–33. Rev. ed. Philadelphia: Fortress, 1971.

Additional Reading

Aland, Kurt, ed. *Martin Luther's 95 Theses*. St. Louis: Concordia, 1967.

Bainton, Roland. *Here I Stand: A Life of Martin Luther.* Nashville: Abingdon, 1950.

Iserloh, Erwin. *The Theses Were Not Posted: Luther Between Reform and Reformation*. Boston: Beacon, 1968.

Luther, Martin. *Explanations of the Ninety-Five Theses* (1518). In *Luther's Works, 31: Career of the Reformer I*, ed. Harold J. Grimm, 77–252. Rev. ed. Philadelphia: Fortress, 1971.

Oberman, Heiko A. *Luther: Man Between God and the Devil.* New Haven: Yale University Press, 1989.

Watson, Philip S. *Let God Be God! An Interpretation of the Theology of Martin Luther*. Philadelphia: Fortress, 1970 (orig. 1947).

The Ninety-Five Theses or Disputation on the Power and Efficacy of Indulgences

Out of love and zeal for truth and the desire to bring it to light, the following theses will be publicly discussed at Wittenberg under the chairmanship of the reverend father Martin Luther, master of arts and sacred theology and regularly appointed lecturer on these subjects at that place. He requests that those who cannot be present to debate orally with us will do so by letter.

In the name of our Lord Jesus Christ. Amen.

1. When our Lord and Master Jesus Christ said, "Repent" [Matt. 4:17], he willed the entire life of believers to be one of repentance.

2. This word cannot be understood as referring to the sacrament of penance, that is, confession and satisfaction, as administered by the clergy.

3. Yet it does not mean solely inner repentance; such inner repentance is worthless unless it produces various outward mortifications of the flesh.

4. The penalty of sin remains as long as the hatred of self, that is, true inner repentance, until our entrance into the kingdom of heaven.

5. The pope neither desires nor is able to remit any penalties except those imposed by his own authority or that of the canons.

6. The pope cannot remit any guilt, except by declaring and showing that it has been remitted by God; or, to be sure, by remitting guilt in cases reserved to his judgment. If his right to grant remission in these cases were disregarded, the guilt would certainly remain unforgiven.

7. God remits guilt to no one unless at the same time he humbles him in all things and makes him submissive to his vicar, the priest.

8. The penitential canons are imposed only on the living, and, according to the canons themselves, nothing should be imposed on the dying.

9. Therefore the Holy Spirit through the pope is kind to us insofar as the pope in his decrees always makes exception of the article of death and of necessity.

10. Those priests act ignorantly and wickedly who, in the case of the dying, reserve canonical penalties for purgatory.

11. Those tares of changing the canonical penalty to the penalty of purgatory were evidently sown while the bishops slept [Matt. 13:25].

12. In former times canonical penalties were imposed, not after, but before absolution, as tests of true contrition.

13. The dying are freed by death from all penalties, are already dead as far as the canon laws are concerned, and have a right to be released from them.

14. Imperfect piety or love on the part of the dying person necessarily brings with it great fear; and the smaller the love, the greater the fear.

15. This fear or horror is sufficient in itself, to say nothing of other things, to constitute the penalty of purgatory, since it is very near the horror of despair.

16. Hell, purgatory, and heaven seem to differ the same as despair, fear, and assurance of salvation.

17. It seems as though for the souls in purgatory fear should necessarily decrease and love increase.

18. Furthermore, it does not seem proved, either by reason or Scripture, that souls in purgatory are outside the state of merit, that is, unable to grow in love.

19. Nor does it seem proved that souls in purgatory, at least not all of them, are certain and assured of their own salvation, even if we ourselves may be entirely certain of it.

20. Therefore the pope, when he uses the words "plenary remission of all penalties," does not actually mean "all penalties," but only those imposed by himself.

21. Thus those indulgence preachers are in error who say that a man is absolved from every penalty and saved by papal indulgences.

22. As a matter of fact, the pope remits to souls in purgatory no penalty which, according to canon law, they should have paid in this life.

23. If remission of all penalties whatsoever could be granted to anyone at all, certainly it would be granted only to the most perfect, that is, to very few.

24. For this reason most people are necessarily deceived by that indiscriminate and high-sounding promise of release from penalty.

25. That power which the pope has in general over purgatory corresponds to the power which any bishop or curate has in a particular way in his own diocese or parish.

26. The pope does very well when he grants remission to souls in purgatory, not by the power of the keys, which he does not have, but by way of intercession for them.

27. They preach only human doctrines who say that as soon as the money clinks into the money chest, the soul flies out of purgatory.

28. It is certain that when money clinks in the money chest, greed and avarice can be increased; but when the church intercedes, the result is in the hands of God alone.

29. Who knows whether all souls in purgatory wish to be redeemed, since we have exceptions in Saint Severinus and Saint Paschal, as related in a legend.

30. No one is sure of the integrity of his own contrition, much less of having received plenary remission.

31. The man who actually buys indulgences is as rare as he who is really penitent; indeed, he is exceedingly rare.

32. Those who believe that they can be certain of their salvation because they have indulgence letters will be eternally damned, together with their teachers.

33. Men must especially be on their guard against those who say that the pope's pardons are that inestimable gift of God by which man is reconciled to him.

34. For the graces of indulgences are concerned only with the penalties of sacramental satisfaction established by man.

35. They who teach that contrition is not necessary on the part of those who intend to buy souls out of purgatory or to buy confessional privileges preach unchristian doctrine.

36. Any truly repentant Christian has a right to full remission of penalty and guilt, even without indulgence letters.

37. Any true Christian, whether living or dead, participates in all the blessings of Christ and the church; and this is granted him by God, even without indulgence letters.

38. Nevertheless, papal remission and blessings are by no means to be disregarded, for they are, as I have said [thesis 6], the proclamation of the divine remission.

39. It is very difficult, even for the most learned theologians, at one and the same time to commend to the people the bounty of indulgences and the need of true contrition.

40. A Christian who is truly contrite seeks and loves to pay penalties for his sins; the bounty of indulgences, however, relaxes penalties and causes men to hate them—at least it furnishes occasion for hating them.

41. Papal indulgences must be preached with caution, lest people erroneously think that they are preferable to other good works of love.

42. Christians are to be taught that the pope does not intend that the buying of indulgences should in any way be compared with works of mercy.

43. Christians are to be taught that he who gives to the poor or lends to the needy does a better deed than he who buys indulgences.

44. Because love grows by works of love, man thereby becomes better. Man does not, however, become better by means of indulgences but is merely freed from penalties.

45. Christians are to be taught that he who sees a needy man and passes him by, yet gives his money for indulgences, does not buy papal indulgences but God's wrath.

46. Christians are to be taught that, unless they have more than they need, they must reserve enough for their family needs and by no means squander it on indulgences.

47. Christians are to be taught that the buying of indulgences is a matter of free choice, not commanded.

48. Christians are to be taught that the pope, in granting indulgences, needs and thus desires their devout prayer more than their money.

49. Christians are to be taught that papal indulgences are useful only if they do not put their trust in them, but very harmful if they lose their fear of God because of them.

50. Christians are to be taught that if the pope knew the exactions of the indulgence preachers, he would rather that the basilica of Saint Peter were burned to ashes than built up with the skin, flesh, and bones of his sheep.

51. Christians are to be taught that the pope would and should wish to give of his own money, even though he had to sell the basilica of Saint Peter, to many of those from whom certain hawkers of indulgences cajole money.

52. It is vain to trust in salvation by indulgence letters, even though the indulgence commissary, or even the pope, were to offer his soul as security.

53. They are enemies of Christ and the pope who forbid altogether the preaching of the Word of God in some churches in order that indulgences may be preached in others.

54. Injury is done the Word of God when, in the same sermon, an equal or larger amount of time is devoted to indulgences than to the Word.

55. It is certainly the pope's sentiment that if indulgences, which are a very insignificant thing, are celebrated with one bell, one procession, and one ceremony, then the gospel, which is the very greatest thing, should be preached with a hundred bells, a hundred processions, a hundred ceremonies.

56. The treasures of the church, out of which the pope distributes indulgences, are not sufficiently discussed or known among the people of Christ.

57. That indulgences are not temporal treasures is certainly clear, for many indulgence sellers do not distribute them freely but only gather them.

58. Nor are they the merits of Christ and the saints, for, even without the pope, the latter always work for grace for the inner man, and the cross, death, and hell for the outer man.

59. Saint Laurence said that the poor of the church were the treasures of the church, but he spoke according to the usage of the word in his own time.

60. Without want of consideration we say that the keys of the church, given by the merits of Christ, are that treasure;

61. For it is clear that the pope's power is of itself sufficient for the remission of penalties and cases reserved by himself.

62. The true treasure of the church is the most holy gospel of the glory and grace of God.

63. But this treasure is naturally most odious, for it makes the first to be last [Matt. 20:16].

64. On the other hand, the treasure of indulgences is naturally most acceptable, for it makes the last to be first.

65. Therefore the treasures of the gospel are nets with which one formerly fished for men of wealth.

66. The treasures of indulgences are nets with which one now fishes for the wealth of men.

67. The indulgences which the demagogues acclaim as the

greatest graces are actually understood to be such only insofar as they promote gain.

68. They are nevertheless in truth the most significant graces when compared with the grace of God and the piety of the cross.

69. Bishops and curates are bound to admit the commissaries of indulgences with all reverence.

70. But they are much more bound to strain their eyes and ears lest these men preach their own dreams instead of what the pope has commissioned.

71. Let him who speaks against the truth of papal indulgences be anathema and accursed;

72. But let him who guards against the lust and license of the indulgence preachers be blessed;

73. Just as the pope justly thunders against those who by any means whatsoever contrive to harm the sale of indulgences.

74. But much more does he intend to thunder against those who use indulgences as a pretext to contrive harm to holy love and truth.

75. To consider papal indulgences so great that they could absolve a man even if he had done the impossible and had violated the mother of God is madness.

76. We say on the contrary that papal indulgences cannot remove the very least of venial sins as far as guilt is concerned.

77. To say that even Saint Peter, if he were now pope, could not grant greater graces is blasphemy against Saint Peter and the pope.

78. We say on the contrary that even the present pope, or any pope whatsoever, has greater graces at his disposal, that is, the gospel, spiritual powers, gifts of healing, and the like, as it is written in 1 Corinthians 12 [:28].

79. To say that the cross emblazoned with the papal coat of arms, and set up by the indulgence preachers, is equal in worth to the cross of Christ is blasphemy.

80. The bishops, curates, and theologians who permit such talk to be spread among the people will have to answer for this.

81. This unbridled preaching of indulgences makes it difficult even for learned men to rescue the reverence which is due the pope from slander or from the shrewd questions of the laity,

82. Such as: "Why does not the pope empty purgatory for the sake of holy love and the dire need of the souls that are there if he redeems an infinite number of souls for the sake of miserable money with which to build a church? The former reasons would be most just; the latter most trivial."

83. Again, "Why are funeral and anniversary masses for the dead continued and why does he not return or permit the withdrawal of the endowments founded for them, since it is wrong to pray for the redeemed?"

84. Again, "What is this new piety of God and the pope that for a consideration of money they permit a man who is impious and their enemy to buy out of purgatory the pious soul of a friend of God and do not rather, because of the need of that pious and beloved soul, free it for pure love's sake?"

85. Again, "Why are the penitential canons, long since abrogated and dead in actual fact and through disuse, now satisfied by the granting of indulgences as though they were still alive and in force?"

86. Again, "Why does not the pope, whose wealth is today greater than the wealth of the richest Crassus, build this one basilica of Saint Peter with his own money rather than with the money of poor believers?"

87. Again, "What does the pope remit or grant to those who by perfect contrition already have a right to full remission and blessings?"

88. Again, "What greater blessing could come to the church than if the pope were to bestow these remissions and blessings on every believer a hundred times a day, as he now does but once?"

89. "Since the pope seeks the salvation of souls rather than money by his indulgences, why does he suspend the indulgences and pardons previously granted when they have equal efficacy?"

90. To repress these very sharp arguments of the laity by force alone, and not to resolve them by giving reasons, is to expose the church and the pope to the ridicule of their enemies and to make Christians unhappy.

91. If, therefore, indulgences were preached according to the spirit and intention of the pope, all these doubts would be readily resolved. Indeed, they would not exist.

92. Away then with all those prophets who say to the people of Christ, "Peace, peace," and there is no peace! [Jer. 6:14].

93. Blessed be all those prophets who say to the people of Christ, "Cross, cross," and there is no cross!

94. Christians should be exhorted to be diligent in following Christ, their head, through penalties, death, and hell;

95. And thus be confident of entering into heaven through many tribulations rather than through the false security of peace [Acts 14:22].

2

The Sixty-Seven Articles
of Ulrich Zwingli (1523)

Ulrich Zwingli (1484–1531), pioneer of Protestantism in Switzerland, is sometimes called the "third man" of the Reformation after Luther and Calvin. Whatever the ranking for posterity, Zwingli was a very important actor in the drama of his times. He received a fine education at the University of Basel and other centers of the Renaissance, he was ordained a priest, and he devoted himself to eager study of Renaissance scholarship (especially Erasmus's Greek New Testament of 1516). Sometime after 1516, while serving as the parish priest in Einsiedeln, Zwingli underwent an evangelical experience of God's grace similar in some ways to Luther's experience at about the same time. Zwingli's theology, however, was only marginally influenced by Luther. More directly it grew from his experiences in Einsiedeln, where pilgrimages to a shrine for the virgin Mary troubled him deeply, and especially in Zurich, where in early 1519 he became the people's (or preaching) priest at the city's main church. There his sermons and lectures from the New Testament took on an increasingly reforming tone, both against abuses in the Catholic Church and toward the reconstitution of faith and practice. Zwingli led the city of Zurich into Protestantism and exerted great influence with other Swiss cantons as a promoter of "Reformed" (as distinct from Lutheran) faith.

Zwingli was a man of activity and controversy his entire life. Before he died on the field of battle while fighting against Zurich's Catholic foes, he published several influential works outlining a full agenda for reform. Not all Protestants, however, took kindly to his teaching. Luther and his followers contended that Zwingli's formulation of the Lord's supper made it into merely an ineffective symbol. Anabaptists, some of whom had earlier been his pupils and friends, complained that Zwingli's own principles should have led him to repudiate the baptism of infants. And Zwingli was also criticized for letting the Zurich city council gain too much control over the church's affairs.

Early in his career as a Reformer Zwingli sketched out his position on many of the controversial issues of the day in his Sixty-Seven Articles. With some justice, this document can be considered the first Protestant confession. Unlike Luther's Ninety-Five Theses, it spoke to a full range of doctrines and practices. It also devoted considerable attention to foundational principles of the new Protestant movement.

Zwingli prepared his articles for a public disputation on January 29, 1523, at which he was to debate the general vicar of the bishop of Constance. When the vicar chose not to contest the articles before the crowd of six hundred or so that had gathered, the Zurich city council approved Zwingli's positions as its own and directed the ministers of the canton to preach only what could be supported from the Scriptures. Zwingli's articles became the first in a long line of important Swiss Reformed confessions that would include the Ten Confessions of Berne (1528), the First Helvetic Confession (1536), and the Second Helvetic Confession (1566).

The articles emphasize the sole supremacy of Scripture (especially in the introduction and conclusion). They uphold the centrality of Christ and his work (3, 6, 19, 22, 50, 54). They define the church in spiritual instead of institutional categories (8). They criticize the evil effects of tradition (11, 23–27). They stress preaching as the heart of public ministry (14, 62). They carefully define the authority of the state as superior in its own sphere to the church (35–43). And they strike out vigorously against what Zwingli thought were Catholic errors concerning the Mass (18), prohibition of clerical marriage (28–29), and purgatory (57–60). Zwingli and, even more, other Swiss Protestants would later modify some of these assertions. But the major thrust of the Sixty-Seven Articles defined a basic Reformed stance which, with variations, continues as an influential Protestant position to this very day.

Text

Schaff, Philip. *The Creeds of Christendom*, 3:197–207. 6th ed. New York: Harper and Brothers, 1931. (Editor's translation)

Additional Reading

Bromiley, Geoffrey W., ed. *Zwingli and Bullinger*. Philadelphia: Westminster, 1953.

Cochrane, Arthur C., ed. *Reformed Confessions of the 16th Century*. Philadelphia: Westminster, 1966.

Furcha, E. J., and H. Wayne Pipkin, eds. *Prophet, Pastor, Protestant: The Work of Huldrych Zwingli after Five Hundred Years*. Alison Park, Pa.: Pickwick, 1984.

Potter, G. R. *Zwingli*. New York: Cambridge University Press, 1976.

Schaff, Philip. *The Creeds of Christendom*, 1:363–64. 6th ed. New York: Harper and Brothers, 1931.

Stephens, W. P. *The Theology of Huldrych Zwingli*. New York: Oxford University Press, 1986.

The Sixty-Seven Articles of Ulrich Zwingli (1523)

I, Ulrich Zwingli, confess that I have preached in the worthy city of Zurich these sixty-seven articles or opinions on the basis of Scripture, which is called *theopneustos* (that is, inspired by God). I offer to defend and vindicate these articles with Scripture. But if I have not understood Scripture correctly, I am ready to be corrected, but only from the same Scripture.

1. All who say that the gospel is nothing without the confirmation of the church make a mistake and blaspheme God.

2. The sum of the gospel is that our Lord Jesus Christ, true Son of God, has made known to us the will of his heavenly Father, redeemed us from death by his innocence, and reconciled us to God.

3. Therefore, Christ is the only way to salvation for all who have been, who are, and who will be.

4. Whoever seeks or points out any other way to God is a murderer of souls and a thief.

5. Therefore, all who give equal or greater honor to any other teaching beside the gospel make a mistake and show that they do not know what the gospel is.

6. For Jesus Christ is the Pioneer and Captain promised and given by God to the whole human race.

7. He is an everlasting salvation and the head of all believers, who are his body. But without him that body is dead and can do nothing.

8. From this follows, first, that all who live in this head are members and children of God. This is the church or the communion of saints, the bride of Christ, the *ecclesia catholica* [universal church].

9. Second, just as parts of the body can do nothing without the leading of the head, so in the body of Christ no one can do anything without its head, Christ.

10. Just as when the parts of the body do something without the head—tear themselves up, wound, and damage themselves—so also when the members of Christ are so bold as to attempt something without their head, Christ, they are senseless and end up attacking themselves and burdening each other with unwise laws.

11. From this we see that so-called ecclesiastical traditions with their pomp, imperiousness, social standing, titles, and laws are a source of all kinds of madness since they do not agree with the head.

12. Therefore, they rage on, but not for the sake of the head. By God's grace, attention has been drawn to this fact in our day. They will not be allowed to rage on forever, but will be brought to listen to the head alone.

13. Where people heed the Word of God, they learn the will of God plainly and clearly, they are drawn to him by his Spirit, and they are converted to him.

14. Therefore, all Christians should exercise the greatest diligence to see that only the gospel of Christ is preached everywhere.

15. For in believing the gospel we are saved, and in believing not we are condemned, for all truth is clearly contained in it.

16. In the gospel we learn that the teachings and traditions of men are of no use for salvation.

Notice, Pope, What Follows!

17. That Christ is the only, everlasting High Priest can be determined by the fact that those who have passed themselves off as high priests oppose, and even repudiate, the honor and power of Christ.

Of the Mass

18. Christ, who has once offered himself as a sacrifice, is for eternity a perpetually enduring and efficacious sacrifice for the sins of all believers. Therefore we conclude that the Mass is not a sacrifice but a memorial of the one sacrifice and a seal of redemption that Christ made good for us.

Intercession of the Saints

19. Christ is the only Mediator between God and us.

20. God wants to give us all things in his name. From this follows that from now on we need no other mediation except his mediation.

21. When we pray for one another on earth, we do so in such a way that we are confident all things will be given to us only through Christ.

Good Works

22. Christ is our righteousness. Therefore, we conclude that works are good insofar as they are of Christ, but insofar as they are only our own, they are not right and good.

How the Prosperity of the Clergy Should Be Christ

23. Christ condemns the prosperity and splendor of the world. Therefore, we conclude that those who accumulate wealth for themselves in his name slander him monstrously when they make him a pretense for their own greed and wantonness.

Prohibition of Foods

24. Christians are not obligated to do works that God has not commanded. They may eat all foods at all times. From this we learn that decretals regulating cheese and bread are a Roman fraud.

Of Festivals and Pilgrimages

25. Time and place have been made subject to Christ, not the Christian to them. From this is to be learned that those who bind Christians to times and places rob them of their proper freedom.

Cowls, Badges, and the Like

26. Nothing is more displeasing to God than hypocrisy. From this we conclude that everything which makes itself out to be splendid before men is a great hypocrisy and infamy. So much for monks' cowls, badges, tonsures, and the like.

Orders and Sects

27. All Christians are brothers of Christ one with another and should call no one on earth father. So much for orders, sects, cliques, and the like.

The Marriage of Clergy

28. Everything that God permits or has not forbidden is proper. From this we learn that marriage is proper for all people.

The Impure Priest Should Take a Wife

29. All those who are in the church sin if they do not make themselves secure through marriage once they understand that God has granted marriage to them for the sake of purity.

Vows of Purity

30. Those who take a vow of chastity assume madly or childishly too much. From this is to be learned that those who make such vows are treating godly people wantonly.

Of Excommunication

31. No private person may excommunicate anyone else, but the church—that is, the communion of those among whom the one subject to excommunication lives—along with its guardians may act as a bishop.

32. The only one who should be excommunicated is a person who commits a public scandal.

Of Unclaimed Goods

33. Unclaimed goods should not be given to temples, cloisters, monks, priests, or nuns, but to the needy, if it is impossible to return them to their rightful owner.

Of Authorities

34. The so-called spiritual estate has no justification in the teaching of Christ for its splendor.

Secular Authority from God

35. But secular authority does have rightful power and is supported from the teaching and action of Christ.

36. Everything that the so-called spiritual estate claims by right or for the protection of its rights belongs properly to the secular authorities, if they have a mind to be Christians.

37. To these authorities all Christians are obliged to be obedient, with no exceptions;

38. So long as the authorities do not command anything in opposition to God.

39. Therefore all secular laws should be conformed to the divine will, which is to say, that they should protect the oppressed, even if the oppressed make no complaint.

40. Only these secular authorities have the power to put someone to death without provoking God. But only those should be executed who perpetrated a public scandal, unless God has decreed otherwise.

41. If secular rulers properly serve with counsel and assistance the ones for whom God has given them responsibility, they in turn are obligated to offer them bodily sustenance.

42. But if rulers act unfaithfully and not according to the guiding principles of Christ, they may be replaced by God.

43. The sum of the matter is that the best and most secure government exists where the ruler governs with God alone, but the most evil and insecure where the ruler governs according to his own heart.

Of Prayer

44. True worshipers call upon God in spirit and in truth, without a lot of fuss before men.

45. Hypocrites do their deeds to be seen before men; they receive their reward in this age.

46. It must therefore follow that singing or clamoring in church, carried on without devotion and only for the praise of self, is done either for renown from men or profit.

Of Offense

47. A person should choose to suffer physical death before offending a Christian or bringing a Christian into disgrace.

48. The one who takes offense out of imbecility or ignorance, without cause, should not be allowed to remain sick or mean-spirited; rather, such a one should be nurtured to recognize what is really sin and what is not.

49. I know of no greater offense than that priests are not allowed to have lawful wives, while they are allowed to pay concubines. What a disgrace!

Of the Forgiveness of Sins

50. God alone forgives sins, only through Christ Jesus his Son, our Lord.

51. Whoever ascribes this power to the creature takes away God's glory and gives it to someone who is not God. This is truly idolatry.

52. Therefore, confession to a priest or a neighbor should not be done for the forgiveness of sins, but for the sake of receiving counsel.

53. Assigned works of satisfaction (except excommunication) are the product of human counsel; they do not take away sin; and they are imposed on others in order to terrorize them.

The Sorrow of Christ Atones for Sins

54. Christ has borne all of our sorrow and labor. Whoever adds works of penance, which belongs to Christ alone, makes a mistake and blasphemes God.

Withholding Forgiveness

55. Whoever refuses to remit any sin from a repentant person is not acting in the place of God or Peter, but of the devil.

56. Whoever forgives sin only for money is a comrade of Simon and Balaam, and is the true apostle of the devil.

Of Purgatory

57. The true holy Scripture knows nothing of a purgatory after this life.

58. The judgment of the departed is known to God alone.

59. And the less God has caused to make known to us about it, the less we should try to find out about it.

60. I do not condemn it if a person concerned about the dead calls upon God to show them mercy. Yet to fix the time for this (seven years for a mortal sin) and to lie about such matters for the sake of gain is not human but diabolical.

Of the Priesthood and Its Ordination

61. Of the kind of ordination that priests in recent times have invented, the holy Scripture knows nothing.

62. Scripture recognizes no priests except those who proclaim God's Word.

63. Scripture asks that honor be offered to those who preach the Word, that is, that they be given physical sustenance.

Of Dealing with Misdeeds

64. Those who acknowledge their misdeeds should not be required to suffer for anything else, but should be allowed to die in peace. Thereafter any goods they leave to the church should be administered in a Christian way.

65. God will certainly deal with those who refuse to acknowledge their misdeeds. Therefore, we should not do them any bodily harm, unless they are leading others astray so obviously that it cannot be ignored.

66. All spiritual leaders should humble themselves, and seek to exalt only the cross of Christ rather than their own purses. Otherwise they will perish. The example is on the cross.

67. If anyone wishes to discuss with me taxes, tithes, unbaptized children, or confirmation, I am ready to provide an answer.

But let no one undertake to argue with sophistry or human wisdom, but let Scripture be the judge (Scripture breathes the Spirit of God), so that you can either find the truth or, if you have found it, hold on to it.

Amen. God grant it!

3

The Schleitheim
Confession (1527)

The reform of the church begun by Luther in Wittenberg
and Zwingli in Zurich blossomed rapidly into a multifaceted
affair. Almost as soon as these "magisterial" (or established)
Reformers announced their programs to correct abuses or to
promote new standards in church and society, other voices of
protest began asking why these leaders did not go further. The
"radical reformation," to use a term made famous by historian
George H. Williams, is the collective category often provided
for these ardent questioners as a whole. Among them could be
found all sorts of proposals: attacks on the sacraments and
other traditions of the church as well as contentions for
Unitarianism, special revelations from the Spirit, and violent
revolution. But in this radical reformation were also those
harkening more directly to the main themes of the best-known
Reformers, themes like the supremacy of Scripture and the
priesthood of all believers. Among these more sober "radicals,"
the evangelical Anabaptists were most prominent and have
been most enduring.

Anabaptism arose first among followers of Zwingli as part of
the reform in Zurich. (The name "Anabaptist," meaning "rebap-
tism," identified these Protestants by what was in the sixteenth
century one of their most radical convictions, that only adults

Reprinted by permission of Herald Press, Scottdale, Pa. 15683 from *The
Doctrines of the Mennonites*, ed. John C. Wenger (1952).

who had made their own profession of faith should be baptized.) Their leaders—Conrad Grebel, Felix Mantz, and George Blaurock—criticized Zwingli for failing to follow his own counsel of grounding all doctrines and practices on the Bible. Scripture, these "Swiss Brethren" taught, should be interpreted as simply and straightforwardly as possible. So interpreted, they could discern no obvious defense for many hereditary church practices, including the baptism of infants, the establishment of the church by the state, the Christian's participation in warfare, and reliance on the state to punish heretics.

To Zwingli, as well as to most other Protestants and Catholics of the era, these proposals were as dangerous as they were absurd. They seemed to undercut time-tested pillars of Christian life that most Protestants felt could be squared with the Bible. They also appeared to threaten the stability of European society. If all were free to believe any interpretation of the Bible they chose to believe, if the church together with the state could not define the correct interpretation of Scripture, then chaos and the destruction of Christianity would be the only result. Few patriotic Americans in the 1950s ever feared the communist menace as much as Protestants and Roman Catholics in the sixteenth century feared these ideas of the Anabaptists.

And so, as frightened communities often do, they lashed out with terror as their weapon. Of the three early leaders of the Swiss Brethren, Conrad Grebel died of the plague in 1526 after spending time in prison, Felix Mantz was put to death in 1527, and George Blaurock was burned at the stake in 1529. But when the early Anabaptist leadership was decimated, others arose to take their place. These new leaders would eventually include Menno Simons (1496–1561) and Jacob Hutter (d. 1536), who founded Anabaptist communions that survive to this day. In Switzerland it was a former Benedictine monk from southern Germany, Michael Sattler, who pulled the distraught remnants of the Anabaptist movement together. Sattler's work, although of short duration, was vital. In early 1527 he gathered Swiss Brethren at Schleitheim in the canton of Schaffhausen, and then after deliberating with this body, he composed on February 24, 1527, the confession of Anabaptist faith that follows. It is not a confession in the sense of ever being officially adopted by a denomination, nor did it attempt to set out doctrines for the entirety of the Christian faith. Rather, it explained the specific convictions that set these Anabaptists apart from what the document calls "the papists and antipapists" (that is, the Catholics and the Protestants). Its principal conclusions were all derived from an intense study of the Bible, especially the New Testament: infant baptism was "the highest and chief abomination of the pope"; Christians must separate completely from the world; it was wrong for believers to take up arms, even in self-defense. Such conclusions were too much for most of even the Protestant Reformers of the sixteenth century. They are minority convictions in the Christian church today. But they also remain potent testimonies to the courage of little-known believers who were faithful to the New Testament as they read it, even unto death.

Three months after he wrote this confession, Michael Sattler was burned at the stake for his beliefs.

Text

John C. Wenger. *The Doctrine of the Mennonites*. Scottdale, Pa.: Mennonite Publishing House, 1952.

Additional Reading

Estep, William R. *The Anabaptist Story*. Rev. ed. Grand Rapids: Eerdmans, 1975.

Klaassen, Walter, ed. *Anabaptism in Outline*. Scottdale, Pa.: Herald, 1981.

Williams, George H. *The Radical Reformation*. Philadelphia: Westminster, 1962.

Yoder, John H. *The Legacy of Michael Sattler*. Scottdale, Pa.: Herald, 1973.

The Schleitheim Confession
Brotherly Union of a Number of Children of God Concerning Seven Articles

May joy, peace, and mercy from our Father through the atonement of the blood of Christ Jesus, together with the gifts of the Spirit—who is sent from the Father to all believers for their strength and comfort and their perseverance in all tribulation until the end, Amen—be to all those who love God, who are the children of light, and who are scattered everywhere as it has been ordained of God our Father, where they are with one mind assembled together in one God and Father of us all: Grace and peace of heart be with you all, Amen.

Beloved brethren and sisters in the Lord: First and supremely we are always concerned for your consolation and the assurance of your conscience (which was previously misled) so that you may not always remain foreigners to us and by right almost completely excluded, but that you may turn again to the true implanted members of Christ, who have been armed through patience and knowledge of themselves, and have therefore again been united with us in the strength of a godly Christian spirit and zeal for God.

It is also apparent with what cunning the devil has turned us aside, so that he might destroy and bring to an end the work of God which in mercy and grace has been partly begun in us. But Christ, the true Shepherd of our souls, who has begun this in us, will certainly direct the same and teach [us] to his honor and our salvation, Amen.

Dear brethren and sisters, we who have been assembled in the Lord at Schleitheim on the Border, make known in points and articles to all who love God that as concerns us we are of one mind to abide in the Lord as God's obedient children, [his] sons and daughters, we who have been and shall be separated from the world in everything, [and] completely at peace. To

God alone be praise and glory without the contradiction of any brethren. In this we have perceived the oneness of the Spirit of our Father and of our common Christ with us. For the Lord is the Lord of peace and not of quarreling, as Paul points out. That you may understand in what articles this has been formulated you should observe and note [the following].

A very great offense has been introduced by certain false brethren among us, so that some have turned aside from the faith, in the way they intend to practice and observe the freedom of the Spirit and of Christ. But such have missed the truth and to their condemnation are given over to the lasciviousness and self-indulgence of the flesh. They think faith and love may do and permit everything, and nothing will harm them nor condemn them, since they are believers.

Observe, you who are God's members in Christ Jesus, that faith in the heavenly Father through Jesus Christ does not take such form. It does not produce and result in such things as these false brethren and sisters do teach. Guard yourselves and be warned of such people, for they do not serve our Father, but their father, the devil.

But you are not that way. For they that are Christ's have crucified the flesh with its passions and lusts. You understand me well and [know] the brethren whom we mean. Separate yourselves from them for they are perverted. Petition the Lord that they may have the knowledge which leads to repentance, and [pray] for us that we may have constancy to persevere in the way which we have espoused, for the honor of God and of Christ, his Son, Amen.

The articles which we discussed and on which we were of one mind are these: 1. Baptism; 2. The Ban [Excommunication]; 3. Breaking of Bread; 4. Separation from the Abomination; 5. Pastors in the Church; 6. The Sword; and 7. The Oath.

First. Observe concerning baptism: Baptism shall be given to all those who have learned repentance and amendment of life, and who believe truly that their sins are taken away by Christ, and to all those who walk in the resurrection of Jesus Christ, and wish to be buried with him in death, so that they may be resurrected with him, and to all those who with this significance request it [baptism] of us and demand it for themselves. This excludes all infant baptism, the highest and chief abomination of the pope. In this you have the foundation and testimony of the apostles (Matt. 28; Mark 16; Acts 2, 8, 16, 19). This we wish to hold simply, yet firmly and with assurance.

Second. We are agreed as follows on the ban: The ban shall be employed with all those who have given themselves to the Lord, to walk in his commandments, and with all those who are baptized into the one body of Christ and who are called brethren or sisters, and yet who slip sometimes and fall into error and sin, being inadvertently overtaken. The same shall be admonished twice in secret and the third time openly disciplined or banned according to the command of Christ (Matt. 18). But this shall be done according to the regulation of the Spirit (Matt. 5) before the breaking of bread, so that we may break and eat one bread, with one mind and in one love, and may drink of one cup.

Third. In the breaking of bread we are of one mind and are agreed [as follows]: All those who wish to break one bread in remembrance of the broken body of Christ, and all who wish to drink of one drink as a remembrance of the shed blood of Christ, shall be united beforehand by baptism in one body of Christ which is the church of God and whose head is Christ. For as Paul points out we cannot at the same time be partakers of the Lord's table and the table of devils; we cannot at the same time drink the cup of the Lord and the cup of the devil. That is, all those who have fellowship with the dead works of darkness have no part in the light. Therefore all who follow the devil and the world have no part with those who are called unto God out of the world. All who lie in evil have no part in the good.

Therefore it is and must be [thus]: Whoever has not been called by one God to one faith, to one baptism, to one Spirit, to one body, with all the children of God's church, cannot be made [into] one bread with them, as indeed must be done if one is truly to break bread according to the command of Christ.

Fourth. We are agreed [as follows] on separation: A separation shall be made from the evil and from the wickedness which the devil planted in the world; in this manner, simply that we shall not have fellowship with them [the wicked] and not run with them in the multitude of their abominations. This is the way it is: Since all who do not walk in the obedience of faith, and have not united themselves with God so that they wish to do his will, are a great abomination before God, it is not possible for anything to grow or issue from them except abominable things. For truly all creatures are in but two classes, good and bad, believing and unbelieving, darkness and light, the world and those who [have come] out of the world, God's temple and idols, Christ and Belial; and none can have part with the other.

To us then the command of the Lord is clear when he calls upon us to be separate from the evil and thus he will be our God and we shall be his sons and daughters.

He further admonishes us to withdraw from Babylon and the earthly Egypt that we may not be partakers of the pain and suffering which the Lord will bring upon them.

From this we should learn that everything that is not united with our God and Christ cannot be other than n abomination which we should shun and flee from. By this is meant all popish and antipopish works and church services, meetings and church attendance, drinking houses, civic affairs, the commitments [made in] unbelief and other things of that kind, which are highly regarded by the world and yet are carried on in flat contradiction to the command of God, in accordance with all the unrighteousness which is in the world. From all these things we shall be separated and have no part with them for they are nothing but an abomination, and they are the cause of our being hated before our Christ Jesus, who has set us free from the slavery of the flesh and fitted us for the service of God through the Spirit whom he has given us.

Therefore there will also unquestionably fall from us the unchristian, devilish weapons of force—such as sword, armor, and the like, and all their use [either] for friends or against one's enemies—by virtue of the word of Christ, Resist not [him that is] evil.

Fifth. We are agreed as follows on pastors in the church of God: The pastor in the church of God shall, as Paul has prescribed, be one who out-and-out has a good report of those who are outside the faith. This office shall be to read, to admonish and teach, to warn, to discipline, to ban in the church, to lead out in prayer for the advancement of all the brethren and sisters, to lift up the bread when it is to be broken, and in all things to see to the care of the body of Christ, in order that it may be built up and developed, and the mouth of the slanderer be stopped.

This one moreover shall be supported of the church which has chosen him, wherein he may be in need, so that he who serves the gospel may live of the gospel as the Lord has ordained. But if a pastor should do something requiring discipline, he shall not be dealt with except [on the testimony of] two or three witnesses. And when they sin they shall be disciplined before all in order that the others may fear.

But should it happen that through the cross this pastor should be banished or led to the Lord [through martyrdom] another shall be ordained in his place in the same hour so that God's little flock and people may not be destroyed.

Sixth. We are agreed as follows concerning the sword: The sword is ordained of God outside the perfection of Christ. It punishes and puts to death the wicked, and guards and protects the good. In the Law the sword was ordained for the punishment of the wicked and for their death, and the same [sword] is [now] ordained to be used by the worldly magistrates.

In the perfection of Christ, however, only the ban is used for a warning and for the excommunication of the one who has sinned, without putting the flesh to death—simply the warning and the command to sin no more.

Now it will be asked by many who do not recognize [this as] the will of Christ for us, whether a Christian may or should employ the sword against the wicked for the defense and protection of the good, or for the sake of love.

Our reply is unanimously as follows: Christ teaches and commands us to learn of him, for he is meek and lowly in heart and so shall we find rest to our souls. Also Christ says to the heathenish woman who was taken in adultery, not that one should stone her according to the Law of his Father (and yet he says, As the Father has commanded me, thus I do), but in mercy and forgiveness and warning, to sin no more. Such [an attitude] we also ought to take completely according to the rule of the ban.

Second, it will be asked concerning the sword, whether a Christian shall pass sentence in worldly disputes and strife such as unbelievers have with one another. This is our united answer. Christ did not wish to decide or pass judgment between brother and brother in the case of the inheritance, but refused to do so. Therefore we should do likewise.

Third, it will be asked concerning the sword, Shall one be a magistrate if one should be chosen as such? The answer is as follows: They wished to make Christ king, but he fled and did not view it as the arrangement of his Father. Thus shall we do as he did, and follow him, and so shall we not walk in darkness. For he himself says, He who wishes to come after me, let him deny himself and take up his cross and follow me. Also, he himself forbids [employment of] the force of the sword, saying, The worldly princes lord it over them . . . but not so shall it be with you. Further, Paul says, Whom God did foreknow he also did predestinate to be conformed to the image of his Son. Also Peter says, Christ has suffered (not ruled) and left us an example, that you should follow his steps.

Finally it will be observed that it is not appropriate for a Christian to serve as a magistrate because of these points: The government magistracy is according to the flesh, but the Christian's is according to the Spirit; their houses and dwelling remain in this world, but the Christian's are in heaven; their citizenship is in this world, but the Christian's citizenship is in heaven; the weapons of their conflict and war are carnal and against the flesh only, but the Christian's weapons are spiritual, against the fortification of the devil. The worldlings are armed with steel and iron, but the Christian is armed with the armor of God, with truth, righteousness, peace, faith, salvation, and the Word of God. In brief, as is the mind of Christ toward us, so shall the mind of the members of the body of Christ be through him in all things, that there may be no schism in the body through which it would be destroyed. For every kingdom divided against itself will be destroyed. Now since Christ is as it is written of him, his members must also be the same, that his body may remain complete and united to its own advancement and upbuilding.

Seventh. We are agreed as follows concerning the oath: The oath is a confirmation among those who are quarreling or making promises. In the Law it is commanded to be performed in God's name, but only in truth, not falsely. Christ, who teaches the perfection of the Law, prohibits all swearing to his [followers], whether true or false—neither by heaven, nor by the earth, nor by Jerusalem, nor by our head—and that for the reason which he shortly thereafter gives, For you are not able to make one hair white or black. So you see it is for this reason that all swearing is forbidden: we cannot fulfill that which we promise when we swear, for we cannot change [even] the very least thing on us.

Now there are some who do not give credence to the simple command of God, but object with this question: Well now, did not God swear to Abraham by himself (since he was God) when he promised him that he would be with him and that he would be his God if he would keep his commandments—why then should I not also swear when I promise to someone? Answer: Hear what the Scripture says: God, since he wished more abundantly to show unto the heirs the immutability of his counsel, inserted an oath, that by two immutable things (in which it is impossible for God to lie) we might have a strong consolation. Observe the meaning of this Scripture: What God forbids you to do, he has power to do, for everything is possible for him. God swore an oath to Abraham, says the Scripture, so that he might show that his counsel is immutable. That is, no one can withstand or thwart his will; therefore he can keep his oath. But we can do nothing, as is said above by Christ, to keep or perform [our oaths]: therefore we shall not swear at all.

Then others further say as follows: It is not forbidden of God to swear in the New Testament, when it is actually commanded in the Old, but it is forbidden only to swear by heaven, earth, Jerusalem, and our head. Answer: Hear the Scripture, he who swears by heaven swears by God's throne and by him who sitteth thereon. Observe: it is forbidden to swear by heaven, which is only the throne of God. How much more is it forbidden [to swear] by God himself! Ye fools and blind, which is greater, the throne or him that sitteth thereon?

Further some say, Because evil is now [in the world, and] because man needs God for [the establishment of] the truth, so did the apostles Peter and Paul also swear. Answer: Peter and Paul only testify of that which God promised to Abraham with the oath. They themselves promise nothing, as the example indicates clearly. Testifying and swearing are two different things. For when a person swears he is in the first place promising future things, as Christ was promised to Abraham

whom we a long time afterwards received. But when a person
bears testimony he is testifying about the present, whether it
is good or evil, as Simeon spoke to Mary about Christ and testified, Behold this [child] is set for the fall and rising of many
in Israel, and for a sign which shall be spoken against.

Christ also taught us along the same line when he said, Let
your communication be Yea, yea; Nay, nay; for whatsoever is
more than these cometh of evil. He says, Your speech or word
shall be yea and nay. [However] when one does not wish to
understand, he remains closed to the meaning. Christ is simply Yea and Nay, and all those who seek him will understand
his Word. Amen.

Dear brethren and sisters in the Lord: These are the articles
of certain brethren who had heretofore been in error and who
had failed to agree in the true understanding, so that many
weaker consciences were perplexed, causing the name of God
to be greatly slandered. Therefore there has been a great need
for us to become of one mind in the Lord, which has come to
pass. To God be praise and glory!

Now since you have so well understood the will of God
which has been made known by us, it will be necessary for you
to achieve perseveringly, without interruption, the known will
of God. For you know well what the servant who sinned knowingly heard as his recompense.

Everything which you have unwittingly done and confessed
as evildoing is forgiven you through the believing prayer which
is offered by us in our meeting for all our shortcomings and
guilt. [This state is yours] through the gracious forgiveness of
God and through the blood of Jesus Christ. Amen.

Keep watch on all who do not walk according to the sim-
plicity of the divine truth which is stated in this letter from [the
decisions of] our meeting, so that everyone among us will be
governed by the rule of the ban and henceforth the entry of
false brethren and sisters among us may be prevented.

Eliminate from you that which is evil and the Lord will be
your God and you will be his sons and daughters.

Dear brethren, keep in mind what Paul admonishes
Timothy when he says, The grace of God that bringeth salvation hath appeared to all men, teaching us that, denying
ungodliness and worldly lusts, we should live soberly, righ-

teously, and godly, in this present world; looking for that blessed hope, and the glorious appearing of the great God and our Savior Jesus Christ; who gave himself for us, that he might redeem us from all iniquity, and purify unto himself a people of his own, zealous of good works. Think on this and exercise yourselves therein and the God of peace will be with you.

May the name of God be hallowed eternally and highly praised, Amen. May the Lord give you his peace, Amen.

The Acts of Schleitheim on the Border [Canton Schaffhausen, Switzerland], on Matthias' [Day], Anno MDXXVII.

4

Martin Luther's
Small Catechism (1529)

Luther wrote his Small Catechism, a simple manual of instruction in the Christian faith, after one of the greatest disappointments of his life. In 1527 and 1528, Luther and his associates were asked by their prince to inspect the churches of the region. The results were profoundly disappointing. Ignorance reigned among clergy and laity alike, and the schools were in ruins. To meet the need for popular instruction Luther immediately drew up wall charts containing simple explanations of the Ten Commandments, the Lord's Prayer, and the Apostles' Creed. When his colleagues delayed in their own efforts at providing educational materials, Luther pulled together his placards and published them as a short, simple exposition of the faith. Many other catechisms would be written by Lutheran pastors and theologians in the sixteenth century, but this one remained the norm.

Luther intended his catechism to be an aid to family worship. In its preface he condemns parents who, by neglecting the Christian education of their children, have become the

Reprinted from Book of Concord, edited by Theodore G. Tappert, copyright © 1959 Fortress Press, by permission of Augsburg Fortress.

"worst enemies of God and man." Almost all of the catechism's sections begin with remarks directed at the head of the house (e.g., "The Ten Commandments in the plain form in which the head of the family shall teach it to his household"). Such instructions suggest that Luther was coming to see more clearly the need for order, discipline, and regular practice in the new Protestant movement.

The catechism contains nine sections, each a series of questions and answers. These sections treat—as was common with most catechisms of the period—the Ten Commandments, the Apostles' Creed, the Lord's Prayer, baptism, confession and absolution, and the Lord's supper. They also include instructions for morning and evening prayers, grace at meals, and a "Table of Duties" made up of scriptural passages "selected for various estates and conditions of men, by which they may be admonished to do their respective duties." These expositions, it is worth noting, are remarkably free of the polemics that Luther employed so vigorously in many of his other writings.

Much of the influence of Lutheranism around the world can be traced to the success of this catechism in expressing the profound truths of the faith in a language that all can understand. Unlike some Reformed confessions, Luther's Small Catechism lays out the Ten Commandments before describing the work of Christ, thus emphasizing Luther's conviction that the primary purpose of God's Law is to drive the sinner to Christ. The catechism's exposition of the creed focuses on the free gift of salvation in Christ. And its sections on baptism and the Lord's supper expound the views—mediating between Roman Catholic sacramentalism and Protestant mere symbolism—which Luther developed fully in lengthy theological works.

The Small Catechism became part of the *Book of Concord*, which was assembled in Germany in 1580 as an effort to end doctrinal strife. Among the other documents included in this authoritative collection of Lutheran confessions was Luther's Large Catechism, a series of sermons, directed this time as much to pastors as to the laity, that expounded the Ten Commandments, the Apostles' Creed, the Lord's Prayer, and the sacraments at greater length.

Text

The Book of Concord: The Confessions of the Evangelical Lutheran Church. Translated and edited by Theodore G. Tappert, 338–56. Philadelphia: Fortress, 1959.

Additional Reading

Bornkamm, Heinrich. *Luther in Mid-Career, 1521–1530.* Philadelphia: Fortress, 1983.

Luther, Martin. "The Large Catechism." In *The Book of Concord: The Confessions of the Evangelical Lutheran Church,* trans. and ed. Theodore G. Tappert, 357–461. Philadelphia: Fortress, 1959.

Reu, Johann Michael. *Dr. Martin Luther's Small Catechism: A History of Its Origin, Its Distribution, and Its Use.* Chicago: Wartburg, 1929.

Strauss, Gerald. *Luther's House of Learning: Indoctrination of the Young in the German Reformation.* Baltimore: Johns Hopkins University Press, 1978.

Enchiridion [i.e., Handbook] The Small Catechism of Dr. Martin Luther for Ordinary Pastors and Preachers

[Preface]

Grace, mercy, and peace in Jesus Christ, our Lord, from Martin Luther to all faithful, godly pastors and preachers.

The deplorable conditions which I recently encountered when I was a visitor constrained me to prepare this brief and simple catechism or statement of Christian teaching. Good God, what wretchedness I beheld! The common people, especially those who live in the country, have no knowledge whatever of Christian teaching, and unfortunately many pastors are quite incompetent and unfitted for teaching. Although the people are supposed to be Christian, are baptized, and receive the holy sacrament, they do not know the Lord's Prayer, the Creed, or the Ten Commandments, they live as if they were pigs and irrational beasts, and now that the gospel has been restored they have mastered the fine art of abusing liberty.

How will you bishops answer for it before Christ that you have so shamefully neglected the people and paid no attention at all to the duties of your office? May you escape punishment for this! You withhold the cup in the Lord's supper and insist on the observance of human laws, yet you do not take the slightest interest in teaching the people the Lord's Prayer, the Creed, the Ten Commandments, or a single part of the Word of God. Woe to you forever!

I therefore beg of you for God's sake, my beloved brethren who are pastors and preachers, that you take the duties of your office seriously, that you have pity on the people who are entrusted to your care, and that you help me to teach the catechism to the people, especially those who are young. Let those who lack the qualifications to do better at least take this booklet and these forms and read them to the people word for word in this manner:

In the first place, the preacher should take the utmost care to avoid changes or variations in the text and wording of the Ten Commandments, the Creed, the Lord's Prayer, the sacraments, and the like. On the contrary, he should adopt one form, adhere to it, and use it repeatedly year after year. Young and inexperienced people must be instructed on the basis of a uniform, fixed text and form. They are easily confused if a teacher employs one form now and another form—perhaps with the intention of making improvements—later on. In this way all the time and labor will be lost.

This was well understood by our good fathers, who were accustomed to using the same form in teaching the Lord's Prayer, the Creed, and the Ten Commandments. We, too, should teach these things to the young and unlearned in such a way that we do not alter a single syllable or recite the catechism differently from year to year. Choose the form that pleases you, therefore, and adhere to it henceforth. When you preach to intelligent and educated people, you are at liberty to exhibit your learning and to discuss these topics from different angles and in such a variety of ways as you may be capable of. But when you are teaching the young, adhere to a fixed and unchanging form and method. Begin by teaching them the Ten Commandments, the Creed, the Lord's Prayer, and the like, following the text word for word so that the young may repeat these things after you and retain them in their memory.

If any refuse to receive your instructions, tell them that they deny Christ and are no Christians. They should not be admitted to the sacrament, be accepted as sponsors in baptism, or be allowed to participate in any Christian privileges. On the contrary, they should be turned over to the pope and his officials, and even to the devil himself. In addition, parents and employers should refuse to furnish them with food and drink and should notify them that the prince is disposed to banish such rude people from his land.

Although we cannot and should not compel anyone to believe, we should nevertheless insist that the people learn to know how to distinguish between right and wrong according to the standards of those among whom they live and make their living. For anyone who desires to reside in a city is bound to know and observe the laws under whose protection he lives, no matter whether he is a believer or, at heart, a scoundrel or knave.

In the second place, after the people have become familiar with the text, teach them what it means. For this purpose, take the explanations in this booklet, or choose any other brief and fixed explanations which you may prefer, and adhere to them without changing a single syllable, as stated above with reference to the text. Moreover, allow yourself ample time, for it is not necessary to take up all the parts at once. They can be presented one at a time. When the learners have a proper understanding of the first commandment, proceed to the second commandment, and so on. Otherwise they will be so overwhelmed that they will hardly remember anything at all.

In the third place, after you have thus taught this brief catechism, take up a large catechism so that the people may have a richer and fuller understanding. Expound every commandment, petition, and part, pointing out their respective obligations, benefits, dangers, advantages, and disadvantages, as you will find all of this treated at length in the many books written for this purpose. Lay the greatest weight on those commandments or other parts which seem to require special attention

among the people where you are. For example, the seventh
commandment, which treats of stealing, must be emphasized
when instructing laborers and shopkeepers, and even farmers
and servants, for many of these are guilty of dishonesty and
thievery. So, too, the fourth commandment must be stressed
when instructing children and the common people in order
that they may be encouraged to be orderly, faithful, obedient,
and peaceful. Always adduce many examples from the
Scriptures to show how God punished and blessed.

You should also take pains to urge governing authorities
and parents to rule wisely and educate their children. They
must be shown that they are obliged to do so, and that they are
guilty of damnable sin if they do not do so, for by such neglect
they undermine and lay waste both the kingdom of God and
the kingdom of the world and are the worst enemies of God
and man. Make very plain to them the shocking evils they
introduce when they refuse their aid in the training of children
to become pastors, preachers, notaries, and the like, and tell
them that God will inflict awful punishments on them for these
sins. It is necessary to preach about such things. The extent to
which parents and governing authorities sin in this respect is
beyond telling. The devil also has a horrible purpose in mind.

Finally, now that the people are freed from the tyranny of
the pope, they are unwilling to receive the sacrament and they
treat it with contempt. Here, too, there is need of exhortation,
but with this understanding: No one is to be compelled to
believe or to receive the sacrament, no law is to be made concerning it, and no time or place should be appointed for it. We
should so preach that, of their own accord and without any
law, the people will desire the sacrament and, as it were, compel us pastors to administer it to them. This can be done by
telling them: It is to be feared that anyone who does not desire
to receive the sacrament at least three or four times a year
despises the sacrament and is no Christian, just as he is no
Christian who does not hear and believe the gospel. Christ did
not say, "Omit this," or "Despise this," but he said, "Do this, as
often as you drink it." Surely he wishes that this be done and
not that it be omitted and despised. "*Do* this," he said.

He who does not highly esteem the sacrament suggests
thereby that he has no sin, no flesh, no devil, no world, no
death, no hell. That is to say, he believes in none of these,

although he is deeply immersed in them and is held captive by
the devil. On the other hand, he suggests that he needs no
grace, no life, no paradise, no heaven, no Christ, no God, nothing good at all. For if he believed that he was involved in so
much that is evil and was in need of so much that is good, he
would not neglect the sacrament in which aid is afforded
against such evil and in which such good is bestowed. It is not
necessary to compel him by any law to receive the sacrament,
for he will hasten to it of his own accord, he will feel constrained to receive it, he will insist that you administer it to
him.

Accordingly you are not to make a law of this, as the pope
has done. All you need to do is clearly to set forth the advantage and disadvantage, the benefit and loss, the blessing and
danger connected with this sacrament. Then the people will
come of their own accord and without compulsion on your
part. But if they refuse to come, let them be, and tell them that
those who do not feel and acknowledge their great need and
God's gracious help belong to the devil. If you do not give such
admonitions, or if you adopt odious laws on the subject, it is
your own fault if the people treat the sacrament with contempt. How can they be other than negligent if you fail to do
your duty and remain silent? So it is up to you, dear pastor and
preacher! Our office has become something different from
what it was under the pope. It is now a ministry of grace and
salvation. It subjects us to greater burdens and labors, dangers
and temptations, with little reward or gratitude from the
world. But Christ himself will be our reward if we labor faithfully. The Father of all grace grant it! To him be praise and
thanks forever, through Christ, our Lord. Amen.

[I]
The Ten Commandments in the plain form in which the head of the family shall teach them to his household

The First

"You shall have no other gods."
What does this mean?
Answer: We should fear, love, and trust in God above all
things.

The Second

"You shall not take the name of the Lord your God in vain."
What does this mean?
Answer: We should fear and love God, and so we should not use his name to curse, swear, practice magic, lie, or deceive, but in every time of need call upon him, pray to him, praise him, and give him thanks.

The Third

"Remember the Sabbath day, to keep it holy."
What does this mean?
Answer: We should fear and love God, and so we should not despise his Word and the preaching of the same, but deem it holy and gladly hear and learn it.

The Fourth

"Honor your father and your mother."
What does this mean?
Answer: We should fear and love God, and so we should not despise our parents and superiors, nor provoke them to anger, but honor, serve, obey, love, and esteem them.

The Fifth

"You shall not kill."
What does this mean?
Answer: We should love and fear God, and so we should not endanger our neighbor's life, nor cause him any harm, but help and befriend him in every necessity of life.

The Sixth

"You shall not commit adultery."
What does this mean?
Answer: We should fear and love God, and so we should lead a chaste and pure life in word and deed, each one loving and honoring his wife or her husband.

The Seventh

"You shall not steal."
What does this mean?
Answer: We should fear and love God, and so we should not

rob our neighbor of his money or his property, nor bring them into our possession by dishonest trade or by dealing in shoddy wares, but help him to improve and protect his income and property.

The Eighth

"You shall not bear false witness against your neighbor."
What does this mean?

Answer: We should fear and love God, and so we should not tell lies about our neighbor, nor betray, slander, or defame him, but should apologize for him, speak well of him, and interpret charitably all that he does.

The Ninth

"You shall not covet your neighbor's house."
What does this mean?

Answer: We should fear and love God, and so we should not seek by craftiness to gain possession of our neighbor's inheritance or home, nor to obtain them under pretext of legal right, but be of service and help to him so that he may keep what is his.

The Tenth

"You shall not covet your neighbor's wife, or his manservant, or his maidservant, or his ox, or his ass, or anything that is your neighbor's."
What does this mean?

Answer: We should fear and love God, and so we should not abduct, estrange, or entice away our neighbor's wife, servants, or cattle, but encourage them to remain and discharge their duty to him.

[Conclusion]

What does God declare concerning all these commandments?

Answer: He says, "I the Lord your God am a jealous God, visiting the iniquity of the fathers upon the children to the third and the fourth generation of those who hate me, but showing steadfast love to thousands of those who love me and keep my commandments."

What does this mean?

Answer: God threatens to punish all who transgress these commandments. We should therefore fear his wrath and not disobey these commandments. On the other hand, he promises grace and every blessing to all who keep them. We should therefore love him, trust in him, and cheerfully do what he has commanded.

[II]
The Creed in the plain form in which the head of the family shall teach it to his household

The First Article: Creation

"I believe in God, the Father almighty, Maker of heaven and earth."
What does this mean?
Answer: I believe that God has created me and all that exists; that he has given me and still sustains my body and soul, all my limbs and senses, my reason and all the faculties of my mind, together with food and clothing, house and home, family and property; that he provides me daily and abundantly with all the necessities of life, protects me from all danger, and preserves me from all evil. All this he does out of his pure, fatherly, and divine goodness and mercy, without any merit or worthiness on my part. For all of this I am bound to thank, praise, serve, and obey him. This is most certainly true.

The Second Article: Redemption

"And in Jesus Christ, his only Son, our Lord: who was conceived by the Holy Spirit, born of the virgin Mary, suffered under Pontius Pilate, was crucified, dead, and buried: he descended into hell, the third day he rose from the dead, he ascended into heaven, and is seated on the right hand of God, the Father almighty, whence he shall come to judge the living and the dead."
What does this mean?
Answer: I believe that Jesus Christ, true God, begotten of the Father from eternity, and also true man, born of the virgin Mary, is my Lord, who has redeemed me, a lost and condemned creature, delivered me and freed me from all sins, from death, and from the power of the devil, not with silver and gold but with his holy and precious blood and with his

innocent sufferings and death, in order that I may be his, live under him in his kingdom, and serve him in everlasting righteousness, innocence, and blessedness, even as he is risen from the dead and lives and reigns to all eternity. This is most certainly true.

The Third Article: Sanctification

"I believe in the Holy Spirit, the holy Christian church, the communion of saints, the forgiveness of sins, the resurrection of the body, and the life everlasting. Amen."
What does this mean?
Answer: I believe that by my own reason or strength I cannot believe in Jesus Christ, my Lord, or come to him. But the Holy Spirit has called me through the gospel, enlightened me with his gifts, and sanctified and preserved me in true faith, just as he calls, gathers, enlightens, and sanctifies the whole Christian church on earth and preserves it in union with Jesus Christ in the one true faith. In this Christian church he daily and abundantly forgives all my sins, and the sins of all believers, and on the last day he will raise me and all the dead and will grant eternal life to me and to all who believe in Christ. This is most certainly true.

[III]
The Lord's Prayer in the plain form in which the head of the family shall teach it to his household

[*Introduction*]

"Our Father who art in heaven."
What does this mean?
Answer: Here God would encourage us to believe that he is truly our Father and we are truly his children in order that we may approach him boldly and confidently in prayer, even as beloved children approach their dear father.

The First Petition

"Hallowed be thy name."
What does this mean?
Answer: To be sure, God's name is holy in itself, but we pray in this petition that it may also be holy for us.

How is this done?

Answer: When the Word of God is taught clearly and purely and we, as children of God, lead holy lives in accordance with it. Help us to do this, dear Father in heaven! But whoever teaches and lives otherwise than as the Word of God teaches, profanes the name of God among us. From this preserve us, heavenly Father!

The Second Petition

"Thy kingdom come."

What does this mean?

Answer: To be sure, the kingdom of God comes of itself, without our prayer, but we pray in this petition that it may also come to us.

How is this done?

Answer: When the heavenly Father gives us his Holy Spirit so that by his grace we may believe his holy Word and live a godly life, both here in time and hereafter forever.

The Third Petition

"Thy will be done, on earth as it is in heaven."

What does this mean?

Answer: To be sure, the good and gracious will of God is done without our prayer, but we pray in this petition that it may also be done by us.

How is this done?

Answer: When God curbs and destroys every evil counsel and purpose of the devil, of the world, and of our flesh which would hinder us from hallowing his name and prevent the coming of his kingdom, and when he strengthens us and keeps us steadfast in his Word and in faith even to the end. This is his good and gracious will.

The Fourth Petition

"Give us this day our daily bread."

What does this mean?

Answer: To be sure, God provides daily bread, even to the wicked, without our prayer, but we pray in this petition that God may make us aware of his gifts and enable us to receive our daily bread with thanksgiving.

What is meant by daily bread?

Answer: Everything required to satisfy our bodily needs, such as food and clothing, house and home, fields and flocks, money and property; a pious spouse and good children, trustworthy servants, godly and faithful rulers, good government; seasonable weather, peace and health, order and honor; true friends, faithful neighbors, and the like.

The Fifth Petition

"And forgive us our debts, as we also have forgiven our debtors."

What does this mean?

Answer: We pray in this petition that our heavenly Father may not look upon our sins, and on their account deny our prayers, for we neither merit nor deserve those things for which we pray. Although we sin daily and deserve nothing but punishment, we nevertheless pray that God may grant us all things by his grace. And assuredly we on our part will heartily forgive and cheerfully do good to those who may sin against us.

The Sixth Petition

"And lead us not into temptation."

What does this mean?

Answer: God tempts no one to sin, but we pray in this petition that God may so guard and preserve us that the devil, the world, and our flesh may not deceive us or mislead us into unbelief, despair, and other great and shameful sins, but that, although we may be so tempted, we may finally prevail and gain the victory.

The Seventh Petition

"But deliver us from evil."

What does this mean?

Answer: We pray in this petition, as in a summary, that our Father in heaven may deliver us from all manner of evil, whether it affect body or soul, property or reputation, and that at last, when the hour of death comes, he may grant us a blessed end and graciously take us from this world of sorrow to himself in heaven.

[*Conclusion*]

"*Amen.*"

What does this mean?

Answer: It means that I should be assured that such petitions are acceptable to our heavenly Father and are heard by him, for he himself commanded us to pray like this and promised to hear us. "Amen, amen" means "Yes, yes, it shall be so."

[IV]
The Sacrament of Holy Baptism in the plain form in which the head of the family shall teach it to his household

First

What is baptism?

Answer: Baptism is not merely water, but it is water used according to God's command and connected with God's Word.

What is this Word of God?

Answer: As recorded in Matthew 28:19, our Lord Christ said, "Go therefore and make disciples of all nations, baptizing them in the name of the Father and of the Son and of the Holy Spirit."

Second

What gifts or benefits does baptism bestow?

Answer: It effects forgiveness of sins, delivers from death and the devil, and grants eternal salvation to all who believe, as the Word and promise of God declare.

What is this Word and promise of God?

Answer: As recorded in Mark 16:16, our Lord Christ said, "He who believes and is baptized will be saved; but he who does not believe will be condemned."

Third

How can water produce such great effects?

Answer: It is not the water that produces these effects, but the Word of God connected with the water, and our faith which relies on the Word of God connected with the water. For without the Word of God the water is merely water and no baptism. But when connected with the Word of God it is a baptism, that is, a gracious water of life and a washing of regeneration in the Holy Spirit, as Saint Paul wrote to Titus (3:5–8), "He saved us by the washing of regeneration and renewal in the Holy Spirit, which he poured out upon us richly through Jesus Christ our Savior, so that we might be justified by his grace and become heirs in hope of eternal life. The saying is sure."

Fourth

What does such baptizing with water signify?

Answer: It signifies that the old Adam in us, together with all sins and evil lusts, should be drowned by daily sorrow and repentance and be put to death, and that the new man should come forth daily and rise up, cleansed and righteous, to live forever in God's presence.

Where is this written?

Answer: In Romans 6:4, Saint Paul wrote, "We were buried therefore with him by baptism into death, so that as Christ was raised from the dead by the glory of the Father, we too might walk in newness of life."

[V]
[Confession and Absolution] How Plain People Are to Be Taught to Confess

What is confession?

Answer: Confession consists of two parts. One is that we confess our sins. The other is that we receive absolution or forgiveness from the confessor as from God himself, by no means doubting but firmly believing that our sins are thereby forgiven before God in heaven.

What sins should we confess?

Answer: Before God we should acknowledge that we are guilty of all manner of sins, even those of which we are not aware, as we do in the Lord's Prayer. Before the confessor, however, we should confess only those sins of which we have knowledge and which trouble us.

What are such sins?

Answer: Reflect on your condition in the light of the Ten Commandments: whether you are a father or mother, a son or daughter, a master or servant; whether you have been disobedient, unfaithful, lazy, ill-tempered, or quarrelsome; whether you have harmed anyone by word or deed; and whether you have stolen, neglected, or wasted anything, or done other evil.

Please give me a brief form of confession.

Answer: You should say to the confessor: "Dear pastor, please hear my confession and declare that my sins are forgiven for God's sake."

"Proceed."

"I, a poor sinner, confess before God that I am guilty of all sins. In particular I confess in your presence that, as a manservant or maidservant, I am unfaithful to my master, for here and there I have not done what I was told. I have made my master angry, caused him to curse, neglected to do my duty, and caused him to suffer loss. I have also been immodest in word and deed. I have quarreled with my equals. I have grumbled and sworn at my mistress. For all this I am sorry and pray for grace. I mean to do better."

A master or mistress may say: "In particular I confess in your presence that I have not been faithful in training my children, servants, and spouse to the glory of God. I have cursed. I have set a bad example by my immodest language and actions. I have injured my neighbor by speaking evil of him, overcharging him, giving him inferior goods and short measure." Masters and mistresses should add whatever else they have done contrary to God's commandments and to their action in life.

If, however, anyone does not feel that his conscience is burdened by such or by greater sins, he should not worry, nor should he search for and invent other sins, for this would turn confession into torture; he should simply mention one or two sins of which he is aware. For example, "In particular I confess that I once cursed. On one occasion I also spoke indecently. And I neglected this or that." Let this suffice.

If you have knowledge of no sin at all (which is quite unlikely), you should mention none in particular, but receive forgiveness upon the general confession which you make to God in the presence of the confessor.

Then the confessor shall say: "God be merciful to you and strengthen your faith. Amen."

Again he shall say: "Do you believe that this forgiveness is the forgiveness of God?"

Answer: "Yes, I do."

Then he shall say: "Be it done for you as you have believed. According to the command of our Lord Jesus Christ, I forgive you your sins in the name of the Father and of the Son and of the Holy Spirit. Amen. Go in peace."

A confessor will know additional passages of the Scriptures with which to comfort and to strengthen the faith of those whose consciences are heavily burdened or who are distressed and sorely tried. This is intended simply as an ordinary form of confession for plain people.

[VI]
The Sacrament of the Altar in the plain form in which the head of the family shall teach it to his household

What is the sacrament of the altar?

Answer: Instituted by Christ himself, it is the true body and blood of our Lord Jesus Christ, under the bread and wine, given to us Christians to eat and drink.

Where is this written?

Answer: The holy evangelists Matthew, Mark, and Luke, and also Saint Paul, write thus: "Our Lord Jesus Christ, on the night when he was betrayed, took bread, and when he had given thanks, he broke it, and gave it to the disciples and said, 'Take, eat; this is my body which is given for you. Do this in remembrance of me.' In the same way also he took the cup, after supper, and when he had given thanks he gave it to them, saying, 'Drink of it, all of you. This cup is the new covenant in my blood, which is poured out for many for the forgiveness of sins. Do this, as often as you drink it, in remembrance of me.'"

What is the benefit of such eating and drinking?

Answer: We are told in the words "for you" and "for the forgiveness of sins." By these words the forgiveness of sins, life, and salvation are given to us in the sacrament, for where there is forgiveness of sins, there are also life and salvation.

How can bodily eating and drinking produce such great effects?

Answer: The eating and drinking do not in themselves produce them, but the words "for you" and "for the forgiveness of sins." These words, when accompanied by the bodily eating and drinking, are the chief thing in the sacrament, and he who believes these words has what they say and declare: the forgiveness of sins.

Who, then, receives this sacrament worthily?

Answer: Fasting and bodily preparation are a good external discipline, but he is truly worthy and well prepared who believes these words "for you" and "for the forgiveness of sins." On the other hand, he who does not believe these words, or doubts them, is unworthy and unprepared, for the words "for you" require truly believing hearts.

[VII]
[Morning and Evening Prayers] How the head of the family shall teach his household to say morning and evening prayers

In the morning, when you rise, make the sign of the cross and say, "In the name of God, the Father, the Son, and the Holy Spirit. Amen."

Then, kneeling or standing, say the Apostles' Creed and the Lord's Prayer. Then you may say this prayer:

"I give thee thanks, heavenly Father, through thy dear Son Jesus Christ, that thou hast protected me through the night from all harm and danger. I beseech thee to keep me this day, too, from all sin and evil, that in all my thoughts, words, and deeds I may please thee. Into thy hands I commend my body and soul and all that is mine. Let thy holy angel have charge of me, that the wicked one may have no power over me. Amen."

After singing a hymn (possibly a hymn on the Ten Commandments) or whatever your devotion may suggest, you should go to your work joyfully.

In the evening, when you retire, make the sign of the cross and say, "In the name of God, the Father, the Son, and the Holy Spirit. Amen."

Then, kneeling or standing, say the Apostles' Creed and the Lord's Prayer. Then you may say this prayer:

"I give thee thanks, heavenly Father, through thy dear Son Jesus Christ, that thou hast this day graciously protected me. I beseech thee to forgive all my sin and the wrong which I have done. Graciously protect me during the coming night. Into thy hands I commend my body and soul and all that is mine. Let thy holy angels have charge of me, that the wicked one may have no power over me. Amen."

Then quickly lie down and sleep in peace.

[VIII]
[Grace at Table] How the head of the family shall teach his household to offer blessing and thanksgiving at table

[*Blessing before Eating*]

When children and the whole household gather at the table, they should reverently fold their hands and say:

"The eyes of all look to thee, O Lord, and thou givest them their food in due season. Thou openest thy hand; thou satisfiest the desire of every living thing."

(It is to be observed that "satisfying the desire of every living thing" means that all creatures receive enough to eat to make them joyful and of good cheer. Greed and anxiety about food prevent such satisfaction.)

Then the Lord's Prayer should be said, and afterwards this prayer:

"Lord God, heavenly Father, bless us, and these thy gifts which of thy bountiful goodness thou hast bestowed on us, through Jesus Christ our Lord. Amen."

[*Thanksgiving after Eating*]

After eating, likewise, they should fold their hands reverently and say:

"O give thanks to the Lord, for he is good; for his steadfast love endures forever. He gives to the beasts their food, and to the young ravens which cry. His delight is not in the strength of the horse, nor his pleasure in the legs of a man; but the Lord takes pleasure in those who fear him, in those who hope in his steadfast love."

Then the Lord's Prayer should be said, and afterwards this prayer:

"We give thee thanks, Lord God, our Father, for all thy benefits, through Jesus Christ our Lord, who lives and reigns forever. Amen."

[IX]
Table of Duties consisting of certain passages of the Scriptures, selected for various estates and conditions of men, by which they may be admonished to do their respective duties

Bishops, Pastors, and Preachers

"A bishop must be above reproach, married only once, temperate, sensible, dignified, hospitable, an apt teacher, no drunkard, not violent but gentle, not quarrelsome, and no lover of money. He must manage his own household well, keeping his children submissive and respectful in every way. He must not be a recent convert" (1 Tim. 3:2–6).

Duties Christians Owe Their Teachers and Pastors

"Remain in the same house, eating and drinking what they provide, for the laborer deserves his wages" (Luke 10:7). "The Lord commanded that those who proclaim the gospel should get their living by the gospel" (1 Cor. 9:14). "Let him who is taught the word share all good things with him who teaches. Do not be deceived; God is not mocked" (Gal. 6:6–7). "Let the elders who rule well be considered worthy of double honor, especially those who labor in preaching and teaching; for the Scripture says, 'You shall not muzzle an ox when it is treading out the grain,' and 'The laborer deserves his wages'" (1 Tim. 5:17–18). "We beseech you, brethren, to respect those who labor among you and are over you in the Lord and admonish you, and to esteem them very highly in love because of their work. Be at peace among yourselves" (1 Thess. 5:12–13). "Obey your leaders and submit to them; for they are keeping watch over your souls, as men who will have to give account. Let them do this joyfully, and not sadly, for that would be of no advantage to you" (Heb. 13:17).

Governing Authorities

"Let every person be subject to the governing authorities. For there is no authority except from God, and those that exist have been instituted by God. Therefore he who resists the authorities resists what God has appointed, and those who resist will incur judgment. He who is in authority does not bear the sword in vain; he is the servant of God to execute his wrath on the wrongdoer" (Rom. 13:1–4).

Duties Subjects Owe to Governing Authorities

"Render therefore to Caesar the things that are Caesar's, and to God the things that are God's" (Matt. 22:21). "Let every person be subject to the governing authorities. Therefore one must be subject not only to avoid God's wrath but also for the sake of conscience. For the same reason you also pay taxes, for the authorities are ministers of God, attending to this very thing. Pay all of them their dues, taxes to whom taxes are due, revenue to whom revenue is due, respect to whom respect is due, honor to whom honor is due" (Rom. 13:1, 5–7). "I urge that supplications, prayers, intercessions, and thanksgivings be made for all men, for kings and all who are in high positions, that we may lead a quiet and peaceable life, godly and respectful in every way" (1 Tim. 2:1–2). "Remind them to be submissive to rulers and authorities, to be obedient, to be ready for any honest work" (Titus 3:1). "Be subject for the Lord's sake to every human institution, whether it be to the emperor as supreme, or to governors as sent by him to punish those who do wrong and to praise those who do right" (1 Pet. 2: 13–14).

Husbands

"You husbands, live considerately with your wives, bestowing honor on the woman as the weaker sex, since you are joint heirs of the grace of life, in order that your prayers may not be hindered" (1 Pet. 3:7). "Husbands, love your wives, and do not be harsh with them" (Col. 3:19).

Wives

"You wives, be submissive to your husbands, as Sarah obeyed Abraham, calling him lord. And you are now her children if you do right and let nothing terrify you" (1 Pet. 3:1, 6).

Parents

"Fathers, do not provoke your children to anger, lest they become discouraged, but bring them up in the discipline and instruction of the Lord" (Eph. 6:4; Col. 3:21).

Children

"Children, obey your parents in the Lord, for this is right. 'Honor your father and mother' (this is the first commandment with a promise) 'that it may be well with you and that you may live long on the earth'" (Eph. 6:1–3).

Laborers and Servants, Male and Female

"Be obedient to those who are your earthly masters, with fear and trembling, with singleness of heart, as to Christ; not in the way of eye-service, as men-pleasers, but as servants of Christ, doing the will of God from the heart, rendering service with a good will as to the Lord and not to men, knowing that whatever good anyone does, he will receive the same again from the Lord, whether he is a slave or free" (Eph. 6:5–8).

Masters and Mistresses

"Masters, do the same to them, and forbear threatening, knowing that he who is both their Master and yours is in heaven, and that there is no partiality with him" (Eph. 6:9).

Young Persons in General

"You that are younger, be subject to the elders. Clothe yourselves, all of you, with humility toward one another, for 'God opposes the proud, but gives grace to the humble.' Humble yourselves therefore under the mighty hand of God, that in due time he may exalt you" (1 Pet. 5:5–6).

Widows

"She who is a real widow, and is left all alone, has set her hope on God and continues in supplications and prayers night and day; whereas she who is self-indulgent is dead even while she lives" (1 Tim. 5:5–6).

Christians in General

"The commandments are summed up in this sentence, 'You shall love your neighbor as yourself'" (Rom. 13:9). "I urge that supplications, prayers, intercessions, and thanksgivings be made for all men" (1 Tim. 2:1).

> Let each his lesson learn with care
> And all the household well will fare.

The Augsburg Confession (1530)

In early 1530 the Holy Roman Emperor Charles V called for a meeting (or "diet") of his German electors, other high German nobles, and representatives of imperial cities to be held in the spring at Augsburg. The emperor had not been in Germany since the Diet of Worms (1521), where Luther had made his famous profession that his conscience was captive to the Word of God and so he could not recant what he had written, even at the request of the emperor. Affairs of the church had moved a considerable distance in the intervening period. Lutheran teaching had spread, Catholic resistance was mobilizing, and political discord continued. Charles' purpose in calling for the imperial diet at Augsburg was to unite his quarreling German princes, both to prepare for battle against Turkish invaders and to end strife within the church.

For the latter purpose, leaders of the new Protestant movement prepared statements of their faith in order to provide the emperor a clear picture of their Christian beliefs. Luther's prince, the elector John of Saxony, asked his theologians at Wittenberg to perform this task. They already possessed a brief statement of basic beliefs, prepared the previous year at Schwabach. To that document they added a fuller account of

Protestant differences with Catholics that was prepared during a conference at Torgau.

When the German nobles and theologians arrived in Augsburg, the Protestant leaders decided that it would be best to present a united front. They therefore asked Luther's chief lieutenant, Philip Melanchthon (1497–1560), to draw up a statement, which he did by making use of the documents from Schwabach and Torgau, as well as other earlier professions of Lutheran faith. Luther himself was not able to attend the Augsburg meeting, for he had been declared an outlaw after the Diet of Worms, and so was persona non grata with the emperor. (During the Augsburg diet, Luther took up residence at the Castle Coburg, not too far from Augsburg, and bombarded his colleagues with steady correspondence.)

Melanchthon was moderate by the standards of the day. Since he was still hoping that fellowship could be restored between Protestants and Catholics, he wrote the Augsburg Confession as charitably as he could, often going out of his way to show where Lutheran positions still were identical or very similar to those of the Catholics. (Luther did not entirely approve this conciliatory spirit, for he thought the breach had become irreparable; yet he was largely pleased with the actual confession that Melanchthon prepared.) At the same time, Melanchthon wanted to show the emperor and his Catholic advisors that the Lutherans were not nearly as radical as some of the other groups lumped with them as Protestants. This motive explains particularly the condemnations of the Anabaptists that are sprinkled liberally throughout the first part of the confession (e.g., arts. 5, 9, 12, 16, 17).

At Augsburg, Melanchthon and his fellow Lutherans tinkered with their statement right up to the time when it was presented on Saturday (not Friday as the preface says), June 25, 1530. The text was read aloud in German by Christian Baier, vice-chancellor of the Saxon elector. (Rumor has it that the emperor, who did not know German well, fell asleep during the lengthy reading, as he also did later at the diet when the Catholic response to the Lutheran confession was read.) The Lutherans then presented an official Latin copy with the German to the emperor. Both of these originals have been lost. The translation that follows is based on the German text as reconstructed from the many copies of the confession that were made at the time. The Catholics presented and then published their rebuttal (*Confutatio Confessionis Augustanae*), to which Melanchthon responded in 1531 with a lengthy *Apology for the Augsburg Confession*.

The Augsburg Confession, because of its historical importance and doctrinal weight, rapidly became the definitive confession for Lutherans. It, along with Melanchthon's *Apology*, was included in the *Book of Concord* from 1580 that later Lutherans assembled as a fuller compendium of the faith.

This confession expresses clearly the desire of the Lutherans to base their faith on Scripture and the sole-sufficient work of Christ. Its first twenty-one articles present convictions that the Lutherans hoped could be accepted by the Catholics. The last eight offer lengthier explanations of matters in dispute. Some of the Lutheran assertions in this section, like the discussion of the Mass (art. 24), would be in the minds of Catholic theologians when they wrote their responses at the Council of Trent. Of special note in the confession is Melanchthon's effort to show that Lutheran teaching not only arises from Scripture, but also is compatible with the traditions of the historic church. To that end, the confession frequently appeals to the teachings of Augustine (354–430) and also draws on the great summary of canon law prepared by Gratian, the twelfth-century harmonizer of the church's many decrees, edicts, and canons (official church pronouncements, often from councils). For those who desire further information about these references, the notes prepared by Theodore Tappert for the text reproduced here are helpful.

The Augsburg Confession, as the chief Lutheran official confession, is a vitally important Reformation doctrine. The circumstances of its preparation—by a theologian attempting to mediate between Catholics and Protestants, for political leaders seeking to cement their unity, before an emperor concerned about the security of his domain—also suggests something about the way church doctrine grows out of and speaks to the real circumstances of everyday life.

Text

The Book of Concord: The Confessions of the Evangelical Lutheran Church. Translated and edited by Theodore G. Tappert, 23–96. Philadelphia: Fortress, 1959.

Additional Reading

Burgess, Joseph A., ed. *The Role of the Augsburg Confession: Catholic and Lutheran Views*. Philadelphia: Fortress, 1980.

Gritsch, Eric W., and Robert W. Jenson. *Lutheranism: The Theological Movement and Its Confessional Writings*. Philadelphia: Fortress, 1976.

Manschreck, Clyde L. *Melanchthon, the Quiet Reformer*. New York: Abingdon, 1958.

Maurer, Wilhelm. *Historical Commentary on the Augsburg Confession*. Philadelphia: Fortress, 1986.

Melanchthon, Philip. *Apology of the Augsburg Confession*. In *The Book of Concord: The Confessions of the Evangelical Lutheran Church*, trans. and ed. Theodore G. Tappert, 97–285. Philadelphia: Fortress, 1959.

The Augsburg Confession
A Confession of Faith Presented in Augsburg by Certain Princes and Cities to His Imperial Majesty Charles V in the Year 1530

I will also speak of thy testimonies before kings,
and shall not be put to shame.
—Ps. 119:46

Preface

Most serene, most mighty, invincible Emperor, most gracious Lord:

A short time ago Your Imperial Majesty graciously summoned a diet of the empire to convene here in Augsburg. In the summons Your Majesty indicated an earnest desire to deliber-

ate concerning matters pertaining to the Turk, that traditional
foe of ours and of the Christian religion, and how with continuing help he might effectively be resisted. The desire was also
expressed for deliberation on what might be done about the
dissension concerning our holy faith and the Christian religion,
and to this end it was proposed to employ all diligence amicably and charitably to hear, understand, and weigh the judgments, opinions, and beliefs of the several parties among us, to
unite the same in agreement on one Christian truth, to put
aside whatever may not have been rightly interpreted or
treated by either side, to have all of us embrace and adhere to a
single, true religion and live together in unity and in one fellowship and church, even as we are all enlisted under one
Christ. Inasmuch as we, the undersigned electors and princes
and our associates, have been summoned for these purposes,
together with other electors, princes, and estates, we have com-
plied with the command and can say without boasting that we
were among the first to arrive.

In connection with the matter pertaining to the faith and in
conformity with the imperial summons, Your Imperial Majesty
also graciously and earnestly requested that each of the electors, princes, and estates should commit to writing and present, in German and Latin, his judgments, opinions, and
beliefs with reference to the said errors, dissensions, and
abuses. Accordingly, after due deliberation and counsel, it was
decided last Wednesday that, in keeping with Your Majesty's
wish, we should present our case in German and Latin today
(Friday). Wherefore, in dutiful obedience to Your Imperial
Majesty, we offer and present a confession of our pastors' and
preachers' teaching and of our own faith, setting forth how and
in what manner, on the basis of the holy Scriptures, these
things are preached, taught, communicated, and embraced in
our lands, principalities, dominions, cities, and territories.

If the other electors, princes, and estates also submit a similar written statement of their judgments and opinions, in Latin
and German, we are prepared, in obedience to Your Imperial
Majesty, our most gracious lord, to discuss with them and their
associates, insofar as this can honorably be done, such practical and equitable ways as may restore unity. Thus the matters
at issue between us may be presented in writing on both sides,
they may be discussed amicably and charitably, our differences

may be reconciled, and we may be united in one, true religion, even as we are all under one Christ and should confess and contend for Christ. All of this is in accord with Your Imperial Majesty's aforementioned summons. That it may be done according to divine truth we invoke almighty God in deepest humility and implore him to bestow his grace to this end. Amen.

If, however, our lords, friends, and associates who represent the electors, princes, and estates of the other party do not comply with the procedure intended by Your Imperial Majesty's summons, if no amicable and charitable negotiations take place between us, and if no results are attained, nevertheless we on our part shall not omit doing anything, insofar as God and conscience allow, that may serve the cause of Christian unity. Of this Your Imperial Majesty, our aforementioned friends (the electors, princes, and estates), and every lover of the Christian religion who is concerned about these questions will be graciously and sufficiently assured from what follows in the confession which we and our associates submit.

In the past Your Imperial Majesty graciously gave assurance to the electors, princes, and estates of the empire, especially in a public instruction at the diet in Spires in 1526, that for reasons there stated Your Imperial Majesty was not disposed to render decisions in matters pertaining to our holy faith but would diligently urge it upon the pope to call a council. Again, by means of a written instruction at the last diet in Spires a year ago, the electors, princes, and estates of the empire were, among other things, informed and notified by Your Imperial Majesty's viceroy (His Royal Majesty of Hungary and Bohemia, etc.) and by Your Imperial Majesty's orator and appointed commissioners, that Your Imperial Majesty's viceroy, administrators, and councilors of the imperial government (together with the absent electors, princes, and representatives of the estates) who were assembled at the diet convened in Ratisbon had considered the proposal concerning a general council and acknowledged that it would be profitable to have such a council called. Since the relations between Your Imperial Majesty and the pope were improving and were progressing toward a good, Christian understanding, Your Imperial Majesty was sure that the pope would not refuse to call a general council, and so Your Imperial Majesty graciously offered to promote and bring about the calling of such a general council by the pope, along with Your Imperial Majesty, at the earliest opportunity and to allow no hindrance to be put in the way.

If the outcome should be such as we mentioned above [i.e., with no reconciliation at Augsburg] we offer in full obedience, even beyond what is required, to participate in such a general, free, and Christian council as the electors, princes, and estates have with the highest and best motives requested in all the diets of the empire which have been held during Your Imperial Majesty's reign. We have at various times made our protestations and appeals concerning these most weighty matters, and have done so in legal form and procedure. To these we declare our continuing adherence, and we shall not be turned aside from our position by these or any following negotiations (unless the matters in dissension are finally heard, amicably weighed, charitably settled, and brought to Christian concord in accordance with Your Imperial Majesty's summons) as we herewith publicly witness and assert. This is our confession and that of our associates, and it is specifically stated, article by article, in what follows.

Articles of Faith and Doctrine

1. [God]

We unanimously hold and teach, in accordance with the decree of the Council of Nicea, that there is one divine essence, which is called and which is truly God, and that there are three Persons in this one divine essence, equal in power and alike eternal: God the Father, God the Son, God the Holy Spirit. All three are one divine essence, eternal, without division, without end, of infinite power, wisdom, and goodness, one Creator and Preserver of all things visible and invisible. The word "person" is to be understood as the fathers employed the term in this connection, not as a part or a property of another but as that which exists of itself.

Therefore all the heresies which are contrary to this article are rejected. Among these are the heresy of the Manicheans, who assert that there are two gods, one good and one evil; also that of the Valentinians, Arians, Eunomians, Mohammedans, and others like them; also that of the Samosatenes, old and new, who hold that there is only one Person and sophistically assert that the other two, the Word and the Holy Spirit, are not necessarily distinct Persons but that the Word signifies a physical word or voice and that the Holy Spirit is a movement induced in creatures.

2. [Original Sin]

It is also taught among us that since the fall of Adam all men who are born according to the course of nature are conceived and born in sin. That is, all men are full of evil lust and inclinations from their mothers' wombs and are unable by nature to have true fear of God and true faith in God. Moreover, this inborn sickness and hereditary sin is truly sin and condemns to the eternal wrath of God all those who are not born again through baptism and the Holy Spirit.

Rejected in this connection are the Pelagians and others who deny that original sin is sin, for they hold that natural man is made righteous by his own powers, thus disparaging the sufferings and merit of Christ.

3. [The Son of God]

It is also taught among us that God the Son became man, born of the virgin Mary, and that the two natures, divine and human, are so inseparably united in one person that there is one Christ, true God and true man, who was truly born, suffered, was crucified, died, and was buried in order to be a sacrifice not only for original sin but also for all other sins and to propitiate God's wrath. The same Christ also descended into hell, truly rose from the dead on the third day, ascended into heaven, and sits on the right hand of God, that he may eternally rule and have dominion over all creatures, that through the Holy Spirit he may sanctify, purify, strengthen, and comfort all who believe in him, that he may bestow on them life and every grace and blessing, and that he may protect and defend them against the devil and against sin. The same Lord Christ will return openly to judge the living and the dead, as stated in the Apostles' Creed.

4. [Justification]

It is also taught among us that we cannot obtain forgiveness of sin and righteousness before God by our own merits, works, or satisfactions, but that we receive forgiveness of sin and become righteous before God by grace, for Christ's sake, through faith, when we believe that Christ suffered for us and that for his sake our sin is forgiven and righteousness and eternal life are given to us. For God will regard and reckon this faith as righteousness, as Paul says in Romans 3:21–26 and 4:5.

5. [The Office of the Ministry]

To obtain such faith God instituted the office of the ministry, that is, provided the gospel and the sacraments. Through these, as through means, he gives the Holy Spirit, who works faith, when and where he pleases, in those who hear the gospel. And the gospel teaches that we have a gracious God, not by our own merits but by the merit of Christ, when we believe this.

Condemned are the Anabaptists and others who teach that the Holy Spirit comes to us through our own preparations, thoughts, and works without the external word of the gospel.

6. [The New Obedience]

It is also taught among us that such faith should produce good fruits and good works and that we must do all such good works as God has commanded, but we should do them for God's sake and not place our trust in them as if thereby to merit favor before God. For we receive forgiveness of sin and righteousness through faith in Christ, as Christ himself says, "So you also, when you have done all that is commanded you, say, 'We are unworthy servants'" (Luke 17:10). The fathers also teach thus, for Ambrose says, "It is ordained of God that whoever believes in Christ shall be saved, and he shall have forgiveness of sins, not through works but through faith alone, without merit."

7. [The Church]

It is also taught among us that one holy Christian church will be and remain forever. This is the assembly of all believers among whom the gospel is preached in its purity and the holy sacraments are administered according to the gospel. For it is sufficient for the true unity of the Christian church that the gospel be preached in conformity with a pure understanding of it and that the sacraments be administered in accordance with the divine Word. It is not necessary for the true unity of the

Christian church that ceremonies, instituted by men, should be observed uniformly in all places. It is as Paul says in Ephesians 4:4–5, "There is one body and one Spirit, just as you were called to the one hope that belongs to your call, one Lord, one faith, one baptism."

8. [What the Church Is]

Again, although the Christian church, properly speaking, is nothing else than the assembly of all believers and saints, yet because in this life many false Christians, hypocrites, and even open sinners remain among the godly, the sacraments are efficacious even if the priests who administer them are wicked men, for as Christ himself indicated, "The Pharisees sit on Moses' seat" (Matt. 23:2).

Accordingly the Donatists and all others who hold contrary views are condemned.

9. Baptism

It is taught among us that baptism is necessary and that grace is offered through it. Children, too, should be baptized, for in baptism they are committed to God and become acceptable to him.

On this account the Anabaptists, who teach that infant baptism is not right, are rejected.

10. The Holy Supper of Our Lord

It is taught among us that the true body and blood of Christ are really present in the supper of our Lord under the form of bread and wine and are there distributed and received. The contrary doctrine is therefore rejected.

11. Confession

It is taught among us that private absolution should be retained and not allowed to fall into disuse. However, in confession it is not necessary to enumerate all trespasses and sins, for this is impossible (Ps. 19:12, "Who can discern his errors?").

12. Repentance

It is taught among us that those who sin after baptism receive forgiveness of sin whenever they come to repentance, and absolution should not be denied them by the church.

Properly speaking, true repentance is nothing else than to have contrition and sorrow, or terror, on account of sin, and yet at the same time to believe the gospel and absolution (namely, that sin has been forgiven and grace has been obtained through Christ), and this faith will comfort the heart and again set it at rest. Amendment of life and the forsaking of sin should then follow, for these must be the fruits of repentance, as John says, "Bear fruit that befits repentance" (Matt. 3:8).

Rejected here are those who teach that persons who have once become godly cannot fall again.

Condemned on the other hand are the Novatians who denied absolution to such as had sinned after baptism.

Rejected also are those who teach that forgiveness of sin is not obtained through faith but through the satisfactions made by man.

13. The Use of the Sacraments

It is taught among us that the sacraments were instituted not only to be signs by which people might be identified outwardly as Christians, but that they are signs and testimonies of God's will toward us for the purpose of awakening and strengthening our faith. For this reason they require faith, and they are rightly used when they are received in faith and for the purpose of strengthening faith.

14. Order in the Church

It is taught among us that nobody should publicly teach or preach or administer the sacraments in the church without a regular call.

15. Church Usages

With regard to church usages that have been established by men, it is taught among us that those usages are to be observed which may be observed without sin and which contribute to peace and good order in the church, among them being certain holy days, festivals, and the like. Yet we accompany these observations with instruction so that consciences may not be burdened by the notion that such things are necessary for salvation. Moreover it is taught that all ordinances and traditions instituted by men for the purpose of propitiating God and earning grace are contrary to the gospel and the teaching about faith in Christ. Accordingly monastic vows and other traditions concerning distinctions of foods, days, and the like, by which it is intended to earn grace and make satisfaction for sin, are useless and contrary to the gospel.

16. Civil Government

It is taught among us that all government in the world and all established rule and laws were instituted and ordained by God for the sake of good order, and that Christians may without sin occupy civil offices or serve as princes and judges, render decisions and pass sentence according to imperial and other existing laws, punish evildoers with the sword, engage in just wars, serve as soldiers, buy and sell, take required oaths, possess property, be married, and the like.

Condemned here are the Anabaptists who teach that none of the things indicated above is Christian.

Also condemned are those who teach that Christian perfection requires the forsaking of house and home, wife and child, and the renunciation of such activities as are mentioned above. Actually, true perfection consists alone of proper fear of God and real faith in God, for the gospel does not teach an outward and temporal but an inward and eternal mode of existence and righteousness of the heart. The gospel does not overthrow civil authority, the state, and marriage but requires that all these be kept as true orders of God and that everyone, each according to his own calling, manifest Christian love and genuine good works in his station of life. Accordingly Christians are obliged to be subject to civil authority and obey its commands and laws in all that can be done without sin. But when commands of the civil authority cannot be obeyed without sin, we must obey God rather than men (Acts 5:29).

17. [The Return of Christ to Judgment]

It is also taught among us that our Lord Jesus Christ will return on the last day for judgment and will raise up all the dead, to give eternal life and everlasting joy to believers and the elect but to condemn ungodly men and the devil to hell and eternal punishment.

Rejected, therefore, are the Anabaptists who teach that the devil and condemned men will not suffer eternal pain and torment.

Rejected, too, are certain Jewish opinions which are even now making an appearance and which teach that, before the resurrection of the dead, saints and godly men will possess a worldly kingdom and annihilate all the godless.

18. Freedom of the Will

It is also taught among us that man possesses some measure of freedom of the will which enables him to live an outwardly honorable life and to make choices among the things that reason comprehends. But without the grace, help, and activity of the Holy Spirit man is not capable of making himself acceptable to God, of fearing God and believing in God with his whole heart, or of expelling inborn evil lusts from his heart. This is accomplished by the Holy Spirit, who is given through the Word of God, for Paul says in 1 Corinthians 2:14, "natural man does not receive the gifts of the Spirit of God."

In order that it may be evident that this teaching is no novelty, the clear words of Augustine on free will are here quoted from the third book of his *Hypognosticon*: "We concede that all men have a free will, for all have a natural, innate understanding and reason. However, this does not enable them to act in matters pertaining to God (such as loving God with their whole heart or fearing him), for it is only in the outward acts of this life that they have freedom to choose good or evil. By good I mean what they are capable of by nature: whether or not to labor in the fields, whether or not to eat or drink or visit a friend, whether to dress or undress, whether to build a house, take a wife, engage in a trade, or do whatever else may be good and profitable. None of these is or exists without God, but all things are from him and through him. On the other hand, by his own choice man can also undertake evil, as when he wills to kneel before an idol, commit murder, and the like."

19. The Cause of Sin

It is taught among us that although almighty God has created and still preserves nature, yet sin is caused in all wicked men and despisers of God by the perverted will. This is the will of the devil and of all ungodly men; as soon as God withdraws his support, the will turns away from God to evil. It is as Christ says in John 8:44, "When the devil lies, he speaks according to his own nature."

20. Faith and Good Works

Our teachers have been falsely accused of forbidding good works. Their writings on the Ten Commandments, and other writings as well, show that they have given good and profitable accounts and instructions concerning true Christian estates and works. About these little was taught in former times, when for the most part sermons were concerned with childish and useless works like rosaries, the cult of saints, monasticism, pilgrimages, appointed fasts, holy days, brotherhoods, and the like. Our opponents no longer praise these useless works so highly as they once did, and they have also learned to speak now of faith, about which they did not preach at all in former times. They do not teach now that we become righteous before God by our works alone, but they add faith in Christ and say that faith and works make us righteous before God. This teaching may offer a little more comfort than the teaching that we are to rely solely on our works.

Since the teaching about faith, which is the chief article in the Christian life, has been neglected so long (as all must admit) while nothing but works was preached everywhere, our people have been instructed as follows:

We begin by teaching that our works cannot reconcile us with God or obtain grace for us, for this happens only through faith, that is, when we believe that our sins are forgiven for Christ's sake, who alone is the Mediator who reconciles the Father. Whoever imagines that he can accomplish this by works, or that he can merit grace, despises Christ and seeks his own way to God, contrary to the gospel.

This teaching about faith is plainly and clearly treated by Paul in many passages, especially in Ephesians 2:8–9, "For by grace you have been saved through faith; and this is not your own doing, it is the gift of God—not because of works, lest any man should boast."

That no new interpretation is here introduced can be demonstrated from Augustine, who discusses this question thoroughly and teaches the same thing, namely, that we obtain grace and are justified before God through faith in Christ and not through works. His whole book, *De spiritu et litera*, proves this.

Although this teaching is held in great contempt among untried people, yet it is a matter of experience that weak and terrified consciences find it most comforting and salutary. The conscience cannot come to rest and peace through works, but only through faith, that is, when it is assured and knows that for Christ's sake it has a gracious God, as Paul says in Romans 5:1, "Since we are justified by faith, we have peace with God."

In former times this comfort was not heard in preaching, but poor consciences were driven to rely on their own efforts, and all sorts of works were undertaken. Some were driven by their conscience into monasteries in the hope that there they might merit grace through monastic life. Others devised other works for the purpose of earning grace and making satisfaction for sins. Many of them discovered that they did not obtain peace by such means. It was therefore necessary to preach this doctrine about faith in Christ and diligently apply it in order that men may know that the grace of God is appropriated without merits, through faith alone.

Instruction is also given among us to show that the faith here spoken of is not that possessed by the devil and the ungodly, who also believe the history of Christ's suffering and his resurrection from the dead, but we mean such true faith as believes that we receive grace and forgiveness of sin through Christ.

Whoever knows that in Christ he has a gracious God, truly knows God, calls upon him, and is not, like the heathen, without God. For the devil and the ungodly do not believe this article concerning the forgiveness of sin, and so they are at enmity with God, cannot call upon him, and have no hope of receiving good from him. Therefore, as has just been indicated, the Scriptures speak of faith but do not mean by it such knowledge as the devil and ungodly men possess. Hebrews 11:1 teaches about faith in such a way as to make it clear that faith is not merely a knowledge of historical events but is a confidence in God and in the fulfillment of his promises. Augustine also reminds us that we should understand the word "faith" in the Scriptures to mean confidence in God, assurance that God is gracious to us, and not merely such a knowledge of historical events as the devil also possesses.

It is also taught among us that good works should and must be done, not that we are to rely on them to earn grace but that we may do God's will and glorify him. It is always faith alone that apprehends grace and forgiveness of sin. When through faith the Holy Spirit is given, the heart is moved to do good works. Before that, when it is without the Holy Spirit, the heart is too weak. Moreover, it is in the power of the devil, who drives poor human beings into many sins. We see this in the philosophers who undertook to lead honorable and blameless lives; they failed to accomplish this, and instead fell into many great and open sins. This is what happens when a man is without true faith and the Holy Spirit and governs himself by his own human strength alone.

Consequently this teaching concerning faith is not to be accused of forbidding good works but is rather to be praised for teaching that good works are to be done and for offering help as to how they may be done. For without faith and without Christ human nature and human strength are much too weak to do good works, call upon God, have patience in suffering, love one's neighbor, diligently engage in callings which are commanded, render obedience, avoid evil lusts, and the like. Such great and genuine works cannot be done without the help of Christ, as he himself says in John 15:5, "Apart from me you can do nothing."

21. The Cult of Saints

It is also taught among us that saints should be kept in remembrance so that our faith may be strengthened when we see what grace they received and how they were sustained by faith. Moreover, their good works are to be an example for us, each of us in his own calling. So His Imperial Majesty may in salutary and godly fashion imitate the example of David in making war on the Turk, for both are incumbents of a royal office which demands the defense and protection of their subjects.

However, it cannot be proved from the Scriptures that we are to invoke saints or seek help from them. "For there is one mediator between God and men, Christ Jesus" (1 Tim. 2:5), who is the only Savior, the only High Priest, Advocate, and Intercessor before God (Rom. 8:34). He alone has promised to hear our prayers. Moreover, according to the Scriptures, the highest form of divine service is sincerely to seek and call upon this same Jesus Christ in every time of need. "If anyone sins, we have an advocate with the Father, Jesus Christ the righteous" (1 John 2:1).

This is just about a summary of the doctrines that are preached and taught in our churches for proper Christian instruction, the consolation of consciences, and the amendment of believers. Certainly we should not wish to put our own souls and consciences in grave peril before God by misusing his name or Word, nor should we wish to bequeath to our children and posterity any other teaching than that which agrees with the pure Word of God and Christian truth. Since this teaching is grounded clearly on the holy Scriptures and is not contrary or opposed to that of the universal Christian church, or even of the Roman Church (insofar as the latter's teaching is reflected in the writings of the fathers), we think that our opponents cannot disagree with us in the articles set forth above. Therefore, those who presume to reject, avoid, and separate from our churches as if our teaching were heretical, act in an unkind and hasty fashion, contrary to all Christian unity and love, and do so without any solid basis of divine command or Scripture. The dispute and dissension are concerned chiefly with various traditions and abuses. Since, then, there is nothing unfounded or defective in the principal articles and since this our confession is seen to be godly and Christian, the bishops should in all fairness act more leniently, even if there were some defect among us in regard to traditions, although we hope to offer firm grounds and reasons why we have changed certain traditions and abuses.

Articles about Matters in Dispute, in Which an Account Is Given of the Abuses Which Have Been Corrected

From the above it is manifest that nothing is taught in our churches concerning articles of faith that is contrary to the holy Scriptures or what is common to the Christian church. However, inasmuch as some abuses have been corrected (some of the abuses having crept in over the years and others of them having been introduced with violence), we are obliged by our circumstances to give an account of them and to indicate our reasons for permitting changes in these cases in order that Your Imperial Majesty may perceive that we have not acted in an unchristian and frivolous manner but have been compelled by God's command (which is rightly to be regarded as above all custom) to allow such changes.

22. Both Kinds in the Sacrament

Among us both kinds [i.e., the bread and the wine] are given to laymen in the sacrament. The reason is that there is a clear command and order of Christ, "Drink of it, all of you" (Matt. 26:27). Concerning the chalice Christ here commands with clear words that all should drink of it.

In order that no one might question these words and interpret them as if they apply only to priests, Paul shows in 1 Corinthians 11:20–29 that the whole assembly of the congregation in Corinth received both kinds. This usage continued in the church for a long time, as can be demonstrated from history and from the writings of the fathers. In several places Cyprian mentions that the cup was given to laymen in his time. Saint Jerome also states that the priests who administered the sacrament distributed the blood of Christ to the people. Pope Gelasius himself ordered that the sacrament was not to be divided. Not a single canon can be found which requires the reception of only one kind. Nobody knows when or through whom this custom of receiving only one kind was introduced, although Cardinal Cusanus mentions when the use was approved [in 1215]. It is evident that such a custom, introduced contrary to God's command and also contrary to the ancient canons, is unjust. Accordingly it is not proper to burden the consciences of those who desire to observe the sacrament according to Christ's institution or to compel them to act contrary to the arrangement of our Lord Christ. Because the division of the sacrament is contrary to the institution of Christ, the customary carrying about of the sacrament in procession is also omitted by us.

23. The Marriage of Priests

Among all people, both of high and low degree, there has been loud complaint throughout the world concerning the flagrant immorality and the dissolute life of priests who were not able to remain continent and who went so far as to engage in abominable vices. In order to avoid such unbecoming offense, adultery, and other lechery, some of our priests have entered the married state. They have given as their reason that they have been impelled and moved to take this step by the great distress of their consciences, especially since the Scriptures

clearly assert that the state of marriage was instituted by the
Lord God to avoid immorality, for Paul says, "Because of the
temptation of immorality, each man should have his own wife"
(1 Cor. 7:3), and again, "It is better to marry than to be aflame
with passion" (1 Cor. 7:9). Moreover, when Christ said in
Matthew 19:11, "Not all men can receive this precept," he indicated that few people have the gift of living in celibacy, and he
certainly knew man's nature. God created man as male and
female according to Genesis 1:27. Experience has made it all
too manifest whether or not it lies in human power and ability
to improve or change the creation of God, the supreme
Majesty, by means of human resolutions or vows without a
special gift or grace of God. What good has resulted? What
honest and chaste manner of life, what Christian, upright, and
honorable sort of conduct has resulted in many cases? It is well
known what terrible torment and frightful disturbance of conscience many have experienced on their deathbeds on this
account, and many have themselves acknowledged this. Since
God's Word and command cannot be altered by any human
vows or laws, our priests and other clergy have taken wives to
themselves for these and other reasons and causes.

It can be demonstrated from history and from the writings
of the fathers that it was customary for priests and deacons to
marry in the Christian church of former times. Paul therefore
said in 1 Timothy 3:2, "A bishop must be above reproach, married only once." It was only four hundred years ago that the
priests in Germany were compelled by force to take the vows
of celibacy. At that time there was such serious and strong
resistance that an archbishop of Mayence who had published
the new papal decree was almost killed during an uprising of
the entire body of priests. The decree concerning celibacy was
at once enforced so hastily and indecently that the pope at the
time not only forbade future marriages of priests but also
broke up the marriages which were of long standing. This was
of course not only contrary to all divine, natural, and civil law,
but was also utterly opposed and contrary to the canons which
the popes had themselves made and to the decisions of the
most renowned councils.

Many devout and intelligent people in high station have
expressed similar opinions and the misgiving that such
enforced celibacy and such prohibition of marriage (which

God himself instituted and left free to man) never produced any good but rather gave occasion for many great and evil vices and much scandal. As his biography shows, even one of the popes, Pius II, often said and allowed himself to be quoted as saying that while there may well have been some reasons for prohibiting the marriage of clergymen, there were now more important, better, and weightier reasons for permitting them to be married. There is no doubt that Pope Pius, as a prudent and intelligent man, made this statement because of grave misgivings.

In loyalty to Your Imperial Majesty we therefore feel confident that, as a most renowned Christian emperor, Your Majesty will graciously take into account the fact that, in these last times of which the Scriptures prophesy, the world is growing worse, and men are growing weaker and more infirm.

Therefore it is most necessary, profitable, and Christian to recognize this fact in order that the prohibition of marriage may not cause worse and more disgraceful lewdness and vice to prevail in German lands. No one is able to alter or arrange such matters in a better or wiser way than God himself, who instituted marriage to aid human infirmity and prevent unchastity.

The old canons also state that it is sometimes necessary to relax severity and rigor for the sake of human weakness and to prevent and avoid greater offense.

In this case relaxation would certainly be both Christian and very necessary. How would the marriage of priests and the clergy, and especially of the pastors and others who are to minister to the church, be of disadvantage to the Christian church as a whole? If this hard prohibition of marriage is to continue longer, there may be a shortage of priests and pastors in the future.

As we have observed, the assertion that priests and clergymen may marry is based on God's Word and command. Besides, history demonstrates both that priests were married and that the vow of celibacy has been the cause of so much frightful and unchristian offense, so much adultery, and such terrible, shocking immorality and abominable vice that even some honest men among the cathedral clergy and some of the courtiers in Rome have often acknowledged this and have complained that such vices among the clergy would, on account of their abomination and prevalence, arouse the wrath of God. It is therefore deplorable that Christian marriage has not only been forbidden but has in many places been swiftly punished, as if it were a great crime, in spite of the fact that in the holy Scriptures God commanded that marriage be held in honor. Marriage has also been highly praised in the imperial laws and in all states in which there have been laws and justice. Only in our time does one begin to persecute innocent people simply because they are married—and especially priests, who above all others should be spared—although this is done contrary not only to divine Law but also to canon law. In 1 Timothy 4:1, 3, the apostle Paul calls the teaching that forbids marriage a doctrine of the devil. Christ himself asserts that the devil is a murderer from the beginning (John 8:44). These two statements fit together well, for it must be a doctrine of the devil to forbid marriage and then to be so bold as to maintain such a teaching with the shedding of blood.

However, just as no human law can alter or abolish a command of God, neither can any vow alter a command of God. Saint Cyprian therefore offered the counsel that women who were unable to keep their vows of chastity should marry. He wrote in his eleventh letter, "If they are unwilling or unable to keep their chastity, it is better for them to marry than to fall into the fire through their lusts, and they should see to it that they do not give their brothers and sisters occasion for offense."

In addition, all the canons show great leniency and fairness toward those who have made vows in their youth—and most of the priests and monks entered into their estates ignorantly when they were young.

24. The Mass

We are unjustly accused of having abolished the Mass. Without boasting, it is manifest that the Mass is observed among us with greater devotion and more earnestness than among our opponents. Moreover, the people are instructed often and with great diligence concerning the holy sacrament, why it was instituted, and how it is to be used (namely, as a comfort for terrified consciences) in order that the people may be drawn to the communion and Mass. The people are also given instruction about other false teachings concerning the sacrament. Meanwhile no conspicuous changes have been made in the public ceremonies of the Mass, except that in certain places German hymns are sung in addition to the Latin responses for the instruction and exercise of the people. After all, the chief purpose of all ceremonies is to teach the people what they need to know about Christ.

Before our time, however, the Mass came to be misused in many ways, as is well known, by turning it into a sort of fair, by buying and selling it, and by observing it in almost all churches for a monetary consideration. Such abuses were often condemned by learned and devout men even before our time. Then when our preachers preached about these things and the priests were reminded of the terrible responsibility which should properly concern every Christian (namely, that whoever uses the sacrament unworthily is guilty of the body and blood of Christ), such mercenary masses and private masses, which had hitherto been held under compulsion for the sake of revenues and stipends, were discontinued in our churches.

At the same time the abominable error was condemned according to which it was taught that our Lord Christ had by his death made satisfaction only for original sin, and had instituted the Mass as a sacrifice for other sins. This transformed the Mass into a sacrifice for the living and the dead, a sacrifice by means of which sin was taken away and God was reconciled. Thereupon followed a debate as to whether one mass held for many people merited as much as a special mass held for an individual. Out of this grew the countless multiplication of masses, by the performance of which men expected to get everything they needed from God. Meanwhile faith in Christ and true service of God were forgotten.

Demanded without doubt by the necessity of such circumstances, instruction was given so that our people might know how the sacrament is to be used rightly. They were taught, first of all, that the Scriptures show in many places that there is no sacrifice for original sin, or for any other sin, except the one death of Christ. For it is written in the Epistle to the Hebrews that Christ offered himself once and by this offering made satisfaction for all sin. It is an unprecedented novelty in church doctrine that Christ's death should have made satisfaction only for original sin and not for other sins as well.

Accordingly it is to be hoped that everyone will understand that this error is not unjustly condemned.

In the second place, Saint Paul taught that we obtain grace before God through faith and not through works. Manifestly contrary to this teaching is the misuse of the Mass by those who think that grace is obtained through the performance of this work, for it is well known that the Mass is used to remove sin and obtain grace and all sorts of benefits from God, not only for the priest himself but also for the whole world and for others, both living and dead.

In the third place, the holy sacrament was not instituted to make provision for a sacrifice for sin—for the sacrifice has already taken place—but to awaken our faith and comfort our consciences when we perceive that through the sacrament grace and forgiveness of sin are promised us by Christ. Accordingly the sacrament requires faith, and without faith it is used in vain.

Inasmuch, then, as the Mass is not a sacrifice to remove the sins of others, whether living or dead, but should be a communion in which the priest and others receive the sacrament for themselves, it is observed among us in the following manner: On holy days, and at other times when communicants are present, Mass is held and those who desire it are communicated. Thus the Mass is preserved among us in its proper use, the use which was formerly observed in the church and which can be proved by Saint Paul's statement in 1 Corinthians 11:20–29 and by many statements of the fathers. For Chrysostom reports how the priest stood every day, inviting some to communion and forbidding others to approach. The ancient canons also indicate that one man officiated and communicated the other priests and deacons, for the words of the Nicene canon read, "After the priests the deacons shall receive the sacrament in order from the bishop or priest."

Since, therefore, no novelty has been introduced which did not exist in the church from ancient times, and since no conspicuous change has been made in the public ceremonies of the Mass except that other unnecessary masses which were held in addition to the parochial Mass, probably through abuse, have been discontinued, this manner of holding Mass ought not in fairness be condemned as heretical or unchristian. In times past, even in large churches where there were many people, Mass was not held on every day that the people assembled, for according to the Tripartite History, Book 9, on Wednesday and Friday the Scriptures were read and expounded in Alexandria, and all these services were held without Mass.

25. Confession

Confession has not been abolished by the preachers on our side. The custom has been retained among us of not administering the sacrament to those who have not previously been examined and absolved. At the same time the people are carefully instructed concerning the consolation of the Word of absolution so that they may esteem absolution as a great and precious thing. It is not the voice or word of the man who speaks it, but it is the Word of God, who forgives sin, for it is spoken in God's stead and by God's command. We teach with great diligence about this command and power of the keys and how comforting and necessary it is for terrified consciences. We also teach that God requires us to believe this absolution as much as if we heard God's voice from heaven, that we should joyfully comfort ourselves with absolution, and that we should know that through such faith we obtain forgiveness of sins. In former times the preachers who taught much about confession never mentioned a word concerning these necessary matters but only tormented consciences with long enumerations of sins, with satisfactions, with indulgences, with pilgrimages and the like. Many of our opponents themselves acknowledge that we have written about and treated of true Christian repentance in a more fitting fashion than had been done for a long time.

Concerning confession we teach that no one should be compelled to recount sins in detail, for this is impossible. As the psalmist says, "Who can discern his errors?" Jeremiah also says, "The heart is desperately corrupt; who can understand it?" Our wretched human nature is so deeply submerged in sins that it is unable to perceive or know them all, and if we were to be absolved only from those which we can enumerate we would be helped but little. On this account there is no need to compel people to give a detailed account of their sins. That this was also the view of the fathers can be seen in distinction 1, *De poenitentia*, where these words of Chrysostom are quoted:

"I do not say that you should expose yourself in public or should accuse yourself before others, but obey the prophet who says, 'Show your way to the Lord.' Therefore confess to the Lord God, the true judge, in your prayer, telling him of your sins not with your tongue but in your conscience." Here it can be clearly seen that Chrysostom does not require a detailed enumeration of sins. The marginal note in *De poenitentia*, distinction 5, also teaches that such confession is not commanded by the Scriptures but was instituted by the church. Yet the preachers on our side diligently teach that confession is to be retained for the sake of absolution (which is its chief and most important part), for the consolation of terrified consciences, and also for other reasons.

26. The Distinction of Foods

In former times men taught, preached, and wrote that distinctions among foods and similar traditions which had been instituted by men serve to earn grace and make satisfaction for sin. For this reason new fasts, new ceremonies, new orders, and the like were invented daily, and were ardently and urgently promoted, as if these were a necessary service of God by means of which grace would be earned if they were observed and a great sin committed if they were omitted. Many harmful errors in the church have resulted from this.

In the first place, the grace of Christ and the teaching concerning faith are thereby obscured, and yet the gospel earnestly urges them upon us and strongly insists that we regard the merit of Christ as something great and precious and know that faith in Christ is to be esteemed far above all works. On this account Saint Paul contended mightily against the Law of Moses and against human tradition so that we should learn that we do not become good in God's sight by our works but that it is only through faith in Christ that we obtain grace for Christ's sake. This teaching has been almost completely extinguished by those who have taught that grace is to be earned by prescribed fasts, distinctions among foods, vestments, and the like.

In the second place, such traditions have also obscured the commands of God, for these traditions were exalted far above God's commands. This also was regarded as Christian life: whoever observed festivals in this way, prayed in this way, fasted in this way, and dressed in this way was said to live a spiritual and Christian life. On the other hand, other necessary good works were considered secular and unspiritual: the works which everybody is obliged to do according to his calling—for example, that a husband should labor to support his wife and children and bring them up in the fear of God, that a wife should bear children and care for them, that a prince and magistrates should govern land and people, and the like. Such works, commanded by God, were to be regarded as secular and imperfect, while traditions were to be given the glamorous title of alone being holy and perfect works. Accordingly there was no end or limit to the making of such traditions.

In the third place, such traditions have turned out to be a grievous burden to consciences, for it was not possible to keep all the traditions, and yet the people were of the opinion that they were a necessary service of God. Gerson writes that many fell into despair on this account, and some even committed suicide, because they had not heard anything of the consolation of the grace of Christ. We can see in the writings of the summists [i.e., authors of ethical textbooks] and canonists [i.e., church lawyers] how consciences have been confused, for they undertook to collate the traditions and sought mitigations to relieve consciences, but they were so occupied with such efforts that they neglected all wholesome Christian teachings about more important things, such as faith, consolation in severe trials, and the like. Many devout and learned people before our time have also complained that such traditions caused so much strife in the church that godly people were thereby hindered from coming to a right knowledge of Christ. Gerson and others have complained bitterly about this. In fact, Augustine was also displeased that consciences were burdened with so many traditions, and he taught in this connection that they were not to be considered necessary observances.

Our teachers have not taught concerning these matters out of malice or contempt of spiritual authority, but dire need has compelled them to give instruction about the aforementioned errors which have arisen from a wrong estimation of tradition. The gospel demands that the teaching about faith should and must be emphasized in the church, but this teaching cannot be understood if it is supposed that grace is earned through self-chosen works.

It is therefore taught that grace cannot be earned, God cannot be reconciled, and sin cannot be atoned for by observing the said human traditions. Accordingly they should not be made into a necessary service of God. Reasons for this shall be cited from the Scriptures. In Matthew 15:1–20 Christ defends the apostles for not observing the customary traditions, and he adds, "In vain do they worship me, teaching as doctrines the precepts of men" (v. 9). Since he calls them vain service, they must not be necessary. Thereupon Christ says, "Not what goes into the mouth defiles a man." Paul also says in Romans 14:17, "The kingdom of God does not mean food and drink," and in Colossians 2:16 he says, "Let no one pass judgment on you in questions of food and drink or with regard to a festival." In Acts 15:10–11 Peter says, "Why do you make trial of God by putting a yoke upon the neck of the disciples which neither our fathers nor we have been able to bear? But we believe that we shall be saved through the grace of the Lord Jesus, just as they will." Here Peter forbids the burdening of consciences with additional outward ceremonies, whether of Moses or of another. In 1 Timothy 4:1, 3, such prohibitions as forbid food or marriage are called a doctrine of the devil, for it is diametrically opposed to the gospel to institute or practice such works for the purpose of earning forgiveness of sin or with the notion that nobody is a Christian unless he performs such services.

Although our teachers are, like Jovinian, accused of forbidding mortification and discipline, their writings reveal something quite different. They have always taught concerning the holy cross that Christians are obliged to suffer, and this is true and real rather than invented mortification.

They also teach that everybody is under obligation to conduct himself, with reference to such bodily exercise as fasting and other discipline, so that he does not give occasion to sin, but not as if he earned grace by such works. Such bodily exercise should not be limited to certain specified days but should be practiced continually. Christ speaks of this in Luke 21:34, "Take heed to yourselves lest your hearts be weighed down with dissipation," and again, "This kind of demon cannot be driven out by anything but fasting and prayer." Paul said that he pommeled his body and subdued it, and by this he indicated that it is not the purpose of mortification to merit grace but to keep the body in such a condition that one can perform the duties required by one's calling. Thus fasting in itself is not rejected, but what is rejected is making a necessary service of fasts on prescribed days and with specified foods, for this confuses consciences.

We on our part also retain many ceremonies and traditions (such as the liturgy of the Mass and various canticles, festivals, and the like) which serve to preserve order in the church. At the same time, however, the people are instructed that such outward forms of service do not make us righteous before God and that they are to be observed without burdening consciences, which is to say that it is not a sin to omit them if this is done without causing scandal. The ancient fathers maintained such liberty with respect to outward ceremonies, for in the East they kept Easter at a time different from that in Rome. When some regarded this difference as divisive of the church, they were admonished by others that it was not necessary to maintain uniformity in such customs. Irenaeus said, "Disagreement in fasting does not destroy unity in faith," and there is a statement in distinction 12 that such disagreement in human ordinances is not in conflict with the unity of Christendom. Moreover, the Tripartite History, Book 9, gathers many examples of dissimilar church usages and adds the profitable Christian observation, "It was not the intention of the apostles to institute holy days but to teach faith and love."

27. Monastic Vows

In discussing monastic vows it is necessary to begin by considering what opinions have hitherto been held concerning them, what kind of life was lived in the monasteries, and how many of the daily observances in them were contrary not only to the Word of God but also to papal canons. In the days of Saint Augustine monastic life was voluntary. Later, when true discipline and doctrine had become corrupted, monastic vows were invented, and the attempt was made to restore discipline by means of these vows as if in a well-conceived prison.

In addition to monastic vows many other requirements were imposed, and such fetters and burdens were laid on many before they had attained an appropriate age.

Many persons also entered monastic life ignorantly, for although they were not too young, they had not sufficiently appreciated or understood their strength. All of those who were thus ensnared and entangled were pressed and compelled to remain, in spite of the fact that even the papal canons might have set many of them free. The practice was stricter in women's convents than in those of men, although it would have been seemly to show more consideration to women as the weaker sex. Such severity and rigor displeased many devout people in the past, for they must have seen that both boys and girls were thrust into monasteries to provide for their maintenance. They must also have seen what evils came from this arrangement, what scandals and burdened consciences resulted. Many people complained that in such a momentous matter the canons were not strictly adhered to. Besides, monastic vows gained such a reputation, as is well known, that many monks with even a little understanding were displeased.

It was claimed that monastic vows were equal to baptism, and that by monastic life one could earn forgiveness of sin and justification before God. What is more, they added that monastic life not only earned righteousness and godliness, but also that by means of this life both the precepts and the counsels included in the gospel were kept, and so monastic vows were praised more highly than baptism. They also claimed that more merit could be obtained by monastic life than by all other states of life instituted by God—whether the office of pastor and preacher, of ruler, prince, lord or the like, all of whom serve in their appointed calling according to God's Word and command without invented spirituality. None of these things can be denied, for they are found in their own books.

Furthermore, those who were thus ensnared and inveigled into a monastery learned little about Christ. Formerly the monasteries had conducted schools of holy Scripture and other branches of learning which are profitable to the Christian church, so that pastors and bishops were taken from monasteries. But now the picture is changed. In former times people gathered and adopted monastic life for the purpose of learning Scriptures, but now it is claimed that monastic life is of such a nature that thereby God's grace and righteousness before God are earned. In fact, it is called a state of perfection and is regarded as far superior to the other estates instituted by God. All this is mentioned, without misrepresentation, in order that one may better grasp and understand what our teachers teach and preach.

For one thing, it is taught among us with regard to those who desire to marry that all those who are not suited for celibacy have the power, right, and authority to marry, for vows cannot nullify God's order and command. God's command in 1 Corinthians 7:2 reads, "Because of the temptation to immorality, each man should have his own wife and each woman her own husband." It is not alone God's command that urges, drives, and compels us to do this, but God's creation and order also direct all to marriage who are not endowed with the gift of virginity by a special act of God. This appears from God's own words in Genesis 2:18, "It is not good that the man should be alone; I will make a helper fit for him."

What objection may be raised to this? No matter how much one extols the vow and the obligation, no matter how highly one exalts them, it is still impossible to abrogate God's command. Learned men say that a vow made contrary to papal canons is not binding. How much less must be their obligation, lawfulness, and power when they are contrary to God's command!

If there were no reasons which allowed annulment of the obligation of a vow, the popes could not have dispensed and released men from such obligation, for no man has the right to cancel an obligation which is derived from divine Law. Consequently the popes were well aware that some amelioration ought to be exercised in connection with this obligation and have often given dispensations, as in the case of the king of Aragon [a monk who was released from his vows after his brother, the king, died, leaving him heir to the throne] and many others. If dispensations were granted for the maintenance of temporal interests, how much more should dispensations be granted for necessities of men's souls!

Why, then, do our opponents insist so strongly that vows must be kept without first ascertaining whether a vow is of the proper sort? For a vow must involve what is possible and voluntary and must be uncoerced. Yet it is commonly known to what an extent perpetual chastity lies within human power and ability, and there are few, whether men or women, who have taken monastic vows of themselves, willingly, and after due consideration. Before they came to a right understanding they were persuaded to take monastic vows, and sometimes they have been compelled and forced to do so. Accordingly it is not right to argue so rashly and insistently about the obligation of vows inasmuch as it is generally conceded that it belongs to the very nature and character of a vow that it should be voluntary and should be assumed only after due consideration and counsel.

Several canons and papal regulations annul vows that are made under the age of fifteen years. They hold that before this age one does not possess sufficient understanding to determine or arrange the order of one's whole future life. Another canon concedes still more years to human frailty, for it prohibits the taking of monastic vows before the eighteenth year. On the basis of this provision most monastics have excuse and reason for leaving their monasteries inasmuch as a majority of them entered the cloister in their childhood, before attaining such an age.

Finally, although the breaking of monastic vows might be censured, it would not follow that the marriage of those who broke them should be dissolved. For Saint Augustine says in his *Nuptiarum*, question 27, chapter 1, that such a marriage should not be dissolved, and Saint Augustine is no inconsiderable authority in the Christian church, even though some have subsequently differed from him.

Although God's command concerning marriage frees and releases many from monastic vows, our teachers offer still more reasons why monastic vows are null and void. For all service of God that is chosen and instituted by men to obtain righteousness and God's grace without the command and authority of God is opposed to God and the holy gospel and contrary to God's command. So Christ himself says in Matthew 15:9, "In vain do they worship me, teaching as doctrines the precepts of men." Saint Paul also teaches everywhere that one is not to seek for righteousness in the precepts and services invented by men but that righteousness and godliness in God's sight come from faith and trust when we believe that God receives us into his favor for the sake of Christ, his only Son.

It is quite evident that the monks have taught and preached that their invented spiritual life makes satisfaction for sin and obtains God's grace and righteousness. What is this but to diminish the glory and honor of the grace of Christ and deny the righteousness of faith? It follows from this that the customary vows were an improper and false service of God.

Therefore they are not binding, for an ungodly vow, made contrary to God's command, is null and void. Even the canons teach that an oath should not be an obligation to sin.

Saint Paul says in Galatians 5:4, "You are severed from Christ, you who would be justified by the law; you have fallen away from grace." In the same way, those who would be justified by vows are severed from Christ and have fallen away from God's grace, for they rob Christ, who alone justifies, of his honor and bestow this honor on their vows and monastic life.

One cannot deny that the monks have taught and preached that they were justified and earned forgiveness of sins by their vows and their monastic life and observances. In fact, they have invented a still more indecent and absurd claim, namely, that they could apply their good works to others. If one were inclined to count up all these claims for the purpose of casting them into their teeth, how many items could be assembled which the monks themselves are now ashamed of and wish had never occurred! Besides all this, they persuaded the people that the invented spiritual estate of the orders was Christian perfection. Certainly this is exaltation of works as a means of attaining justification. Now, it is no small offense in the Christian church that the people should be presented with such a service of God, invented by men without the command of God, and should be taught that such a service would make men good and righteous before God. For righteousness of faith, which should be emphasized above all else in the Christian church, is obscured when man's eyes are dazzled with this curious angelic spirituality and sham of poverty, humility, and chastity.

Besides, the commands of God and true and proper service of God are obscured when people are told that monks alone are in a state of perfection. For this is Christian perfection: that we fear God honestly with our whole hearts, and yet have sincere confidence, faith, and trust that for Christ's sake we have a gracious, merciful God; that we may and should ask and pray God for those things of which we have need, and confidently expect help from him in every affliction connected with our particular calling and station in life; and that meanwhile we do good works for others and diligently attend to our calling. True perfection and right service of God consist of these things and not mendicancy, or wearing a black or gray cowl, or the like.

However, the common people, hearing the state of celibacy praised above all measure, draw many harmful conclusions from such false exaltation of monastic life, for it follows that their consciences are troubled because they are married. When the common man hears that only mendicants are perfect, he is uncertain whether he can keep his possessions and engage in business without sin. When the people hear that is only a counsel not to take revenge, it is natural that some should conclude that it is not sinful to take revenge outside of the exercise of their office. Still others think that it is not right at all for Christians, even in the government, to avenge wrong.

Many instances are also recorded of men who forsook wife and child, and also their civil office, to take shelter in a monastery. This, they said, is fleeing from the world and seeking a life more pleasing to God than the other. They were unable to understand that one is to serve God by observing the commands God has given and not by keeping the commands invented by men. That is a good and perfect state of life which has God's command to support it; on the other hand, that is a dangerous state of life which does not have God's command behind it. About such matters it was necessary to give the people proper instruction.

In former times Gerson censured the error of the monks concerning perfection and indicated that it was an innovation of his time to speak of monastic life as a state of perfection.

Thus there are many godless opinions and errors associated with monastic vows: that they justify and render men righteous before God, that they constitute Christian perfection, that they are the means of fulfilling both evangelical counsels and precepts, and that they furnish the works of supererogation which we are not obligated to render to God. Inasmuch as all these things are false, useless, and invented, monastic vows are null and void.

28. The Power of Bishops

Many and various things have been written in former times about the power of bishops, and some have improperly confused the power of bishops with the temporal sword. Out of this careless confusion many serious wars, tumults, and uprisings have resulted because the bishops, under pretext of the power given them by Christ, have not only introduced new forms of worship and burdened consciences with reserved cases [i.e., where bishops claimed sole authority to pronounce absolution] and violent use of the ban, but have also assumed to set up and depose kings and emperors according to their pleasure. Such outrage has long since been condemned by learned and devout people in Christendom. On this account our teachers have been compelled, for the sake of comforting consciences, to point out the difference between spiritual and temporal power, sword, and authority, and they have taught that because of God's command both authorities and powers are to be honored and esteemed with all reverence as the two highest gifts of God on earth.

Our teachers assert that according to the gospel the power of the keys or the power of bishops is a power and command of God to preach the gospel, to forgive and retain sins, and to administer and distribute the sacraments. For Christ sent out the apostles with this command, "As the Father has sent me, even so I send you. Receive the Holy Spirit. If you forgive the sins of any, they are forgiven; if you retain the sins of any, they are retained" (John 20:21–23).

This power of the keys or of bishops is used and exercised only by teaching and preaching the Word of God and by administering the sacraments (to many persons or to individuals, depending on one's calling). In this way are imparted not bodily but eternal things and gifts, namely, eternal righteousness, the Holy Spirit, and eternal life. These gifts cannot be obtained except through the office of preaching and of administering the holy sacraments, for Saint Paul says, "The gospel is the power of God for salvation to everyone who has faith." Inasmuch as the power of the church or of bishops bestows eternal gifts and is used and exercised only through the office of preaching, it does not interfere at all with government or temporal authority. Temporal authority is concerned with matters altogether different from the gospel. Temporal power does not protect the soul, but with the sword and physical penalties it protects body and goods from the power of others.

Therefore, the two authorities, the spiritual and the temporal, are not to be mingled or confused, for the spiritual power has its commission to preach the gospel and administer the sacraments. Hence it should not invade the function of the other, should not set up and depose kings, should not annul temporal laws or undermine obedience to government, should not make or prescribe to the temporal power laws concerning worldly matters. Christ himself said, "My kingship is not of this world," and again, "Who made me a judge or divider over you?" Paul also wrote in Philippians 3:20, "Our commonwealth is in heaven," and in 2 Corinthians 10:4–5, "The weapons of our warfare are not worldly but have divine power to destroy strongholds and every proud obstacle to the knowledge of God."

Thus our teachers distinguish the two authorities and the functions of the two powers, directing that both be held in honor as the highest gifts of God on earth.

In cases where bishops possess temporal authority and the sword, they possess it not as bishops by divine right, but by human, imperial right, bestowed by Roman emperors and kings for the temporal administration of their lands. Such authority has nothing at all to do with the office of the gospel.

According to divine right, therefore, it is the office of the bishop to preach the gospel, forgive sins, judge and condemn doctrine that is contrary to the gospel, and exclude from the Christian community the ungodly whose wicked conduct is manifest. All this is to be done not by human power but by God's Word alone. On this account parish ministers and churches are bound to be obedient to the bishops according to the saying of Christ in Luke 10:16, "He who hears you hears me." On the other hand, if they teach, introduce, or institute anything contrary to the gospel, we have God's command not to be obedient in such cases, for Christ says in Matthew 7:15, "Beware of false prophets." Saint Paul also writes in Galatians 1:8, "Even if we, or an angel from heaven, should preach to you a gospel contrary to that which we preached to you, let him be accursed," and in 2 Corinthians 13:8, "We cannot do anything against the truth, but only for the truth." Again Paul refers to "the authority which the Lord has given me for building up and not for tearing down." Canon law requires the same in part 2, question 7, in the chapters "Sacerdotes" and "Oves."

Saint Augustine also writes in his reply to the letters of Petilian that one should not obey even regularly elected bishops if they err or if they teach or command something contrary to the divine holy Scriptures.

Whatever other power and jurisdiction bishops may have in various matters (for example, in matrimonial cases and in tithes), they have these by virtue of human right. However, when bishops are negligent in the performance of such duties, the princes are obliged, whether they like to or not, to administer justice to their subjects for the sake of peace and to prevent discord and great disorder in their lands.

Besides, there is dispute as to whether bishops have the power to introduce ceremonies in the church or establish regulations concerning foods, holy days, and the different orders of the clergy. Those who attribute such power to bishops cite Christ's saying in John 16:12–13, "I have yet many things to say to you, but you cannot bear them now. When the Spirit of truth comes, he will guide you into all the truth." They also cite the example in Acts 15:20, 29, where the eating of blood and what is strangled was forbidden. Besides, they appeal to the fact that the Sabbath was changed to Sunday—contrary, as they say, to the Ten Commandments. No case is appealed to and urged so insistently as the change of the Sabbath, for thereby they wish to maintain that the power of the church is indeed great because the church has dispensed from and altered part of the Ten Commandments.

Concerning this question our teachers assert that bishops do not have power to institute or establish anything contrary to the gospel, as has been indicated above and as is taught by canon law throughout the whole of the ninth distinction. It is patently contrary to God's command and Word to make laws out of opinions or to require that they be observed in order to make satisfaction for sins and obtain grace, for the glory of Christ's merit is blasphemed when we presume to earn grace by such ordinances. It is also apparent that because of this notion human ordinances have multiplied beyond calculation while the teaching concerning faith and righteousness of faith has almost been suppressed. Almost every day new holy days and fasts have been prescribed, ceremonies and new venerations of saints have been instituted in order that by such works grace and everything good might be earned from God.

Again, those who institute human ordinances also act contrary to God's command when they attach sin to foods, days, and similar things and burden Christendom with the bondage of the law, as if in order to earn God's grace there had to be a service of God among Christians like the Levitical service, and as if God had commanded the apostles and bishops to institute

it, as some have written. It is quite believable that some bishops were misled by the example of the Law of Moses. The
result was that countless regulations came into being—for
example, that it is a mortal sin to do manual work on holy days
(even when it does not give offense to others), that it is a mortal sin to omit the seven hours [of daily prayer prescribed for
monks], that some foods defile the conscience, that fasting is
a work by which God is reconciled, that in a reserved case sin
is not forgiven unless forgiveness is secured from the person
for whom the case is reserved, in spite of the fact that canon
law says nothing of the reservation of guilt but speaks only
about the reservation of ecclesiastical penalties.

Where did the bishops get the right and power to impose
such requirements on Christendom to ensnare men's consciences? In Acts 15:10 Saint Peter forbids putting a yoke on
the neck of the disciples. And Saint Paul said in 2 Corinthians
10:8 that authority was given for building up and not for
tearing down. Why, then, do they multiply sins with such
requirements?

Yet there are clear passages of divine Scripture which forbid the establishment of such regulations for the purpose of
earning God's grace or as if they were necessary for salvation.
Thus Saint Paul says in Colossians 2:16, "Let no one pass judgment on you in questions of food and drink or with regard to a
festival or a new moon or a sabbath. These are only a shadow
of what is to come; but the substance belongs to Christ." Again
in Colossians 2:20–23, "If with Christ you died to the regulations of the world, why do you live as if you still belonged to
the world? Why do you submit to regulations, 'Do not handle,
Do not taste, Do not touch' (referring to things which all perish as they are used), according to human precepts and doctrines? These have an appearance of wisdom." In Titus 1:14
Saint Paul also forbids giving heed to Jewish myths or to commands of men who reject the truth.

Christ himself says concerning those who urge human ordinances on people, "Let them alone; they are blind guides"
(Matt. 15:14). He rejects such service of God and says, "Every
plant which my heavenly Father has not planted will be rooted
up" (Matt. 15:13).

If, then, bishops have the power to burden the churches
with countless requirements and thus ensnare consciences,

why does the divine Scripture so frequently forbid the making and keeping of human regulations? Why does it call them doctrines of the devil? Is it possible that the Holy Spirit warned against them for nothing?

Inasmuch as such regulations as have been instituted as necessary to propitiate God and merit grace are contrary to the gospel, it is not at all proper for the bishops to require such services of God. It is necessary to preserve the teaching of Christian liberty in Christendom, namely, that bondage to the Law is not necessary for justification, as Saint Paul writes in Galatians 5:1, "For freedom Christ has set us free; stand fast, therefore, and do not submit again to a yoke of slavery." For the chief article of the gospel must be maintained, namely, that we obtain the grace of God through faith in Christ without our merits; we do not merit it by services of God instituted by men.

What are we to say, then, about Sunday and other similar church ordinances and ceremonies? To this our teachers reply that bishops or pastors may make regulations so that everything in the churches is done in good order, but not as a means of obtaining God's grace or making satisfaction for sins, nor in order to bind men's consciences by considering these things necessary services of God and counting it a sin to omit their observance even when this is done without offense. So Saint Paul directed in 1 Corinthians 11:5 that women should cover their heads in the assembly. He also directed that in the assembly preachers should not all speak at once, but one after another, in order.

It is proper for the Christian assembly to keep such ordinances for the sake of love and peace, to be obedient to the bishops and parish ministers in such matters, and to observe the regulations in such a way that one does not give offense to another and so that there may be no disorder or unbecoming conduct in the church. However, consciences should not be burdened by contending that such things are necessary for salvation or that it is a sin to omit them, even when no offense is given to others, just as no one would say that a woman commits a sin if without offense to others she goes out with uncovered head.

Of like character is the observance of Sunday, Easter, Pentecost, and similar holy days and usages. Those who consider the appointment of Sunday in place of the Sabbath as a necessary institution are very much mistaken, for the holy Scriptures have abrogated the Sabbath and teach that after the revelation of the gospel all ceremonies of the old Law may be omitted. Nevertheless, because it was necessary to appoint a certain day so that the people might know when they ought to assemble, the Christian church appointed Sunday for this purpose, and it was the more inclined and pleased to do this in order that the people might have an example of Christian liberty and might know that the keeping neither of the Sabbath nor of any other day is necessary.

There are many faulty discussions of the transformation of the Law, of the ceremonies of the New Testament, and of the change of the Sabbath, all of which have arisen from the false and erroneous opinion that in Christendom one must have services of God like the Levitical or Jewish services and that Christ commanded the apostles and bishops to devise new ceremonies which would be necessary for salvation. Such errors were introduced into Christendom when the righteousness of faith was no longer taught and preached with clarity and purity. Some argue that although Sunday must not be kept as of divine obligation, it must nevertheless be kept as almost of divine obligation, and they prescribe the kind and amount of work that may be done on the day of rest. What are such discussions but snares of conscience? For although they undertake to lighten and mitigate human regulations, yet there can be no moderation or mitigation as long as the opinion remains and prevails that their observance is necessary. And this opinion will remain as long as there is no understanding of the righteousness of faith and Christian liberty.

The apostles directed that one should abstain from blood and from what is strangled. Who observes this prohibition now? Those who do not observe it commit no sin, for the apostles did not wish to burden consciences with such bondage but forbade such eating for a time to avoid offense. One must pay attention to the chief article of Christian doctrine, and this is not abrogated by the decree.

Scarcely any of the ancient canons are observed according to the letter, and many of the regulations fall into disuse from day to day even among those who observe such ordinances most jealously. It is impossible to give counsel or help to consciences unless this mitigation is practiced, that one recognizes that such rules are not to be deemed necessary and that disregard of them does not injure consciences.

The bishops might easily retain the obedience of men if they did not insist on the observance of regulations which cannot be kept without sin. Now, however, they administer the sacrament in one kind and prohibit administration in both kinds. Again, they forbid clergymen to marry and admit no one to the ministry unless he first swears an oath that he will not preach this doctrine, although there is no doubt that it is in accord with the holy gospel. Our churches do not ask that the bishops should restore peace and unity at the expense of their honor and dignity (although it is incumbent on the bishops to do this, too, in case of need), but they ask only that the bishops relax certain unreasonable burdens which did not exist in the church in former times and which were introduced contrary to the custom of the universal Christian church. Perhaps there was some reason for introducing them, but they are not adapted to our times. Nor can it be denied that some regulations were adopted from want of understanding. Accordingly the bishops ought to be so gracious as to temper these regulations inasmuch as such changes do not destroy the unity of the Christian churches. For many regulations devised by men have with the passing of time fallen into disuse and are not obligatory, as papal law itself testifies. If, however, this is impossible and they cannot be persuaded to mitigate or abrogate human regulations which are not to be observed without sin, we are bound to follow the apostolic rule which commands us to obey God rather than men.

Saint Peter forbids the bishops to exercise lordship as if they had power to coerce the churches according to their will. It is not our intention to find ways of reducing the bishops' power, but we desire and pray that they may not coerce our consciences to sin. If they are unwilling to do this and ignore our petition, let them consider how they will answer for it in God's sight, inasmuch as by their obstinacy they offer occasion for division and schism, which they should in truth help to prevent.

[Conclusion]

These are the chief articles that are regarded as controversial. Although we could have mentioned many more abuses and wrongs, to avoid prolixity and undue length we have indicated only the principal ones. The others can readily be weighed in the light of these. In the past there have been grave complaints about indulgences, pilgrimages, and misuse of the ban. Parish ministers also had endless quarrels with monks about the hearing of confessions, about burials, about sermons on special occasions, and about countless other matters. All these things we have discreetly passed over for the common good in order that the chief points at issue may better be perceived.

It must not be thought that anything has been said or introduced out of hatred or for the purpose of injuring anybody, but we have related only matters which we have considered it necessary to adduce and mention in order that it may be made very clear that we have introduced nothing, either in doctrine or in ceremonies, that is contrary to holy Scripture or the universal Christian church. For it is manifest and evident (to speak without boasting) that we have diligently and with God's help prevented any new and godless teaching from creeping into our churches and gaining the upper hand in them.

In keeping with the summons, we have desired to present the above articles as a declaration of our confession and the teaching of our preachers. If anyone should consider that it is lacking in some respect, we are ready to present further information on the basis of the divine holy Scripture.

Your Imperial Majesty's most obedient servants:

John, duke of Saxony, elector
George, margrave of Brandenburg
Ernest, duke of Lüneburg
Philip, landgrave of Hesse
John Frederick, duke of Saxony
Francis, duke of Lüneburg
Wolfgang, prince of Anhalt
Mayor and council of Nuremberg
Mayor and council of Reutlingen

6

The Genevan
Confession (1536)

Although the authorship of this confession is debated, its
significance for the Reformation in Geneva is beyond doubt.
In 1536 the city councils of that French-speaking Swiss city
had just proclaimed themselves on the side of the Protestants
after a lengthy controversy with Catholic nobles and bishops.
Geneva had been guided toward reform by William Farel
(1489–1565), an energetic preacher of the new doctrines. Farel
was unusual for his day or any other, however, in that he recognized his own limitations. Now that Geneva had declared for
reform, he knew that the city needed calm, far-sighted guidance rather than the fiery preaching that was his specialty.
Fortunately for Farel, a traveler who seemed to have the
needed qualities passed through Geneva at just the right time.
The Frenchman John Calvin (1509–1564) was still a young
scholar in 1536, but he already had a growing reputation.
Earlier that same year he had published a manual of Christian
doctrine that displayed with admirable clarity the basic teach-

From Calvin: *Theological Treatises* (Volume XXII: The Library of Christian
Classics), translated with introductions and notes by J. K. S. Reid. Published
simultaneously in Great Britain and the U.S.A. by S. C. M. Press, Ltd. and The
Westminster Press in MCMLIV. Used by permission of Westminster/John
Knox Press.

ings of Reformed Protestantism. This was the first edition of his famous *Institutes of the Christian Religion*, a book that would grow in size and richness through successive editions down almost to the end of Calvin's life.

Calvin was in Geneva mostly, it seemed, by accident. He had earlier been forced to leave France because of his support for Protestantism. He had published the *Institutes* in Basel and then had traveled from place to place. Near the beginning of August he set out for Strasbourg, but was forced to detour when his route led through an area being contested by the armies of Francis I of France and Charles V (who besides Holy Roman Emperor was also king of Spain). The detour took Calvin to Geneva, where he planned to stay at most a day or two. Farel made the most of this opportunity. Recognizing that Calvin had the necessary wisdom and self-discipline to guide a reform over the long haul, he urged Calvin to remain in the city. Calvin at first declined, for he desired the life of a scholar more than that of an active reformer. But Farel was insistent. As Calvin himself reported a few weeks later, "he proceeded to utter the imprecation that God would curse my retirement and the tranquility of the studies which I sought, if I should withdraw and refuse to help, when the necessity was so urgent." Calvin, although not without great reluctance, stayed in Geneva. With only one interlude (1538–1541), when he moved to Strasbourg after disagreements with the Genevan town fathers, Calvin would remain in that city for the rest of his life. It would be through his post as minister and teacher there that Calvin came to be regarded as the premier biblical theologian of the Protestant movement.

The short Genevan Confession that follows was presented to the city fathers on November 10, 1536, soon after Calvin had taken up permanent residence in the city. Both Calvin and Farel are recorded as having brought it to the city senate. Earlier witnesses, like Calvin's successor, Theodore Beza, said that Calvin was the author. Later authorities have claimed that it came from Farel. Whatever Calvin's exact role in preparing the document, it does reflect in sharp outline the main themes of his reforming thought. The same reliance on the Bible, the same emphasis on human sinfulness and the need for grace, and the same focus on the work of Christ that mark the *Institutes* are presented in this short confession.

The pattern of the confession follows the Augsburg Confession by first setting forth more strictly theological convictions and then emphasizing themes in dispute with the Catholics. This confession is distinguished from earlier Swiss documents like Zwingli's Sixty-Seven Articles by its tighter argument and more consistent theological perspective. It is distinguished from the Lutherans' Augsburg Confession especially by its sections on the sacraments, where the Genevan Confession treats baptism and the Lord's supper as "representing" spiritual realities rather than communicating them directly. (Calvin's views on the sacraments in later editions of the *Institutes*, however, moved back closer to the Lutherans, at least as formulated by Melanchthon.) The confession's conciseness and sense of authority mark it as a characteristic statement of faith from the second generation of Protestants.

The Genevan Confession of 1536 did not have the impact of Calvin's much longer catechism, which was published in many editions after 1541. Nor did it ever become a widely accepted definition of faith for entire groups of Protestants. Still, it did provide for the earliest stages of the Reformation in Geneva a succinct, forceful statement of the sort of Christian convictions to which Calvin devoted his life.

Text

Calvin: Theological Treatises. Edited by J. K. S. Reid, 26–33. Philadelphia: Westminster, 1954.

Additional Reading

Bouwsma, William J. *John Calvin: A Sixteenth Century Portrait*. New York: Oxford University Press, 1988.

Calvin, John. *The Catechism of the Church of Geneva* (1545 ed.). In *Calvin: Theological Treatises*, ed. J. K. S. Reid, 83–139. Philadelphia: Westminster, 1954.

____. *Institutes of the Christian Religion*. Edited by John T. McNeill and translated by Ford Lewis Battles. 2 vols. Philadelphia: Westminster, 1960.

McNeill, John T. *The History and Character of Calvinism*. New York: Oxford University Press, 1954.

Parker, T. H. L. *John Calvin: A Biography*. Philadelphia: Westminster, 1975.

Confession of Faith which all the citizens and inhabitants of Geneva and the subjects of the country must promise to keep and hold

1. The Word of God

First, we affirm that we desire to follow Scripture alone as the rule of faith and religion, without mixing with it any other thing which might be devised by the opinion of men apart from the Word of God, and without wishing to accept for our spiritual government any other doctrine than what is conveyed to us by the same Word without addition or diminution, according to the command of our Lord.

2. One Only God

Following, then, the lines laid down in the holy Scriptures, we acknowledge that there is one only God, whom we are both to worship and serve, and in whom we are to put all our confidence and hope: having this assurance, that in him alone is contained all wisdom, power, justice, goodness, and pity. And since he is spirit, he is to be served in spirit and in truth. Therefore we think it an abomination to put our confidence or hope in any created thing, to worship anything else than him, whether angels or any other creatures, and to recognize any other Savior of our souls than him alone, whether saints or men living upon earth; and likewise to offer the service, which ought to be rendered to him, in external ceremonies or carnal observances, as if he took pleasure in such things, or to make an image to represent his divinity or any other image for adoration.

3. The Law of God Alike for All

Because there is only one Lord and Master who has dominion over our consciences, and because his will is the only principle of all justice, we confess all our life ought to be ruled in accordance with the commandments of his holy Law in which is contained all perfection of justice, and that we ought to have no other rule of good and just living, nor invent other good works to supplement it than those which are there contained, as follows: Exodus 20: "I am the Lord thy God, who brought thee," and so on.

4. Natural Man

We acknowledge man by nature to be blind, darkened in understanding, and full of corruption and perversity of heart, so that of himself he has no power to be able to comprehend the true knowledge of God as is proper, nor to apply himself to good works. But on the contrary, if he is left by God to what he is by nature, he is only able to live in ignorance and to be abandoned to all iniquity. Hence he has need to be illumined by God, so that he come to the right knowledge of his salvation, and thus to be redirected in his affections and reformed to the obedience of the righteousness of God.

5. Man by Himself Lost

Since man is naturally (as has been said) deprived and destitute in himself of all the light of God, and of all righteousness, we acknowledge that by himself he can only expect the wrath and malediction of God, and hence that he must look outside himself for the means of his salvation.

6. Salvation in Jesus

We confess then that it is Jesus Christ who is given to us by the Father, in order that in him we should recover all of which in ourselves we are deficient. Now all that Jesus Christ has done and suffered for our redemption, we veritably hold without any doubt, as it is contained in the Creed, which is recited in the church, that is to say: I believe in God the Father almighty, and so on.

7. Righteousness in Jesus

Therefore we acknowledge the things which are consequently given to us by God in Jesus Christ: first, that being in our own nature enemies of God and subjects of his wrath and judgment, we are reconciled with him and received again in grace through the intercession of Jesus Christ, so that by his righteousness and guiltlessness we have remission of our sins, and by the shedding of his blood we are cleansed and purified from all our stains.

8. Regeneration in Jesus

Second, we acknowledge that by his Spirit we are regenerated into a new spiritual nature. That is to say that the evil desires of our flesh are mortified by grace, so that they rule us no longer. On the contrary, our will is rendered conformable to God's will, to follow in his way and to seek what is pleasing to him. Therefore we are by him delivered from the servitude of sin, under whose power we were of ourselves held captive, and by this deliverance we are made capable and able to do good works and not otherwise.

9. Remission of Sins Always Necessary for the Faithful

Finally, we acknowledge that this regeneration is so effected in us that, until we slough off this mortal body, there remains always in us much imperfection and infirmity, so that we always remain poor and wretched sinners in the presence of God. And, however much we ought day by day to increase and grow in God's righteousness, there will never be plentitude or perfection while we live here. Thus we always have need of the mercy of God to obtain the remission of our faults and offenses. And so we ought always to look for our righteousness in Jesus Christ and not at all in ourselves, and in him be confident and assured, putting no faith in our works.

10. All Our Good in the Grace of God

In order that all glory and praise be rendered to God (as is his due), and that we be able to have true peace and rest of conscience, we understand and confess that we receive all benefits from God, as said above, by his clemency and pity, without any consideration of our worthiness or the merit of our works, to which is due no other retribution than eternal confusion. Nonetheless our Savior in his goodness, having received us into the communion of his Son Jesus, regards the works that we have done in faith as pleasing and agreeable; not that they merit it at all, but because, not imputing any of the imperfection that is there, he acknowledges in them nothing but what proceeds from his Spirit.

11. Faith

We confess that the entrance which we have to the great treasures and riches of the goodness of God that is vouchsafed to us is by faith; inasmuch as, in certain confidence and assurance of heart, we believe in the promises of the gospel, and receive Jesus Christ as he is offered to us by the Father and described to us by the Word of God.

12. *Invocation of God Only and Intercession of Christ*

As we have declared that we have confidence and hope for salvation and all good only in God through Jesus Christ, so we confess that we ought to invoke him in all necessities in the name of Jesus Christ, who is our Mediator and Advocate with him and has access to him. Likewise we ought to acknowledge that all good things come from him alone, and to give thanks to him for them. On the other hand, we reject the intercession of the saints as a superstition invented by men contrary to Scripture, for the reason that it proceeds from mistrust of the sufficiency of the intercession of Jesus Christ.

13. *Prayer Intelligible*

Moreover since prayer is nothing but hypocrisy and fantasy unless it proceed from the interior affections of the heart, we believe that all prayers ought to be made with clear understanding. And for this reason, we hold the prayer of our Lord to show fittingly what we ought to ask of him: Our Father which art in heaven, . . . but deliver us from evil. Amen.

14. *Sacraments*

We believe that the sacraments which our Lord has ordained in his church are to be regarded as exercises of faith for us, both for fortifying and confirming it in the promises of God and for witnessing before men. Of them there are in the Christian church only two which are instituted by the authority of our Savior: baptism and the supper of our Lord; for what is held in the realm of the pope concerning seven sacraments, we condemn as fable and lie.

15. *Baptism*

Baptism is an external sign by which our Lord testifies that he desires to receive us for his children, as members of his Son Jesus. Hence in it there is represented to us the cleansing from sin which we have in the blood of Jesus Christ, the mortification of our flesh which we have by his death that we may live in him by his Spirit. Now since our children belong to such an alliance with our Lord, we are certain that the external sign is rightly applied to them.

16. The Holy Supper

The supper of our Lord is a sign by which under bread and wine he represents the true spiritual communion which we have in his body and blood. And we acknowledge that according to his ordinance it ought to be distributed in the company of the faithful, in order that all those who wish to have Jesus for their life be partakers of it. Inasmuch as the Mass of the pope was a reprobate and diabolical ordinance subverting the mystery of the holy supper, we declare that it is execrable to us, an idolatry condemned by God; for so much is it itself regarded as a sacrifice for the redemption of souls that the bread is in it taken and adored as God. Besides there are other execrable blasphemies and superstitions implied here, and the abuse of the Word of God which is taken in vain without profit or edification.

17. Human Traditions

The ordinances that are necessary for the internal discipline of the church, and belong solely to the maintenance of peace, honesty, and good order in the assembly of Christians, we do not hold to be human traditions at all, inasmuch as they are comprised under the general command of Paul, where he desires that all be done among them decently and in order. But all laws and regulations made binding on conscience which oblige the faithful to things not commanded by God, or establish another service of God than that which he demands, thus tending to destroy Christian liberty, we condemn as perverse doctrines of Satan, in view of our Lord's declaration that he is honored in vain by doctrines that are the commandment of men. It is in this estimation that we hold pilgrimages, monasteries, distinctions of foods, prohibition of marriage, confessions, and other like things.

18. The Church

While there is only one church of Jesus Christ, we always acknowledge that necessity requires companies of the faithful to be distributed in different places. Of these assemblies each one is called church. But inasmuch as all companies do not assemble in the name of our Lord, but rather to blaspheme and pollute him by their sacrilegious deeds, we believe that the proper mark by which to discern the church of Jesus Christ is that his holy gospel be purely and faithfully preached, proclaimed, heard, and kept, that his sacraments be properly administered, even if there be some imperfections and faults, as there always will be among men. On the other hand, where the gospel is not declared, heard, and received, there we do not acknowledge the form of the church. Hence the churches governed by the ordinances of the pope are rather synagogues of the devil than Christian churches.

19. Excommunication

Because there are always some who hold God and his Word in contempt, who take account of neither injunction, exhortation, nor remonstrance, thus requiring greater chastisement, we hold the discipline of excommunication to be a thing holy and salutary among the faithful, since truly it was instituted by our Lord with good reason. This is in order that the wicked should not by their damnable conduct corrupt the good and dishonor our Lord, and that although proud they may turn to penitence. Therefore we believe that it is expedient according to the ordinance of God that all manifest idolaters, blasphemers, murderers, thieves, lewd persons, false witnesses, sedition-mongers, quarrelers, those guilty of defamation or assault, drunkards, dissolute liers, when they have been duly admonished and if they do not make amendment, be separated from the communion of the faithful until their repentance is known.

20. Ministers of the Word

We recognize no other pastors in the church than faithful pastors of the Word of God, feeding the sheep of Jesus Christ on the one hand with instruction, admonition, consolation, exhortation, deprecation; and on the other resisting all false doctrines and deceptions of the devil, without mixing with the pure doctrine of the Scriptures their dreams or their foolish imaginings. To these we accord no other power or authority but to conduct, rule, and govern the people of God committed to them by the same Word, in which they have power to command, defend, promise, and warn, and without which they neither can nor ought to attempt anything. As we receive the true ministers of the Word of God as messengers and ambassadors of God, it is necessary to listen to them as to himself, and we hold their ministry to be a commission from God necessary in the church. On the other hand we hold that all seductive and false prophets, who abandon the purity of the gospel and deviate to their own inventions, ought not at all to be suffered or maintained, who are not the pastors they pretend, but rather, like ravening wolves, ought to be hunted and ejected from the people of God.

21. Magistrates

We hold the supremacy and dominion of kings and princes as also of other magistrates and officers, to be a holy thing and a good ordinance of God. And since in performing their office they serve God and follow a Christian vocation, whether in defending the afflicted and innocent, or in correcting and punishing the malice of the perverse, we on our part also ought to accord them honor and reverence, to render respect and subservience, to execute their commands, to bear the charges they impose on us, so far as we are able without offense to God. In sum, we ought to regard them as vicars and lieutenants of God, whom one cannot resist without resisting God himself; and their office as a sacred commission from God which has been given them so that they may rule and govern us. Hence we hold that all Christians are bound to pray for the prosperity of the superiors and lords of the country where they live, to obey the statutes and ordinances which do not contravene the commandments of God, to promote welfare, peace, and public good, endeavoring to sustain the honor of those over them and the peace of the people, without contriving or attempting anything to inspire trouble or dissension. On the other hand we declare that all those who conduct themselves unfaithfully toward their superiors, and have not a right concern for the public good of the country where they live, demonstrate thereby their infidelity toward God.

7

The Heidelberg
Catechism (1563)

The city of Heidelberg came over to Protestantism under its prince, Frederick II, in 1545. For most of the next twenty years, however, a series of struggles—first with the forces of the Holy Roman Empire and then among Protestants themselves—kept the religious life of the city in turmoil. Under two successive rulers, Otto Henry and Frederick III, competition between Lutherans and the Reformed was especially keen. A disgraceful incident in 1560 precipitated a crisis. A Lutheran pastor and a Calvinist deacon exchanged vitriolic polemics and then quarreled violently in front of the assembled city at a Sunday celebration of the Lord's supper. Frederick III, in frustration, banished both antagonists from the realm and tried to find a better way. (As sidelight, an influential physician in Heidelberg, Thomas Erastus, urged Frederick to take a more active role in working through the city's religious difficulties. Thereafter, patterns of church-state interaction that relied heavily on the top-down authority of a ruler have been known as "Erastian.")

Reproduced with permission as published in The Heidelberg Catechism (400th Anniversary Edition 1563–1963), copyright 1962, United Church Press, New York, New York.

Frederick's first action was to seek theologians who, this time, could work together. In the end he found a remarkable pair. Caspar Olevianus (1536–1587), a French Reformed Protestant who had studied with Calvin and Beza but who yet read Melanchthon's books with appreciation, became pastor of Heidelberg's main church. Zacharius Ursinus (1534–1583), a native of Breslau in what is now Poland, had begun his theological education with Melanchthon in Wittenberg but had also studied personally with Calvin. Frederick named him professor of theology. Together they made a team of rare compatibility. The two had enjoyed harmonious relationships with both Lutherans and Calvinists. In addition, both were eager to work together to present a common Protestant front. And they both had a gift for pastoral insight.

Frederick wanted the two not only to put the religious affairs of his city back on an even keel. He also wanted them to draw up a statement of belief that could combine the best of Lutheran and Reformed wisdom and that could instruct ordinary people in the fundamentals of the Christian faith. The first edition of the Heidelberg Catechism was published on January 19, 1563, with a nine-page introduction by Prince Frederick. It became immediately popular in those parts of Germany that leaned in the Reformed direction and even had some success in Lutheran areas over the next two decades until growing tensions made it nearly impossible for any person, work, or perspective to straddle the increasingly sharp divide between the Lutherans and the Reformed.

The catechism would go on to have an even greater influence in the Netherlands. From the mid-1560s, Dutch Protestants had been struggling to replace both the political rule of Spain and the spiritual domination of the Catholic Church. The Catholic ruler of Spain, Philip II, was dead set against these aspirations. Persecution, armed struggle, and the martyrdom of many Protestants was the result. In these dire circumstances the Heidelberg Catechism made its appearance in Dutch. A Belgium-born preacher, Peter Dathenus, eventually found asylum with a band of Dutch refugees in Heidelberg where he prepared a translation of the catechism into their language. In 1568 Dathenus returned to the Netherlands with this translation, where it won almost immediate acceptance. By

1586 ministers of the Dutch Protestant church were required
to subscribe to the catechism as an expression of their faith,
and the practice of organizing preaching week-by-week according to the themes and Scripture references of the catechism
was firmly established. (To this day, descendants of these early
Dutch Protestants in at least two American denominations, the
Reformed Church in America and the Christian Reformed
Church, still organize at least some of their preaching according to the outline of the catechism.)

The catechism was a superb statement of faith for a perse-
cuted people. Its stress, from the very first question, on God's
desire to comfort his own, as well as its emphasis on the tran-
scendent goodness of God's providence, brought reassurance
to those who felt that they had been abandoned by all earthly
powers.

The catechism's long life in several denominational families
(including the German Reformed Church in America, which is
now part of the United Church of Christ) owes as much to its
winsome spirit as to the circumstances under which it was first
adopted. Unlike almost all other confessions or catechisms of
the sixteenth century, it is nearly devoid of polemics. (The crit-
icism of the Catholic Mass in question 80 was inserted at the
direct order of Frederick III.) In this absence of harsh
polemics, it resembles Luther's Small Catechism. Perhaps the
gentler spirit of these documents helps explain why they have
been the two most dearly beloved Protestant statements of
faith. Although these two catechisms share much in spirit and
content, they also have their differences. Luther's statements
on the sacraments are somewhat more "realistic" than those in
the Heidelberg Catechism. And the catechism from Olevianus
and Ursinus has a different order. With most other Reformed
statements of Christian faith, teaching on the Ten
Commandments comes after an exposition of the Apostles'
Creed (in Luther's, the Ten Commandments come before the
creed). With this arrangement, the Reformed were stressing
the Law as part of a Christian's joyful service to Christ, where
Lutherans characteristically described it as the force that
drives the sinner to Christ. The positions are not antithetical,
but they do point to different emphases in the two Protestant
traditions.

An ironic sequel followed the fate of the Heidelberg Catechism. In 1576, Frederick III's son, Louis, a staunch Lutheran, became prince. Immediately upon his accession, he removed Olevianus and Ursinus from their positions and ended the use of the Heidelberg Catechism in Heidelberg. By then, however, it had become too late to curtail the appeal of this powerful exposition of Christian faith.

Text

The Heidelberg Catechism. Translated by Allen O. Miller and M. Eugene Osterhaven. Philadelphia: United Church, 1962.

Additional Reading

Barth, Karl. *Learning Jesus Christ Through the Heidelberg Catechism.* Grand Rapids: Eerdmans, 1981.

Burchill, Christopher J. "On the Consolation of a Christian Scholar: Zacharias Ursinus (1534–1583) and the Reformation of Heidelberg." *Journal of Ecclesiastical History* 37 (Oct. 1986): 568–83.

The Commentary of Dr. Zacharias Ursinus on the Heidelberg Catechism. Translated by G. W. Willard. Columbus, Ohio: Scott and Bascom, 1851.

Nevin, John W. *The History and Genesis of the Heidelberg Catechism.* Chambersburg, Pa., 1847.

Plantinga, Cornelius, Jr. *A Place to Stand: A Reformed Study of Creeds and Confessions.* Grand Rapids: Christian Reformed Church, 1979.

Visser, Derk, ed. *Controversy and Conciliation: The Reformation in the Palatine, 1559–1583.* Alison Park, Pa.: Pickwick, 1986.

The Heidelberg Catechism

Question 1. *What is your only comfort, in life and in death?*

That I belong—body and soul, in life and in death—not to myself but to my faithful Savior, Jesus Christ, who at the cost of his own blood has fully paid for all my sins and has completely freed me from the dominion of the devil; that he protects me so well that without the will of my Father in heaven not a hair can fall from my head; indeed, that everything must fit his purpose for my salvation. Therefore, by his Holy Spirit, he also assures me of eternal life, and makes me wholeheartedly willing and ready from now on to live for him.

Question 2. *How many things must you know that you may live and die in the blessedness of this comfort?*

Three. First, the greatness of my sin and wretchedness. Second, how I am freed from all my sins and their wretched consequences. Third, what gratitude I owe to God for such redemption.

Part 1
Man's Sin and Guilt—The Law of God

Question 3. *Where do you learn of your sin and its wretched consequences?*

From the Law of God.

Question 4. *What does the Law of God require of us?*

Jesus Christ teaches this in a summary in Matthew 22:37–40:
"You shall love the Lord your God with all your heart, and with all your soul, and with all your mind. This is the great and first commandment. And a second is like it, you shall love your neighbor as yourself. On these two commandments depend all the Law and the prophets."

Question 5. *Can you keep all this perfectly?*

No, for by nature I am prone to hate God and my neighbor.

Question 6. *Did God create man evil and perverse like this?*

No. On the contrary, God created man good and in his image, that is, in true righteousness and holiness, so that he might rightly know God his Creator, love him with his whole heart, and live with him in eternal blessedness, praising and glorifying him.

Question 7. *Where, then, does this corruption of human nature come from?*

From the fall and disobedience of our first parents, Adam and Eve, in the garden of Eden; whereby our human life is so poisoned that we are all conceived and born in the state of sin.

Question 8. *But are we so perverted that we are altogether unable to do good and prone to do evil?*

Yes, unless we are born again through the Spirit of God.

Question 9. *Is not God unjust in requiring of man in his Law what he cannot do?*

No, for God so created man that he could do it. But man, upon the instigation of the devil, by deliberate disobedience, has cheated himself and all his descendants out of these gifts.

Question 10. *Will God let man get by with such disobedience and defection?*

Certainly not, for the wrath of God is revealed from heaven, both against our inborn sinfulness and our actual sins, and he will punish them according to his righteous judgment in time and in eternity, as he has declared: "Cursed be everyone who does not abide by all things written in the book of the Law, and do them."

Question 11. *But is not God also merciful?*

God is indeed merciful and gracious, but he is also righteous. It is his righteousness which requires that sin committed against the supreme majesty of God be punished with extreme, that is, with eternal punishment of body and soul.

Part 2
Man's Redemption and Freedom—
The Grace of God in Jesus Christ

Question 12. *Since, then, by the righteous judgment of God we have deserved temporal and eternal punishment, how may we escape this punishment, come again to grace, and be reconciled to God?*

God wills that his righteousness be satisfied; therefore, payment in full must be made to his righteousness, either by ourselves or by another.

Question 13. *Can we make this payment ourselves?*

By no means. On the contrary, we increase our debt each day.

Question 14. *Can any mere creature make the payment for us?*

No one. First of all, God does not want to punish any other creature for man's debt. Moreover, no mere creature can bear the burden of God's eternal wrath against sin and redeem others from it.

Question 15. *Then, what kind of mediator and redeemer must we seek?*

One who is a true and righteous man and yet more powerful than all creatures, that is, one who is at the same time true God.

Question 16. *Why must he be a true and righteous man?*

Because God's righteousness requires that man who has sinned should make reparation for sin, but the man who is himself a sinner cannot pay for others.

Question 17. *Why must he at the same time be true God?*

So that by the power of his divinity he might bear as a man the burden of God's wrath, and recover for us and restore to us righteousness and life.

Question 18. *Who is this Mediator who is at the same time true God and a true and perfectly righteous man?*

Our Lord Jesus Christ, who is freely given to us for complete redemption and righteousness.

Question 19. *Whence do you know this?*

From the holy gospel, which God himself revealed in the beginning in the garden of Eden, afterward proclaimed through the holy patriarchs and prophets and foreshadowed through the sacrifices and other rites of the old covenant, and finally fulfilled through his own well-beloved Son.

Question 20. *Will all men, then, be saved through Christ as they became lost through Adam?*

No. Only those who, by true faith, are incorporated into him and accept all his benefits.

Question 21. *What is true faith?*

It is not only a certain knowledge by which I accept as true all that God has revealed to us in his Word, but also a whole-hearted trust which the Holy Spirit creates in me through the gospel, that, not only to others, but to me also God has given the forgiveness of sins, everlasting righteousness, and salvation, out of sheer grace solely for the sake of Christ's saving work.

Question 22. *What, then, must a Christian believe?*

All that is promised us in the gospel, a summary of which is taught us in the articles of the Apostles' Creed, our universally acknowledged confession of faith.

Question 23. *What are these articles?*

I believe in God the Father almighty, Maker of heaven and earth;

And in Jesus Christ, his only-begotten Son, our Lord: who was conceived by the Holy Spirit, born of the virgin Mary; suffered under Pontius Pilate, was crucified, dead, and buried; he descended into hell, the third day he rose again from the dead; he ascended into heaven and sits at the right hand of God the Father almighty; from thence he shall come to judge the living and the dead.

I believe in the Holy Spirit; the holy catholic Church; the communion of saints; the forgiveness of sins; the resurrection of the body; and the life everlasting.

Question 24. *How are these articles divided?*

Into three parts: The first concerns God *the Father* and our *creation*; the second, God *the Son* and our *redemption*; and the third, God *the Holy Spirit* and our *sanctification*.

Question 25. *Since there is only one divine Being, why do you speak of three, Father, Son, and Holy Spirit?*

Because God has thus revealed himself in his Word, that these three distinct Persons are the one, true, eternal God.

Question 26. *What do you believe when you say: "I believe in God the Father almighty, Maker of heaven and earth"?*

That the eternal Father of our Lord Jesus Christ, who out of nothing created heaven and earth with all that is in them, who also upholds and governs them by his eternal counsel and providence, is for the sake of Christ his Son my God and my Father. I trust in him so completely that I have no doubt that he will provide me with all things necessary for body and soul. Moreover, whatever evil he sends upon me in this troubled life he will turn to my good, for he is able to do it, being almighty God, and is determined to do it, being a faithful Father.

Question 27. *What do you understand by the providence of God?*

The almighty and ever-present power of God whereby he still upholds, as it were by his own hand, heaven and earth together with all creatures, and rules in such a way that leaves and grass, rain and drought, fruitful and unfruitful years, food and drink, health and sickness, riches and poverty, and everything else, come to us not by chance but by his fatherly hand.

Question 28. *What advantage comes from acknowledging God's creation and providence?*

We learn that we are to be patient in adversity, grateful in the midst of blessing, and to trust our faithful God and Father for the future, assured that no creature shall separate us from his love, since all creatures are so completely in his hand that without his will they cannot even move.

Question 29. *Why is the Son of God called Jesus, which means "Savior"?*

Because he saves us from our sins, and because salvation is to be sought or found in no other.

Question 30. *Do those who seek their salvation and well-being from saints, by their own efforts, or by other means really believe in the only Savior Jesus?*

No. Rather, by such actions they deny Jesus, the only Savior and Redeemer, even though they boast of belonging to him. It therefore follows that either Jesus is not a perfect Savior, or those who receive this Savior with true faith must possess in him all that is necessary for their salvation.

Question 31. *Why is he called "Christ," that is, the "Anointed One"?*

Because he is ordained by God the Father and anointed with the Holy Spirit to be *our chief Prophet* and *Teacher*, fully revealing to us the secret purpose and will of God concerning our redemption; to be *our only High Priest*, having redeemed us by the one sacrifice of his body and ever interceding for us with the Father; and to be *our eternal King*, governing us by his

Word and Spirit, and defending and sustaining us in the redemption he has won for us.

Question 32. *But why are you called a Christian?*

Because through faith I share in Christ and thus in his anointing, so that I may confess his name, offer myself a living sacrifice of gratitude to him, and fight against sin and the devil with a free and good conscience throughout this life and hereafter rule with him in eternity over all creatures.

Question 33. *Why is he called "God's only-begotten Son," since we also are God's children?*

Because Christ alone is God's own eternal Son, whereas we are accepted for his sake as children of God by grace.

Question 34. *Why do you call him "Our Lord"?*

Because, not with gold or silver but at the cost of his blood, he has redeemed us body and soul from sin and all the dominion of the devil, and has bought us for his very own.

Question 35. *What is the meaning of: "Conceived by the Holy Spirit, born of the virgin Mary"?*

That the eternal Son of God, who is and remains true and eternal God, took upon himself our true manhood from the flesh and blood of the virgin Mary through the action of the Holy Spirit, so that he might also be the true seed of David, like his fellow men in all things, except for sin.

Question 36. *What benefit do you receive from the holy conception and birth of Christ?*

That he is our Mediator, and that, in God's sight, he covers over with his innocence and perfect holiness the sinfulness in which I have been conceived.

Question 37. *What do you understand by the word "suffered"?*

That throughout his life on earth, but especially at the end of it, he bore in body and soul the wrath of God against the sin of the whole human race, so that by his suffering, as the only expiatory sacrifice, he might redeem our body and soul from everlasting damnation, and might obtain for us God's grace, righteousness, and eternal life.

Question 38. *Why did he suffer "under Pontius Pilate" as his judge?*

That he, being innocent, might be condemned by an earthly judge, and thereby set us free from the judgment of God which, in all its severity, ought to fall upon us.

Question 39. *Is there something more in his having been crucified than if he had died some other death?*

Yes, for by this I am assured that he took upon himself the curse which lay upon me, because the death of the cross was cursed by God.

Question 40. *Why did Christ have to suffer "death"?*

Because the righteousness and truth of God are such that nothing else could make reparation for our sins except the death of the Son of God.

Question 41. *Why was he "buried"?*

To confirm the fact that he was really dead.

Question 42. *Since, then, Christ died for us, why must we also die?*

Our death is not a reparation for our sins, but only a dying to sin and an entering into eternal life.

Question 43. *What further benefit do we receive from the sacrifice and death of Christ on the cross?*

That by his power our old self is crucified, put to death, and buried with him, so that the evil passions of our mortal bodies may reign in us no more, but that we may offer ourselves to him as a sacrifice of thanksgiving.

Question 44. *Why is there added: "He descended into hell"?*

That in my severest tribulations I may be assured that Christ my Lord has redeemed me from hellish anxieties and torment by the unspeakable anguish, pains, and terrors which he suffered in his soul both on the cross and before.

Question 45. *What benefit do we receive from "the resurrection" of Christ?*

First, by his resurrection he has overcome death that he might make us share in the righteousness which he has obtained for us through his death. Second, we too are now raised by his power to a new life. Third, the resurrection of Christ is a sure pledge to us of our blessed resurrection.

Question 46. *How do you understand the words: "He ascended into heaven"?*

That Christ was taken up from the earth into heaven before the eyes of his disciples and remains there on our behalf until he comes again to judge the living and the dead.

Question 47. *Then, is not Christ with us unto the end of the world, as he has promised us?*

Christ is true man and true God. As a man he is no longer on earth, but in his divinity, majesty, grace, and Spirit, he is never absent from us.

Question 48. *But are not the two natures in Christ separated from each other in this way, if the humanity is not wherever the divinity is?*

Not at all; for since divinity is incomprehensible and everywhere present, it must follow that the divinity is indeed beyond the bounds of the humanity which it has assumed, and is nonetheless ever in that humanity as well, and remains personally united to it.

Question 49. *What benefit do we receive from Christ's ascension into heaven?*

First, that he is our Advocate in the presence of his Father in heaven. Second, that we have our flesh in heaven as a sure pledge that he, as the head, will also take us, his members, up to himself. Third, that he sends us his Spirit as a counterpledge by whose power we seek what is above, where Christ is, sitting at the right hand of God, and not things that are on earth.

Question 50. *Why is there added: "And sits at the right hand of God"?*

Because Christ ascended into heaven so that he might manifest himself there as the head of his church, through whom the Father governs all things.

Question 51. *What benefit do we receive from this glory of Christ, our head?*

First, that through his Holy Spirit he pours out heavenly gifts upon us, his members. Second, that by his power he defends and supports us against all our enemies.

Question 52. *What comfort does the return of Christ "to judge the living and the dead" give you?*

That in all affliction and persecution I may await with head held high the very Judge from heaven who has already submitted himself to the judgment of God for me and has removed all the curse from me; that he will cast all his enemies and mine into everlasting condemnation, but he shall take me, together with all his elect, to himself into heavenly joy and glory.

Question 53. *What do you believe concerning "the Holy Spirit"?*

First, that, with the Father and the Son, he is equally eternal God; second, that God's Spirit is also given to me, preparing me through a true faith to share in Christ and all his benefits, that he comforts me and will abide with me forever.

Question 54. *What do you believe concerning "the holy catholic church"?*

I believe that, from the beginning to the end of the world, and from among the whole human race, the Son of God, by his Spirit and his Word, gathers, protects, and preserves for himself, in the unity of the true faith, a congregation chosen for eternal life. Moreover, I believe that I am and forever will remain a living member of it.

Question 55. *What do you understand by "the communion of saints"?*

First, that believers one and all, as partakers of the Lord Christ, and all his treasures and gifts, shall share in one fellowship. Second, that each one ought to know that he is obliged to use his gifts freely and with joy for the benefit and welfare of other members.

Question 56. *What do you believe concerning "the forgiveness of sins"?*

That, for the sake of Christ's reconciling work, God will no more remember my sins or the sinfulness with which I have to struggle all my life long; but that he graciously imparts to me the righteousness of Christ so that I may never come into condemnation.

Question 57. *What comfort does "the resurrection of the body" give you?*

That after this life my soul shall be immediately taken up to Christ, its head, and that this flesh of mine, raised by the power of Christ, shall be reunited with my soul, and be conformed to the glorious body of Christ.

Question 58. *What comfort does the article concerning "the life everlasting" give you?*

That, since I now feel in my heart the beginning of eternal joy, I shall possess, after this life, perfect blessedness, which no eye has seen, nor ear heard, nor the heart of man conceived, and thereby praise God forever.

Question 59. *But how does it help you now that you believe all this?*

That I am righteous in Christ before God, and an heir of eternal life.

Question 60. *How are you righteous before God?*

Only by true faith in Jesus Christ. In spite of the fact that my conscience accuses me that I have grievously sinned against all the commandments of God, and have not kept any one of them, and that I am still ever prone to all that is evil, nevertheless, God, without any merit of my own, out of pure grace, grants me the benefits of the perfect expiation of Christ, imputing to me his righteousness and holiness as if I had never committed a single sin or had ever been sinful, having fulfilled myself all the obedience which Christ has carried out for me, if only I accept such favor with a trusting heart.

Question 61. *Why do you say that you are righteous by faith alone?*

Not because I please God by virtue of the worthiness of my faith, but because the satisfaction, righteousness, and holiness of Christ alone are my righteousness before God, and because I can accept it and make it mine in no other way than by faith alone.

Question 62. *But why cannot our good works be our righteousness before God, or at least a part of it?*

Because the righteousness which can stand before the judgment of God must be absolutely perfect and wholly in conformity with the divine Law. But even our best works in this life are all imperfect and defiled with sin.

Question 63. *Will our good works merit nothing, even when it is God's purpose to reward them in this life, and in the future life as well?*

This reward is not given because of merit, but out of grace.

Question 64. *But does not this teaching make people careless and sinful?*

No, for it is impossible for those who are ingrafted into Christ by true faith not to bring forth the fruit of gratitude.

Question 65. *Since, then, faith alone makes us share in Christ and all his benefits, where does such faith originate?*

The Holy Spirit creates it in our hearts by the preaching of the holy gospel, and confirms it by the use of the holy sacraments.

Question 66. *What are the sacraments?*

They are visible, holy signs and seals instituted by God in order that by their use he may the more fully disclose and seal us to the promise of the gospel, namely, that because of the one sacrifice of Christ accomplished on the cross he graciously grants us the forgiveness of sins and eternal life.

Question 67. *Are both the Word and the sacraments designed to direct our faith to the one sacrifice of Jesus Christ on the cross as the only ground of our salvation?*

Yes, indeed, for the Holy Spirit teaches in the gospel and confirms by the holy sacraments that our whole salvation is rooted in the one sacrifice of Christ offered for us on the cross.

Question 68. *How many sacraments has Christ instituted in the New Testament?*

Two, holy baptism and the holy supper.

Question 69. *How does holy baptism remind and assure you that the one sacrifice of Christ on the cross avails for you?*

In this way: Christ has instituted this external washing with water and by it has promised that I am as certainly washed with his blood and Spirit from the uncleanness of my soul and from all my sins, as I am washed externally with water which is used to remove the dirt from my body.

Question 70. *What does it mean to be washed with the blood and Spirit of Christ?*

It means to have the forgiveness of sins from God, through grace, for the sake of Christ's blood which he shed for us in his sacrifice on the cross, and also to be renewed by the Holy Spirit and sanctified as members of Christ, so that we may more and more die unto sin and live in a consecrated and blameless way.

Question 71. *Where has Christ promised that we are as certainly washed with his blood and Spirit as with the water of baptism?*

In the institution of baptism which runs thus: "Go therefore and make disciples of all nations, baptizing them in the name of the Father and of the Son and of the Holy Spirit." "He who believes and is baptized will be saved: but he who does not believe will be condemned." This promise is also repeated where the Scriptures call baptism "the water of rebirth" and the washing away of sins.

Question 72. *Does merely the outward washing with water itself wash away sins?*

No; for only the blood of Jesus Christ and the Holy Spirit cleanse us from all sins.

Question 73. *Then why does the Holy Spirit call baptism the water of rebirth and the washing away of sins?*

God does not speak in this way except for a strong reason. Not only does he teach us by baptism that just as the dirt of the body is taken away by water, so our sins are removed by the blood and Spirit of Christ; but more important still, by the divine pledge and sign he wishes to assure us that we are just as truly washed from our sins spiritually as our bodies are washed with water.

Question 74. *Are infants also to be baptized?*

Yes, because they, as well as their parents, are included in the covenant and belong to the people of God. Since both redemption from sin through the blood of Christ and the gift of faith from the Holy Spirit are promised to these children no less than to their parents, infants are also by baptism, as a sign of the covenant, to be incorporated into the Christian church and distinguished from the children of unbelievers. This was done in the old covenant by circumcision. In the new covenant baptism has been instituted to take its place.

Question 75. *How are you reminded and assured in the holy supper that you participate in the one sacrifice of Christ on the cross and in all his benefits?*

In this way: Christ has commanded me and all believers to eat of this broken bread, and to drink of this cup in remembrance of him. He has thereby promised that his body was offered and broken on the cross for me, and his blood was shed for me, as surely as I see with my eyes that the bread of the Lord is broken for me, and that the cup is shared with me. Also, he has promised that he himself as certainly feeds and nourishes my soul to everlasting life with his crucified body and shed blood as I receive from the hand of the minister and actually taste the bread and the cup of the Lord which are given to me as sure signs of the body and blood of Christ.

Question 76. *What does it mean to eat the crucified body of Christ and to drink his shed blood?*

It is not only to embrace with a trusting heart the whole passion and death of Christ, and by it to receive the forgiveness of sins and eternal life. In addition, it is to be so united more and more to his blessed body by the Holy Spirit dwelling both in Christ and in us that, although he is in heaven and we are on earth, we are nevertheless flesh of his flesh and bone of his bone, always living and being governed by one Spirit, as the members of our bodies are governed by one soul.

Question 77. *Where has Christ promised that he will feed and nourish believers with his body and blood just as surely as they eat of this broken bread and drink of this cup?*

In the institution of the holy supper which reads: The Lord Jesus on the night when he was betrayed took bread, and when he had given thanks, he broke it, and said, "This is my body which is for you. Do this in remembrance of me." In the same way also the cup, after supper, saying, "This cup is the new covenant in my blood. Do this, as often as you drink it, in remembrance of me." For as often as you eat this bread and drink the cup, you proclaim the Lord's death until he comes.

This promise is also repeated by the apostle Paul: When we bless "the cup of blessing," is it not a means of sharing in the blood of Christ? When we break the bread, is it not a means of sharing the body of Christ? Because there is one loaf, we, many as we are, are one body; for it is one loaf of which we all partake.

Question 78. *Do the bread and wine become the very body and blood of Christ?*

No, for as the water in baptism is not changed into the blood of Christ, nor becomes the washing away of sins by itself, but is only a divine sign and confirmation of it, so also in the Lord's supper the sacred bread does not become the body of Christ itself, although, in accordance with the nature and usage of sacraments, it is called the body of Christ.

Question 79. *Then why does Christ call the bread his body, and the cup his blood, or the new covenant in his blood, and why does the apostle Paul call the supper "a means of sharing" in the body and blood of Christ?*

Christ does not speak in this way except for a strong reason. He wishes to teach us by it that as bread and wine sustain this temporal life so his crucified body and shed blood are the true food and drink of our souls for eternal life. Even more, he wishes to assure us by this visible sign and pledge that we come to share in his true body and blood through the working of the Holy Spirit as surely as we receive with our mouth these holy tokens in remembrance of him, and that all his sufferings and his death are our own as certainly as if we had ourselves suffered and rendered satisfaction in our own persons.

Question 80. *What difference is there between the Lord's supper and the papal Mass?*

The Lord's supper testifies to us that we have complete forgiveness of all our sins through the one sacrifice of Jesus Christ which he himself has accomplished on the cross once for all; (and that through the Holy Spirit we are incorporated into Christ, who is now in heaven with his true body at the right hand of the Father and is there to be worshiped). But the Mass teaches that the living and the dead do not have forgiveness of sins through the sufferings of Christ unless Christ is again offered for them daily by the priest (and that Christ is bodily under the form of bread and wine and is therefore to be worshiped in them). Therefore the Mass is fundamentally a complete denial of the once for all sacrifice and passion of Jesus Christ (and as such an idolatry to be condemned). [This question was not in the first edition of the catechism. It was added to the second edition; the material in parentheses is from the third edition.]

Question 81. *Who ought to come to the table of the Lord?*

Those who are displeased with themselves for their sins, and who nevertheless trust that these sins have been forgiven them and that their remaining weakness is covered by the passion and death of Christ, and who also desire more and more to strengthen their faith and improve their life. The impenitent and hypocrites, however, eat and drink judgment to themselves.

Question 82. *Should those who show themselves to be unbelievers and enemies of God by their confession and life be admitted to this supper?*

No, for then the covenant of God would be profaned and his wrath provoked against the whole congregation. According to the ordinance of Christ and his apostles, therefore, the Christian church is under obligation, by the office of the keys, to exclude such persons until they amend their lives.

Question 83. *What is the office of the keys?*

The preaching of the holy gospel and Christian discipline. By these two means the kingdom of heaven is opened to believers and shut against unbelievers.

Question 84. *How is the kingdom of heaven opened and shut by the preaching of the holy gospel?*

In this way: The kingdom of heaven is opened when it is proclaimed and openly testified to believers, one and all, according to the command of Christ, that as often as they accept the promise of the gospel with true faith all their sins are truly forgiven them by God for the sake of Christ's gracious work. On the contrary, the wrath of God and eternal condemnation fall upon all unbelievers and hypocrites as long as they do not repent. It is according to this witness of the gospel that God will judge the one and the other in this life and in the life to come.

Question 85. *How is the kingdom of heaven shut and opened by Christian discipline?*

In this way: Christ commanded that those who bear the Christian name in an unchristian way either in doctrine or in life should be given brotherly admonition. If they do not give up their errors or evil ways, notification is given to the church or to those ordained for this by the church. Then, if they do not change after this warning, they are forbidden to partake of the holy sacraments and are thus excluded from the communion of the church and by God himself from the kingdom of Christ. However, if they promise and show real amendment, they are received again as members of Christ and of the church.

Part 3
Man's Gratitude and Obedience—
New Life Through the Holy Spirit

Question 86. *Since we are redeemed from our sin and its wretched consequences by grace through Christ without any merit of our own, why must we do good works?*

Because just as Christ has redeemed us with his blood he also renews us through his Holy Spirit according to his own image, so that with our whole life we may show ourselves grateful to God for his goodness and that he may be glorified through us; and further, so that we ourselves may be assured of our faith by its fruits and by our reverent behavior may win our neighbors to Christ.

Question 87. *Can those who do not turn to God from their ungrateful, impenitent life be saved?*

Certainly not! Scripture says, "Surely you know that the unjust will never come into possession of the kingdom of God. Make no mistake: no fornicator or idolater, none who are guilty either of adultery or of homosexual perversion, no thieves or grabbers or drunkards or slanderers or swindlers, will possess the kingdom of God."

Question 88. *How many parts are there to the true repentance or conversion of man?*

Two: the dying of the old self and the birth of the new.

Question 89. *What is the dying of the old self?*

Sincere sorrow over our sins and more and more to hate them and to flee from them.

Question 90. *What is the birth of the new self?*

Complete joy in God through Christ and a strong desire to live according to the will of God in all good works.

Question 91. *But what are good works?*

Only those which are done out of true faith, in accordance with the Law of God, and for his glory, and not those based on our own opinion or on the traditions of men.

Question 92. *What is the Law of God?*

God spoke all these words saying:

First Commandment

"I am the Lord your God, who brought you out of the land of Egypt, out of the house of bondage. You shall have no other gods before me."

Second Commandment

"You shall not make yourself a graven image, or any likeness of anything that is in heaven above, or that is in the earth beneath, or that is in the water under the earth; you shall not bow down to them or serve them; for I the Lord your God am a jealous God, visiting the iniquity of the fathers upon the children to the third and the fourth generation of those who hate me, but showing steadfast love to thousands of those who love me and keep my commandments."

Third Commandment

"You shall not take the name of the Lord your God in vain; for the Lord will not hold him guiltless who takes his name in vain."

Fourth Commandment

"Remember the Sabbath day, to keep it holy. Six days you shall labor, and do all your work; but the seventh day is a Sabbath to the Lord your God; in it you shall not do any work, you, or your son, or your daughter, your manservant, or your maidservant, or your cattle, or the sojourner who is within your gates; for in six days the Lord made heaven and earth, the sea, and all that is in them, and rested the seventh day; therefore the Lord blessed the Sabbath day and hallowed it."

Fifth Commandment

"Honor your father and your mother, that your days may be long in the land which the Lord your God gives you."

Sixth Commandment

"You shall not kill."

Seventh Commandment

"You shall not commit adultery."

Eighth Commandment
"You shall not steal."

Ninth Commandment
"You shall not bear false witness against your neighbor."

Tenth Commandment
"You shall not covet your neighbor's house; you shall not covet your neighbor's wife, or his manservant, or his maidservant, or his ox, or his ass, or anything that is your neighbor's."

Question 93. *How are these commandments divided?*

Into two tables, the first of which teaches us in four commandments how we ought to live in relation to God; the other, in six commandments, what we owe to our neighbor.

Question 94. *What does the Lord require in the first commandment?*

That I must avoid and flee all idolatry, sorcery, enchantments, invocation of saints or other creatures because of the risk of losing my salvation. Indeed, I ought properly to acknowledge the only true God, trust in him alone, in humility and patience expect all good from him only, and love, fear, and honor him with my whole heart. In short, I should rather turn my back on all creatures than do the least thing against his will.

Question 95. *What is idolatry?*

It is to imagine or possess something in which to put one's trust in place of or beside the one true God who has revealed himself in his Word.

Question 96. *What does God require in the second commandment?*

That we should not represent him or worship him in any other manner than he has commanded in his Word.

Question 97. *Should we, then, not make any images at all?*

God cannot and should not be pictured in any way. As for creatures, although they may indeed be portrayed, God forbids making or having any likeness of them in order to worship them, or to use them to serve him.

Question 98. *But may not pictures be tolerated in churches in place of books for unlearned people?*

No, for we must not try to be wiser than God who does not want his people to be taught by means of lifeless idols, but through the living preaching of his Word.

Question 99. *What is required in the third commandment?*

That we must not profane or abuse the name of God by cursing, by perjury, or by unnecessary oaths. Nor are we to participate in such horrible sins by keeping quiet and thus giving silent consent. In a word, we must not use the holy name of God except with fear and reverence so that he may be rightly confessed and addressed by us, and be glorified in all our words and works.

Question 100. *Is it, therefore, so great a sin to blaspheme God's name by cursing and swearing that God is angry with those who do not try to prevent and forbid it as much as they can?*

Yes, indeed; for no sin is greater or provokes his wrath more than the profaning of his name. That is why he commanded it to be punished with death.

Question 101. *But may we not swear oaths by the name of God in a devout manner?*

Yes, when the civil authorities require it of their subjects, or when it is otherwise needed to maintain and promote fidelity and truth, to the glory of God and the welfare of our neighbor. Such oath taking is grounded in God's Word and has therefore been rightly used by God's people under the old and new covenants.

Question 102. *May we also swear by the saints and other creatures?*

No; for a lawful oath is a calling upon God, as the only Searcher of hearts, to bear witness to the truth, and to punish me if I swear falsely. No creature deserves such honor.

Question 103. *What does God require in the fourth commandment?*

First, that the ministry of the gospel and Christian education be maintained, and that I diligently attend church, especially on the Lord's day, to hear the Word of God, to participate in the holy sacraments, to call publicly upon the Lord, and to give Christian service to those in need. Second, that I cease from my evil works all the days of my life, allow the Lord to work in me through his Spirit, and thus begin in this life the eternal Sabbath.

Question 104. *What does God require in the fifth commandment?*

That I show honor, love, and faithfulness to my father and mother and to all who are set in authority over me; that I submit myself with respectful obedience to all their careful instruction and discipline; and that I also bear patiently their failures, since it is God's will to govern us by their hand.

Question 105. *What does God require in the sixth commandment?*

That I am not to abuse, hate, injure, or kill my neighbor, either with thought, or by word or gesture, much less by deed, whether by myself or through another, but to lay aside all desire for revenge; and that I do not harm myself or willfully expose myself to danger. This is why the authorities are armed with the means to prevent murder.

Question 106. *But does this commandment speak only of killing?*

In forbidding murder God means to teach us that he abhors the root of murder, which is envy, hatred, anger, and desire for revenge, and that he regards all these as hidden murder.

Question 107. *Is it enough, then, if we do not kill our neighbor in any of these ways?*

No; for when God condemns envy, hatred, and anger, he requires us to love our neighbor as ourselves, to show patience, peace, gentleness, mercy, and friendliness toward him, to prevent injury to him as much as we can, and also to do good to our enemies.

Question 108. *What does the seventh commandment teach us?*

That all unchastity is condemned by God, and that we should therefore detest it from the heart, and live chaste and disciplined lives, whether in holy wedlock or in single life.

Question 109. *Does God forbid nothing more than adultery and such gross sins in this commandment?*

Since both our body and soul are a temple of the Holy Spirit, it is his will that we keep both pure and holy. Therefore he forbids all unchaste actions, gestures, words, thoughts, desires, and whatever may excite another person to them.

Question 110. *What does God forbid in the eighth commandment?*

He forbids not only the theft and robbery which civil authorities punish, but God also labels as theft all wicked tricks and schemes by which we seek to get for ourselves our neighbor's goods, whether by force or under pretext of right, such as false weights and measures, deceptive advertising and merchandizing, counterfeit money, exorbitant interest, or any other means forbidden by God. He also forbids all greed and misuse and waste of his gifts.

Question 111. *But what does God require of you in this commandment?*

That I work for the good of my neighbor wherever I can and may, deal with him as I would have others deal with me, and do my work well so that I may be able to help the poor in their need.

Question 112. *What is required in the ninth commandment?*

That I do not bear false witness against anyone, twist anyone's words, be a gossip or a slanderer, or condemn anyone lightly without a hearing. Rather I am required to avoid, under penalty of God's wrath, all lying and deceit as the works of the devil himself. In judicial and all other matters I am to love the truth, and to speak and confess it honestly. Indeed, insofar as I am able, I am to defend and promote my neighbor's good name.

Question 113. *What is required in the tenth commandment?*

That there should never enter our heart even the least inclination or thought contrary to any commandment of God, but that we should always hate sin with our whole heart and find satisfaction and joy in all righteousness.

Question 114. *But can those who are converted to God keep these commandments perfectly?*

No, for even the holiest of them make only a small beginning in obedience in this life. Nevertheless, they begin with serious purpose to conform not only to some, but to all the commandments of God.

Question 115. *Why, then, does God have the Ten Commandments preached so strictly since no one can keep them in this life?*

First, that all our life long we may become increasingly aware of our sinfulness, and therefore more eagerly seek forgiveness of sins and righteousness in Christ. Second, that we may constantly and diligently pray to God for the grace of the Holy Spirit, so that more and more we may be renewed in the image of God, until we attain the goal of full perfection after this life.

Question 116. *Why is prayer necessary for Christians?*

Because it is the chief part of the gratitude which God requires of us, and because God will give his grace and Holy Spirit only to those who sincerely beseech him in prayer without ceasing, and who thank him for these gifts.

Question 117. *What is contained in a prayer which pleases God and is heard by him?*

First, that we sincerely call upon the one true God, who has revealed himself to us in his Word, for all that he has commanded us to ask of him. Then, that we thoroughly acknowledge our need and evil condition so that we may humble ourselves in the presence of his majesty. Third, that we rest assured that, in spite of our unworthiness, he will certainly hear our prayer for the sake of Christ our Lord, as he has promised us in his Word.

Question 118. *What has God commanded us to ask of him?*

All things necessary for soul and body which Christ the Lord has included in the prayer which he himself taught us.

Question 119. *What is the Lord's Prayer?*

"Our Father who art in heaven, hallowed be thy name. Thy kingdom come, thy will be done, on earth as it is in heaven. Give us this day our daily bread; and forgive us our debts, as we also have forgiven our debtors; and lead us not into temptation, but deliver us from evil, for thine is the kingdom and the power and the glory, forever. Amen."

Question 120. *Why has Christ commanded us to address God: "Our Father"?*

That at the very beginning of our prayer he may awaken in us the childlike reverence and trust toward God which should be the motivation of our prayer, which is that God has become our Father through Christ and will much less deny us what we ask him in faith than our human fathers will refuse us earthly things.

Question 121. *Why is there added: "Who art in heaven"?*

That we may have no earthly conception of the heavenly majesty of God, but that we may expect from his almighty power all things that are needed for body and soul.

Question 122. *What is the first petition?*

"Hallowed be thy name." That is: help us first of all to know thee rightly, and to hallow, glorify, and praise thee in all thy works through which there shine thine almighty power, wisdom, goodness, righteousness, mercy, and truth. And so order our whole life in thought, word, and deed that thy name may never be blasphemed on our account, but may always be honored and praised.

Question 123. *What is the second petition?*

"Thy kingdom come." That is: so govern us by thy Word and Spirit that we may more and more submit ourselves unto thee. Uphold and increase thy church. Destroy the works of the devil, every power that raises itself against thee, and all wicked schemes thought up against thy holy Word, until the full coming of thy kingdom in which thou shalt be all in all.

Question 124. *What is the third petition?*

"Thy will be done, on earth, as it is in heaven." That is: grant that we and all men may renounce our own will and obey thy will, which alone is good, without grumbling, so that everyone may carry out his office and calling as willingly and faithfully as the angels in heaven.

Question 125. *What is the fourth petition?*

"Give us this day our daily bread." That is: be pleased to provide for all our bodily needs so that thereby we may acknowledge that thou art the only source of all that is good, and that without thy blessing neither our care and labor nor thy gifts can do us any good. Therefore, may we withdraw our trust from all creatures and place it in thee alone.

Question 126. *What is the fifth petition?*

"And forgive us our debts, as we also have forgiven our debtors." That is: be pleased, for the sake of Christ's blood, not to charge to us, miserable sinners, our many transgressions, nor the evil which still clings to us. We also find this witness of thy grace in us, that it is our sincere intention heartily to forgive our neighbor.

Question 127. *What is the sixth petition?*

"And lead us not into temptation, but deliver us from evil." That is: since we are so weak that we cannot stand by ourselves for one moment, and besides, since our sworn enemies, the devil, the world, and our own sin, ceaselessly assail us, be pleased to preserve and strengthen us through the power of thy Holy Spirit so that we may stand firm against them, and not be defeated in this spiritual warfare, until at last we obtain complete victory.

Question 128. *How do you close this prayer?*

"For thine is the kingdom and the power and the glory, forever." That is: we ask all this of thee because, as our King, thou art willing and able to give us all that is good since thou hast power over all things, and that by this not we ourselves but thy holy name may be glorified forever.

Question 129. *What is the meaning of the little word "Amen"?*

Amen means: this shall truly and certainly be. For my prayer is much more certainly heard by God than I am persuaded in my heart that I desire such things from him.

Canons and Decrees
of the Council of Trent
(1545–1563)

Early in the Reformation leading Catholics joined Protestants in calling for a general council to reform abuses in the church and to thrash out the doctrinal uncertainties of the age. Little progress was made toward such a goal, however, until the late 1530s. Deepening division between Protestants and Roman Catholics was one of the reasons for the delay, but so were the extraordinarily complicated political relations of the day. Leaders of several Catholic nations, directors of important factions in the church, succeeding popes, and the Holy Roman Emperor all had vested interests in making sure that a council would result (at least from each one's own perspective) in more good than harm. Pope Paul III initially called for the council to be held at Mantua in northern Italy in 1537, but was frustrated by political uncertainties. After several other false starts, he asked for bishops and other high officials to convene in 1542 at Trent, one of the emperor's cities that was

From *Canons and Decrees of the Council of Trent*, edited by H. J. Schroeder, by permission of TAN Books and Publishers, Inc., P.O. Box 424, Rockford, IL 61105.

relatively close to Rome. The gathering did not get under way, however, until December 1545.

The council would continue for eighteen years. It met for eight sessions in 1545–1547, an additional six sessions in 1551–1552, and a final eleven sessions in 1562–1563. During the exceedingly brief tenure of Marcellus II (April 1555) and the reactionary pontificate of Paul IV (1555–1559), it did not meet at all. At these and other times, it seemed to many observers that it was on the point of collapse. But fueled, as such ventures so often have been, by a singular combination of high-minded Christian idealism and petty-minded political manipulation, the council persevered to its conclusion.

The result was an official statement of Catholic teaching that gave the church a more detailed definition of its own beliefs than it had ever had. The purposes of the council, which are spelled out in some detail in the decree from the first session, were, in effect, two: reform abuses in the church and answer the Protestants. The emperor, Charles V, wanted to take up the abuses first. Pope Paul III was determined to settle questions of doctrine. The compromise that resulted was to treat both together.

Italian bishops working in concert with the pope played the leading part at Trent. But representatives from France and, in the last sitting especially, from Spain also made a vigorous contribution. A few Protestants showed up as guests, but none exercised much influence. Martin Luther, who died in 1546 shortly after the opening of the council, groused that the meeting was too little and too late. John Calvin lived to write strenuous rebuttals to Trent's early decrees. A notable Lutheran theologian, Martin Chemnitz (1522–1586), published the earliest and perhaps most effective Protestant response.

The excerpts from Trent's canons and decrees that appear below come mainly from the doctrinal portions. If the council had restricted itself to such measures, it would appear to be merely the agent of a "Counter-Reformation," for many of these affirmations are aimed directly at the errors which, from a Catholic perspective, were being promoted by the kind of Protestant statements found elsewhere in this book. But if space had permitted the inclusion of excerpts from the canons and decrees respecting internal reform of the church, it would have been obvious why Trent functioned also as a cornerstone for the "Catholic Reformation." Included in these disciplinary reforms were correctives which many Catholics, as well as Protestants, had long desired. Among other reforms, the council forbade nonresidency, or the absence of bishops and priests from their assigned fields of labor. It banned the office of indulgence seller. It also gave bishops tighter control over all church activities in their dioceses, including the actions of monks, nuns, and friars. And, most momentously, it decreed that every diocese should erect a seminary for the training of priests. This last provision eventually produced a priesthood that was much better educated and much better equipped to communicate the Catholic faith to the people as a whole. It also set up a machinery for promoting the rulings of Trent itself as well as the form of theology (more scholastic and Thomistic than biblical and Augustinian) that the council reinforced.

Having recognized the importance of Trent for church reform, however, it is still true that the council administered a stinging rebuke to the doctrines of the Protestants. Thus, as illustrated below, the council affirmed that church tradition was a coordinate authority with Scripture; that only the teaching officers of the church had the right to interpret the Bible; that the Old Latin Vulgate was the official text of Scripture; that there were seven sacraments; that it was appropriate to keep the cup from the laity at communion; that the Mass or Eucharist was a propitiatory sacrifice of Christ (although not replacing the definitive sacrifice on the cross); that the bread and wine of the Eucharist were transubstantiated into the true body and blood of Christ; that it was good to venerate the transubstantiated bread and wine; that purgatory did indeed exist; and that it was useful to invoke the aid of the saints.

The council's longest decree, from its sixth session of January 1547, concerned justification. In sixteen substantial chapters and thirty-three anathematizing canons the council said a few things that would have pleased some Protestants: for example, that there is no salvation outside of Christ and that justification begins with "the predisposing grace of God through Jesus Christ." But much else contradicted the main teaching to be found in virtually all the confessions and catechisms of the Protestants. Against Luther, Calvin, Cranmer, and the movements associated with these leading Protestants, Trent affirmed the lingering power of human free will. It insisted that faith must be shaped by acts of charity. It defined the sacrament of penance as the only way for postbaptismal sins to be forgiven. And it denied that people could have certain knowledge of their own justification. That these judgments were stated with full reference to the Scriptures and the traditions of the church that Protestants thought supported *their* beliefs on justification only illustrated how hard and fast the breach had become after only two generations of Protestant teaching. In fact, it has taken most of the nearly 450 years since the Council of Trent to even begin to overcome the barrier created by Protestant objections to Catholic practices and Catholic responses to these Protestant objections.

In our increasingly secular world the clash of beliefs for which Protestants and Catholics once fought (and sometimes died) may not seem as stark as they did in the sixteenth century. Yet the differences between them were by no means trivial. Until the Second Vatican Council of the 1960s, the decisions at Trent effectively ended fruitful doctrinal discussion with Protestants. For that reason alone the council's decisions deserve the most serious attention from the Christian heirs of the sixteenth century, regardless of where they may now stand on the issues that called forth such a momentous clash almost half a millennium ago.

The excerpts below are taken from H. J. Schroeder's translation of the original Latin. Scripture references are inserted in parentheses while editorial insertions are in brackets. Biblical passages are from authorized Catholic translations and so may sound as strange in Protestant ears as Protestant translations did to Catholics in the day before ecumenical cooperation on versions of the Bible. The selections represent about 15 percent of the total pronouncements of the council. As an aid to reading these excerpts, the following may help: A "decree" is simply an authoritative pronouncement. A "canon" (from the Greek meaning "straight rod or bar") is an official rule for the church's life or discipline, except when it is applied to Scripture (where it then means the established list of biblical books) or to the Mass (where it is the formal prayer by which the elements of bread and wine are consecrated). In the decree on justification, the word "justice" is sometimes used where Protestants would say "justification." This is a small difference in vocabulary that nonetheless speaks volumes about the space that separated Protestants and Catholics in the sixteenth century.

Text

> Canons and Decrees of the Council of Trent: Original Text with English Translations. Translated and edited by H. J. Schroeder, 11, 17–20, 29–46, 51–55, 72–78, 144–50, 214–17. St. Louis: B. Herder, 1941.

Additional Reading

Chemnitz, Martin. Examination of the Council of Trent (1565–1573). Translated by Fred Kramer. St. Louis: Concordia, 1971, 1979.

Dickens, A. G. The Counter-Reformation. New York: Norton, 1979.

O'Connell, Marvin R. The Counter Reformation, 1559–1610. New York: Harper and Row, 1974.

Jedin, Hubert. A History of the Council of Trent. St. Louis: B. Herder, 1957– .

"U.S. Lutheran—Roman Catholic Dialogue: Justification by Faith." Origins: NC Documentary Service, Oct. 1983.

Canons and Decrees of the Council of Trent

First Session of the Holy Ecumenical and General Council of Trent celebrated under the sovereign pontiff, Paul III, on the thirteenth day of December in the year of the Lord 1545

Decree Concerning the Opening of the Council

Does it please you, for the praise and glory of the holy and undivided Trinity, Father, Son, and Holy Ghost, for the advance and exaltation of the Christian faith and religion, for the extirpation of heresies, for the peace and unity of the Church, for the reform of the clergy and Christian people, for the suppression and destruction of the enemies of the Christian name, to decree and declare that the holy and general Council of Trent begins and has begun?

They answered: It pleases us.

Fourth Session celebrated on the eighth day of April 1546

Decree Concerning the Canonical Scriptures

The holy, ecumenical, and general Council of Trent, lawfully assembled in the Holy Ghost, the same three legates of the apostolic see presiding, keeps this constantly in view, namely, that the purity of the gospel may be preserved in the church after the errors have been removed. This [gospel], of old promised through the Prophets in the holy Scriptures, our Lord Jesus Christ, the Son of God, promulgated first with his own mouth, and then commanded it to be preached by his apostles to every creature (Matt. 28:19–20; Mark 16:15) as the source at once of all saving truth and rules of conduct. It also clearly perceives that these truths and rules are contained in the written books and in the unwritten traditions, which, received by the apostles from the mouth of Christ himself, or from the apostles themselves, the Holy Ghost dictating, have come down to us, transmitted as it were from hand to hand. Following, then, the examples of the orthodox fathers, it receives and venerates with a feeling of piety and reverence all the books both of the Old and New Testaments, since one God is the Author of both; also the traditions, whether they relate to faith or to morals, as having been dictated either orally by Christ or by the Holy Ghost, and preserved in the Catholic Church in unbroken succession. It has thought it proper, moreover, to insert in this decree a list of the sacred books, lest a doubt might arise in the mind of someone as to which are the books received by this council. They are the following: of the Old Testament, the five books of Moses, namely, Genesis, Exodus, Leviticus, Numbers, Deuteronomy; Josue, Judges, Ruth, the four books of Kings, two of Paralipomenon [i.e., Chronicles], the first and second of Esdras, the latter of which is called Nehemias, Tobias, Judith, Esther, Job, the Davidic Psalter of 150 Psalms, Proverbs,

Ecclesiastes, the Canticle of Canticles, Wisdom, Ecclesiasticus, Isaias, Jeremias, with Baruch, Ezechiel, Daniel, the twelve minor Prophets, namely, Osee, Joel, Amos, Abdias, Jonas, Micheas, Nahum, Habacuc, Sophonias, Aggeus, Zacharias, Malachias; two books of Machabees, the first and second. Of the New Testament, the four Gospels, according to Matthew, Mark, Luke, and John; the Acts of the Apostles written by Luke the Evangelist; fourteen Epistles of Paul the apostle, to the Romans, two to the Corinthians, to the Galatians, to the Ephesians, to the Philippians, to the Colossians, two to the Thessalonians, two to Timothy, to Titus, to Philemon, to the Hebrews; two of Peter the apostle, three of John the apostle, one of James the apostle, one of Jude the apostle, and the Apocalypse of John the apostle. If anyone does not accept as sacred and canonical the aforesaid books in their entirety and with all their parts, as they have been accustomed to be read in the Catholic Church and as they are contained in the old Latin Vulgate Edition, and knowingly and deliberately rejects the aforesaid traditions, let him be anathema. Let all understand, therefore, in what order and manner the council, after having laid the foundation of the confession of faith, will proceed, and who are the chief witnesses and supports to whom it will appeal in confirming dogmas and in restoring morals in the church.

Decree Concerning the Edition and Use
of the Sacred Books

Moreover, the same holy council considering that not a little advantage will accrue to the church of God if it be made known which of all the Latin editions of the sacred books now in circulation is to be regarded as authentic, ordains and declares that the old Latin Vulgate Edition, which, in use for so many hundred years, has been approved by the church, be in public lectures, disputations, sermons, and expositions held as authentic, and that no one dare or presume under any pretext whatsoever to reject it.

Furthermore, to check unbridled spirits, it decrees that no one relying on his own judgment shall, in matters of faith and morals pertaining to the edification of Christian doctrine, distorting the holy Scriptures in accordance with his own conceptions, presume to interpret them contrary to that sense which holy mother church, to whom it belongs to judge of their true sense and interpretation, has held and holds, or even contrary to the unanimous teaching of the fathers, even though such interpretations should not at any time be published. Those who act contrary to this shall be made known by the ordinaries [i.e., authoritative church officers] and punished in accordance with the penalties prescribed by the law.

And wishing, as is proper, to impose a restraint in this matter on printers also, who, now without restraint, thinking what pleases them is permitted them, print without the permission of ecclesiastical superiors the books of the holy Scriptures and the notes and commentaries thereon of all persons indiscriminately, often with the name of the press omitted, often also under a fictitious press-name, and what is worse, without the name of the author, and also indiscreetly have for sale such books printed elsewhere, [this council] decrees and ordains that in the future the holy Scriptures, especially the old Vulgate Edition, be printed in the most correct manner possible, and that it shall not be lawful for anyone to print or to have printed any books whatsoever dealing with sacred doctrinal matters without the name of the author, or in the future to sell them, or even to have them in possession, unless they have first been examined and approved by the ordinary, under penalty of anathema and fine prescribed by the last Council of the Lateran. If they be regulars they must in addition to this examination and approval obtain permission also from their own superiors after these have examined the books in accordance with their own statutes. Those who lend or circulate them in manuscript before they have been examined and approved, shall be subject to the same penalties as the printers, and those who have them in their possession or read them, shall, unless they make known the authors, be themselves regarded as the authors. The approbation of such books, however, shall be given in writing and shall appear authentically at the beginning of the book, whether it be written or printed, and all this, that is, both the examination and approbation, shall be done gratuitously, so that what ought to be approved may be approved and what ought to be condemned may be condemned.

Furthermore, wishing to repress that boldness whereby the words and sentences of the holy Scriptures are turned and twisted to all kinds of profane usages, namely, to things scurrilous, fabulous, vain, to flatteries, detractions, superstitions, godless and diabolical incantations, divinations, the casting of lots and defamatory libels, to put an end to such irreverence and contempt, and that no one may in the future dare use in any manner the words of holy Scripture for these and similar purposes, it is commanded and enjoined that all people of this kind be restrained by the bishops as violators and profaners of the Word of God, with the penalties of the law and other penalties that they may deem fit to impose.

Sixth Session celebrated on the thirteenth day of January 1547

Decree Concerning Justification

Introduction

Since there is being disseminated at this time, not without the loss of many souls and grievous detriment to the unity of the church, a certain erroneous doctrine concerning justification, the holy, ecumenical, and general Council of Trent, lawfully assembled in the Holy Ghost, the most reverend John Maris, bishop of Praeneste de Monte, and Marcellus, priest of the Holy Cross in Jerusalem, cardinals of the holy Roman Church and legates apostolic *a latere* [i.e., commissioned from the pope], presiding in the name of our most holy Father and Lord in Christ, Paul III, by the providence of God, the pope, intends, for the praise and glory of almighty God, for the tranquility of the church and the salvation of souls, to expound to all the faithful of Christ the true and salutary doctrine of justification, which the *Sun of justice* (Mal. 4:2), Jesus Christ, *the author and finisher of our faith* (Heb. 12:2) taught, which the apostles transmitted and which the Catholic Church under the inspiration of the Holy Ghost has always retained; strictly forbidding that anyone henceforth presume to believe, preach, or teach otherwise than is defined and declared in the present decree.

Chapter 1

The Impotency of Nature and of the Law to Justify Man. The holy council declares first, that for a correct and clear understanding of the doctrine of justification, it is necessary that each one recognize and confess that since all men had lost innocence in the prevarication of Adam (Rom. 5:12; 1 Cor. 15:22), having become unclean (Isa. 64:6), and, as the apostle says, *by nature children of wrath* (Eph. 2:3), as has been set forth in the decree on original sin, they were so far *the servants of sin* (Rom. 6:17, 20) and under the power of the devil and of death, that not only the Gentiles by the force of nature, but not even the Jews by the very letter of the Law of Moses, were able to be liberated or to rise therefrom, although free will, weakened as it was in its powers and downward bent, was by no means extinguished in them.

Chapter 2

The Dispensation and Mystery of the Advent of Christ. Whence it came to pass that the heavenly Father, *the Father of mercies and the God of all comfort, when the blessed fullness of the time was come* (Gal. 4:4), sent to men Jesus Christ, his own Son, who had both before the Law and during the time of the Law been announced and promised to many of the holy fathers (Gen. 49:10, 18), *that he might redeem the Jews who were under the law* (Gal. 4:5), and *that the Gentiles who followed not after justice* (Rom. 9:30) might attain to justice, and that all men might receive the adoption of sons. Him God has *proposed* as a propitiator *through faith in his blood* (Rom. 3:25) *for our sins, and not for our sins only, but also for those of the whole world* (1 John 2:2).

Chapter 3

Who Are Justified Through Christ. But although *he died for all* (2 Cor. 5:15), yet all do not receive the benefit of his death, but those only to whom the merit of his passion is communicated; because as truly as men would not be born unjust, if they were not born through propagation of the seed of Adam, since by that propagation they contract through him, when they are conceived, injustice as their own, so if they were not born again in Christ, they would never be justified, since in that new birth there is bestowed upon them, through the merit of his passion, the grace by which they are made just. For this benefit the apostle exhorts us always *to give thanks to the Father, who hath made us worthy to be partakers of the lot of the saints in light, and hath delivered us from the power of darkness, and hath translated us into the kingdom of the Son of his love, in whom we have redemption and remission of sins* (Col. 1:12–14).

Chapter 4

A Brief Description of the Justification of the Sinner and Its Mode in the State of Grace. In which words is given a brief description of the justification of the sinner, as being a translation from that state in which man is born a child of the first Adam, to the state of grace and of the adoption of the sons of God through the second Adam, Jesus Christ our Savior. This translation however cannot, since the promulgation of the gospel, be effected except through the laver [i.e., washing] of regeneration or its desire, as it is written: *Unless a man be born again of water and the Holy Ghost, he cannot enter into the kingdom of God* (John 3:5).

Chapter 5

The Necessity of Preparation for Justification in Adults, and Whence It Proceeds. It is furthermore declared that in adults the beginning of that justification must proceed from the predisposing grace of God through Jesus Christ, that is, from his vocation, whereby, without any merits on their part, they are called; that they who by sin had been cut off from God, may be disposed through his quickening and helping grace to convert themselves to their own justification by freely assenting to and cooperating with that grace; so that, while God touches the heart of man through the illumination of the Holy Ghost, man himself neither does absolutely nothing while receiving that inspiration, since he can also reject it, nor yet is he able by his own free will and without the grace of God to move himself to justice in his sight. Hence, when it is said in the sacred writings: *Turn ye to me, and I will turn to you* (Zech. 1:3), we are reminded of our liberty; and when we reply: *Convert us, O Lord, to thee, and we shall be converted* (Lam. 5:21), we confess that we need the grace of God.

Chapter 6

The Manner of Preparation. Now, they [the adults] are disposed to that justice when, aroused and aided by divine grace, receiving *faith by hearing* (Rom. 10:17), they are moved freely toward God, believing to be true what has been divinely revealed and promised, especially that the sinner is justified by God *by his grace, through the redemption that is in Christ Jesus* (Rom. 3:24); and when, understanding themselves to be sinners, by turning themselves from the fear of divine justice, by which they are salutarily aroused, to consider the mercy of God, are raised to hope, trusting that God will be propitious to them for Christ's sake; and they begin to love him as the fountain of all justice, and on that account are moved against sin by a certain hatred and detestation, that is, by that repentance that must be performed before baptism; finally, when they resolve to receive baptism, to begin a new life, and to keep the commandments of God. Of this disposition it is written: *He that cometh to God, must believe that he is, and is a rewarder to them that seek him* (Heb. 11:6); and *Be of good faith, son, thy sins are forgiven thee* (Matt. 9:2; Mark 2:5); and *The fear of the Lord driveth out sin* (Ecclus. 1:27); and *Do penance, and be baptized every one of you in the name of Jesus Christ, for the remission of your sins, and you shall receive the gift of the Holy Ghost* (Acts 2:38); and *Going, therefore, teach ye all nations, baptizing them, in the name of the Father, and of the Son, and of the Holy Ghost, teaching them to observe all things whatsoever I have commanded you* (Matt. 28:19–20a); finally, *Prepare your hearts unto the Lord.*

Chapter 7

In What the Justification of the Sinner Consists, and What Are Its Causes. This disposition or preparation is followed by justification itself, which is not only a remission of sins but also the sanctification and renewal of the inward man through the voluntary reception of the grace and gifts whereby an unjust man becomes just and from being an enemy becomes a friend, that he may be *an heir according to hope of life everlasting* (Titus 3:7). The causes of this justification are: the final cause is the glory of God and of Christ and life everlasting; the efficient cause is the merciful God who *washes and sanctifies* gratuitously, signing and anointing *with the holy Spirit of promise, who is the pledge of our inheritance* (Eph. 1:13–14); the meritorious cause is his most beloved only begotten, our Lord Jesus Christ, who, *when we were enemies* (Rom. 5:10), *for the exceed-*

ing charity wherewith he loved us (Eph. 2:4), merited for us justification by his most holy passion on the wood of the cross and made satisfaction for us to God the Father; the instrumental cause is the sacrament of baptism, which is the sacrament of faith, without which no man was ever justified; finally, the single formal cause is the justice of God, not that by which he himself is just, but that by which he makes us just, that, namely, with which we being endowed by him, are *renewed in the spirit of our mind* (Eph. 4:23), and not only are we reputed but we are truly called and are just, receiving justice within us, each one according to his own measure, which the Holy Ghost distributes to everyone as he wills, and according to each one's disposition and cooperation. For although no one can be just except he to whom the merits of the passion of our Lord Jesus Christ are communicated, yet this takes place in that justification of the sinner, when by the merit of the most holy passion, *the charity of God is poured forth by the Holy Ghost in the hearts* (Rom. 5:5) of those who are justified and inheres in them; whence man through Jesus Christ, in whom he is ingrafted, receives in that justification, together with the remission of sins, all these infused at the same time, namely, faith, hope, and charity. For faith, unless hope and charity be added to it, neither unites man perfectly with Christ nor makes him a living member of his body. For which reason it is most truly said that *faith without works is dead* (James 2:17, 20) and of no profit, and *in Christ Jesus neither circumcision availeth anything nor uncircumcision, but faith that worketh by charity* (Gal. 5:6; 6:15). This faith, conformably to apostolic tradition, catechumens ask of the church before the sacrament of baptism, when they ask for the faith that gives eternal life, which without hope and charity faith cannot give. Whence also they hear immediately the words of Christ: *If thou wilt enter into life, keep the commandments* (Matt. 19:17). Wherefore, when receiving true and Christian justice, they are commanded, immediately on being born again, to preserve it pure and spotless, as *the first robe* (Luke 15:22) given them through Christ Jesus in place of that which Adam by his disobedience lost for himself and for us, so that they may bear it before the tribunal of our Lord Jesus Christ and may have life eternal.

Chapter 8

How the Gratuitous Justification of the Sinner by Faith Is to Be Understood. But when the apostle says that man is justified by faith and freely, these words are to be understood in that sense in which the uninterrupted unanimity of the Catholic Church has held and expressed them, namely, that we are therefore said to be justified by faith, because faith is the beginning of human salvation, the foundation and root of all justification, *without which it is impossible to please God* (Heb. 11:6) and to come to the fellowship of his sons; and we are therefore said to be justified gratuitously, because none of those things that precede justification, whether faith or works, merit the grace of justification. For, *if by grace, it is not now by works, otherwise,* as the apostle says, *grace is no more grace* (Rom. 11:6).

Chapter 9

Against the Vain Confidence of Heretics. But although it is necessary to believe that sins neither are remitted nor ever have been remitted except gratuitously by divine mercy for Christ's sake, yet it must not be said that sins are forgiven or have been forgiven to anyone who boasts of his confidence and certainty of the remission of his sins, resting on that alone, although among heretics and schismatics this vain and ungodly confidence may be and in our troubled times indeed is found and preached with untiring fury against the Catholic Church. Moreover, it must not be maintained, that they who are truly justified must needs, without any doubt whatever, convince themselves that they are justified, and that no one is absolved from sins and justified except he that believes with certainty that he is absolved and justified, and that absolution and justification are effected by this faith alone, as if he who does not believe this, doubts the promises of God and the efficacy of the death and resurrection of Christ. For as no pious person ought to doubt the mercy of God, the merit of Christ and the virtue and efficacy of the sacraments, so each one, when he considers himself and his own weakness and indisposition, may have fear and apprehension concerning his own grace, since no one can know with the certainty of faith, which cannot be subject to error, that he has obtained the grace of God.

Chapter 10

The Increase of the Justification Received. Having, therefore, been thus justified and made the friends and *domestics of God* (Eph. 2:19), advancing *from virtue to virtue,* they are *renewed,* as the apostle says, *day by day,* that is, *mortifying the members* (Col. 3:5) of their flesh, and presenting them as instruments of justice unto sanctification (Rom. 6:13, 19), they, through the observance of the commandments of God and of the church, faith cooperating with good works, increase in that justice received through the grace of Christ and are further justified, as it is written: *He that is just, let him be justified still* (Apoc. 22:11); and, *Be not afraid to be justified even to death* (Ecclus. 18:22); and again, *Do you see that by works a man is justified, and not by faith only?* (James 2:24). This increase of justice holy church asks for when she prays: "Give unto us, O Lord, an increase of faith, hope and charity" (Thirteenth Sunday after Pentecost).

Chapter 11

The Observance of the Commandments and the Necessity and Possibility Thereof. But no one, however much justified, should consider himself exempt from the observance of the commandments; no one should use that rash statement, once forbidden by the fathers under anathema, that the observance of the commandments of God is impossible for one that is justified. For God does not command impossibilities, but by commanding admonishes thee to do what thou canst and to pray for what thou canst not, and aids thee that thou mayest be able. *His commandments are not heavy,* and *his yoke is sweet and burden light* (Matt. 11:30). For they who are the sons of God love Christ, but they who love him, keep his commandments, as he himself testifies (John 14:23); which, indeed, with the divine help they can do. For although during this mortal life, men, however holy and just, fall at times into at least light and daily sins, which are also called venial, they do not on that account cease to be just, for that petition of the just, *forgive us our trespasses* (Matt. 6:12), is both humble and true; for which reason the just ought to feel themselves the more obliged to walk in the way of justice, for *being now freed from sin and made servants of God* (Rom. 6:18, 22), they are able, *living soberly, justly and godly* (Titus 2:12), to proceed onward through Jesus Christ, by whom they have access unto this grace (Rom. 5:1). For God does not forsake those who have been once justified by his grace, unless he be first forsaken by them. Wherefore, no one ought to flatter himself with faith alone, thinking that by faith alone he is made an heir and will obtain the inheritance, even though *he suffer* not *with Christ, that he may be also glorified with him* (Rom. 8:17). For even Christ himself, as the apostle says, *whereas he was the Son of God he learned obedience by the things which he suffered, and being consummated, he became to all who obey him the cause of eternal salvation* (Heb. 5:8–9). For which reason the same apostle admonishes those justified, saying: *Know you not that they who run in the race, all run indeed, but one receiveth the prize? So run that you may obtain. I therefore so run, not as at an uncertainty; I so fight, not as one beating the air, but I chastise my body and bring it into subjection; lest perhaps when I have preached to others, I myself should become a castaway* (1 Cor. 9:24, 26–27). So also the prince of the apostles, Peter: *Labor the more, that by good works you may make sure your calling and election. For doing these things, you shall not sin at any time* (2 Pet. 1:10). From which it is clear that they are opposed to the orthodox teaching of religion who maintain that the just man sins, venially at least, in every good work; or, what is more intolerable, that he merits eternal punishment; and they also who assert that the just sin in all works, if, in order to arouse their sloth and to encourage themselves to run the race, they, in addition to this, that above all God may be glorified, have in view also the eternal reward, since it is written: *I have inclined my heart to do thy justifications on account of the reward* (Ps. 119:112); and of Moses the apostle says that *he looked unto the reward* (Heb. 11:26).

Chapter 12

Rash Presumption of Predestination Is to Be Avoided. No one, moreover, so long as he lives this mortal life, ought in regard to the sacred mystery of divine predestination, so far presume as to state with absolute certainty that he is among the number of the predestined, as if it were true that the one justified either cannot sin anymore, or, if he does sin, that he ought to promise himself an assured repentance. For except by special revelation, it cannot be known whom God has chosen to himself.

Chapter 13

The Gift of Perseverance. Similarly with regard to the gift of perseverance, of which it is written: *He that shall persevere to the end, he shall be saved* (Matt. 10:22; 24:13), which cannot be obtained from anyone except from him who is able to make him stand who stands (Rom. 14:4), that he may stand perseveringly, and to raise him who falls, let no one promise himself herein something as certain with an absolute certainty, although all ought to place and repose the firmest hope in God's help. For God, unless men themselves fail in his grace, as *he has begun a good work, so will he perfect it, working to will and to accomplish* (Phil. 1:6; 2:13). Nevertheless, let those who think themselves to stand, take heed lest they fall, and with fear and trembling work out their salvation (Phil. 2:12), in labors, in watchings, in almsdeeds, in prayer, in fasting and chastity. For knowing that they are born again unto the hope of glory, and not as yet unto glory, they ought to fear for the combat that yet remains with the flesh, with the world, and with the devil, in which they cannot be victorious unless they be with the grace of God obedient to the apostle who says: *We are debtors, not to the flesh, to live according to the flesh; for if you live according to the flesh, you shall die, but if by the spirit you mortify the deeds of the flesh, you shall live* (Rom. 8:12–13).

Chapter 14

The Fallen and Their Restoration. Those who through sin have forfeited the received grace of justification, can again be justified when, moved by God, they exert themselves to obtain through the sacrament of penance the recovery, by the merits of Christ, of the grace lost. For this manner of justification is restoration for those fallen, which the holy fathers have aptly called a second plank after the shipwreck of grace lost. For on behalf of those who fall into sins after baptism, Christ Jesus instituted the sacrament of penance when he said: *Receive ye the Holy Ghost, whose sins you shall forgive, they are forgiven them, and whose you shall retain, they are retained* (John 20:22–23). Hence, it must be taught that the repentance of a Christian after his fall is very different from that at his baptism, and that it includes not only a determination to avoid sins and a hatred of them, or *a contrite and humble heart*, but also the sacramental confession of those sins, at least in desire, to be made in its season, and sacerdotal absolution, as well as satisfaction by fasts, alms, prayers, and other devout exercises of the spiritual life, not indeed for the eternal punishment, which is, together with the guilt, remitted either by the sacrament or by the desire of the sacrament, but for the temporal punishment which, as the sacred writings teach, is not always wholly remitted, as is done in baptism, to those who, ungrateful to the grace of God which they have received, have grieved the Holy Ghost (Eph. 4:30) and have not feared to *violate the temple of God* (1 Cor. 3:17). Of which repentance it is written: *Be mindful whence thou art fallen; do penance, and do the first works* (Apoc. 2:5); and again, *The sorrow that is according to God worketh penance, steadfast unto salvation* (2 Cor. 7:10); and again, *Do penance, and bring forth fruits worthy of penance* (Matt. 3:2; 4:17; Luke 3:8).

Chapter 15

By Every Mortal Sin Grace Is Lost, but Not Faith. Against the subtle wits of some also, who *by pleasing speeches and good works seduce the hearts of the innocent* (Rom. 16:18), it must be maintained that the grace of justification once received is lost not only by infidelity, whereby also faith itself is lost, but also by every other mortal sin, although in this case faith is not lost; thus defending the teaching of the divine Law which excludes from the kingdom of God not only unbelievers, but also the faithful [who are] *fornicators, adulterers, effeminate, liars with mankind, thieves, covetous, drunkards, railers, extortioners,* and all others who commit deadly sins, from which with the help of divine grace they can refrain, and on account of which they are cut off from the grace of Christ.

Chapter 16

The Fruits of Justification, That Is, the Merit of Good Works, and the Nature of That Merit. Therefore, to men justified in this manner, whether they have preserved uninterruptedly the grace received or recovered it when lost, are to be pointed out the words of the apostle: *Abound in every good work, knowing that your labor is not in vain in the Lord* (1 Cor. 15:58). *For God*

*is not unjust, that he should forget your work, and the love
which you have shown in his name* (Heb. 6:10); and, *Do not
lose your confidence, which hath a great reward* (Heb. 10:35).
Hence, to those who work well *unto the end* (Matt. 10:22) and
trust in God, eternal life is to be offered, both as a grace merci-
fully promised to the sons of God through Christ Jesus, and as
a reward promised by God himself, to be faithfully given to
their good works and merits (Rom. 6:22). For this is the crown
of justice which after his fight and course the apostle declared
was laid up for him, to be rendered to him by the just Judge,
and not only to him, but also to all that love his coming (2 Tim.
4:8). For since Christ Jesus himself, as the head into the members and the vine into the branches (John 15:1–2), continually
infuses strength into those justified, which strength always pre-
cedes, accompanies, and follows their good works, and without which they could not in any manner be pleasing and meritorious before God, we must believe that nothing further is
wanting to those justified to prevent them from being considered to have, by those very works which have been done in
God, fully satisfied the divine Law according to the state of this
life and to have truly merited eternal life, to be obtained in its
[due] time, provided they depart [this life] in grace (Apoc.
14:13), since Christ our Savior says: *If anyone shall drink of the
water that I will give him, he shall not thirst forever; but it shall
become in him a fountain of water springing up unto life everlasting* (John 4:13–14). Thus, neither is our own justice established as our own from ourselves (Rom 10:3; 2 Cor. 3:5), nor is
the justice of God ignored or repudiated, for that justice which
is called ours, because we are justified by its inherence in us,
that same is [the justice] of God, because it is infused into us
by God through the merit of Christ. Nor must this be omitted,
that although in the sacred writings so much is attributed to
good works, that even *he that shall give a drink of cold water to
one of his least ones,* Christ promises, *shall not lose his reward*
(Matt. 10:42; Mark 9:40); and the apostle testifies that, *That
which is at present momentary and light of our tribulation,
worketh for us above measure exceedingly an eternal weight of
glory* (2 Cor. 4:17); nevertheless, far be it that a Christian
should either trust or glory in himself and not in the Lord,
whose bounty toward all men is so great that he wishes the
things that are his gifts to be their merits. And since *in many*

things we all offend (James 3:2), each one ought to have before his eyes not only the mercy and goodness but also the severity and judgment [of God]; neither ought anyone to judge himself, even though he be not conscious to himself of anything (1 Cor. 4:3–4); because the whole life of man is to be examined and judged not by the judgment of man but of God, *who will bring to light the hidden things of darkness, and will make manifest the counsels of the hearts, and then shall every man have praise from God* (1 Cor. 4:5), who, as it is written, *will render to every man according to his works* (Matt. 16:27; Rom. 2:6; Apoc. 22:12).

After this Catholic doctrine on justification, which whosoever does not faithfully and firmly accept cannot be justified, it seemed good to the holy council to add these canons, that all may know not only what they must hold and follow, but also what to avoid and shun.

Canons Concerning Justification

Canon 1. If anyone says that man can be justified before God by his own works, whether done by his own natural powers or through the teaching of the Law (cf. *supra*, chaps. 1, 3), without divine grace through Jesus Christ, let him be anathema.

Can. 2. If anyone says that divine grace through Christ Jesus is given for this only, that man may be able more easily to live justly and to merit eternal life, as if by free will without grace he is able to do both, although with hardship and difficulty, let him be anathema.

Can. 3. If anyone says that without the predisposing inspiration of the Holy Ghost and without his help, man can believe, hope, love, or be repentant as he ought (Rom. 5:5), so that the grace of justification may be bestowed upon him, let him be anathema.

Can. 4. If anyone says that man's free will moved and aroused by God, by assenting to God's call and action, in no way cooperates toward disposing and preparing itself to obtain the grace of justification, that it cannot refuse its assent if it wishes, but that, as something inanimate, it does nothing whatever and is merely passive, let him be anathema.

Can. 5. If anyone says that after the sin of Adam man's free will was lost and destroyed, or that it is a thing only in name, indeed a name without a reality, a fiction introduced into the church by Satan, let him be anathema.

Can. 6. If anyone says that it is not in man's power to make his ways evil, but that the works that are evil as well as those that are good God produces, not permissively only but also *proprie et per se* [i.e., personally and by himself], so that the treason of Judas is no less his own proper work than the vocation of Saint Paul, let him be anathema.

Can. 7. If anyone says that all works done before justification, in whatever manner they may be done, are truly sins, or merit the hatred of God; that the more earnestly one strives to dispose himself for grace, the more grievously he sins, let him be anathema.

Can. 8. If anyone says that the fear of hell (Matt. 10:28; Luke 12:5), whereby, by grieving for sins, we flee to the mercy of God or abstain from sinning, is a sin or makes sinners worse, let him be anathema.

Can. 9. If anyone says that the sinner is justified by faith alone (*supra*, chaps. 7–8), meaning that nothing else is required to cooperate in order to obtain the grace of justification, and that it is not in any way necessary that he be prepared and disposed by the action of his own will, let him be anathema.

Can. 10. If anyone says that men are justified without the justice of Christ (Gal. 2:16; *supra*, chap. 7), whereby he merited for us, or by that justice are formally just, let him be anathema.

Can. 11. If anyone says that men are justified either by the sole imputation of the justice of Christ or by the sole remission of sins, to the exclusion of the grace and *the charity which is poured forth in their hearts by the Holy Ghost* (Rom. 5:5), and remains in them, or also that the grace by which we are justified is only the good will of God, let him be anathema.

Can. 12. If anyone says that justifying faith is nothing else than confidence in divine mercy (*supra*, chap. 9), which remits sins for Christ's sake, or that it is this confidence alone that justifies us, let him be anathema.

Can. 13. If anyone says that in order to obtain the remission of sins it is necessary for every man to believe with certainty and without any hesitation arising from his own weakness and indisposition that his sins are forgiven him, let him be anathema.

Can. 14. If anyone says that man is absolved from his sins and justified because he firmly believes that he is absolved and justified (*supra*, chap. 9), or that no one is truly justified except him who believes himself justified, and that by this faith alone absolution and justification are effected, let him be anathema.

Can. 15. If anyone says that a man who is born again and justified is bound *ex fide* to believe that he is certainly in the number of the predestined (ibid., chap. 12), let him be anathema.

Can. 16. If anyone says that he will for certain, with an absolute and infallible certainty, have that great gift of perseverance even to the end, unless he shall have learned this by a special revelation (ibid., chap. 13), let him be anathema.

Can. 17. If anyone says that the grace of justification is shared by those only who are predestined to life, but that all others who are called are called indeed but receive not grace, as if they are by divine power predestined to evil, let him be anathema.

Can. 18. If anyone says that the commandments of God are, even for one that is justified and constituted in grace (ibid., chap. 11), impossible to observe, let him be anathema.

Can. 19. If anyone says that nothing besides faith is commanded in the gospel, that other things are indifferent, neither commanded nor forbidden, but free; or that the Ten Commandments in no way pertain to Christians, let him be anathema.

Can. 20. If anyone says that a man is justified and however perfect is not bound to observe the commandments of God and the church, but only to believe, as if the gospel were a bare and absolute promise of eternal life without the condition of observing the commandments, let him be anathema.

Can. 21. If anyone says that Christ Jesus was given by God to men as a redeemer in whom to trust, and not also as a legislator whom to obey, let him be anathema.

Can. 22. If anyone says that the one justified either can without the special help of God persevere in the justice received (*supra*, chap. 13), or that with that help he cannot, let him be anathema.

Can. 23. If anyone says that a man once justified can sin no more, nor lose grace (ibid., chap. 14), and that therefore he who falls and sins was never truly justified; or on the contrary, that he can during his whole life avoid all sins, even those that are venial, except by a special privilege from God, as the church holds in regard to the blessed virgin, let him be anathema.

Can. 24. If anyone says that the justice received is not preserved and also not increased before God through good works (ibid., chap. 10), but that those works are merely the fruits and signs of justification obtained, but not the cause of its increase, let him be anathema.

Can. 25. If anyone says that in every good work the just man sins at least venially (ibid., chap. 11 at the end), or, what is more intolerable, mortally, and hence merits eternal punishment, and that he is not damned for this reason only, because God does not impute these works unto damnation, let him be anathema.

Can. 26. If anyone says that the just ought not for the good works done in God (ibid., chap. 16) to expect and hope for an eternal reward from God through his mercy and the merit of Jesus Christ, if by doing well and by keeping the divine commandments they persevere to the end (Matt. 24:13), let him be anathema.

Can. 27. If anyone says that there is no mortal sin except that of unbelief (*supra*, chap. 15), or that grace once received is not lost through any other sin however grievous and enormous except by that of unbelief, let him be anathema.

Can. 28. If anyone says that with the loss of grace through sin faith is also lost with it, or that the faith which remains is not a true faith, although it is not a living one, or that he who has faith without charity is not a Christian, let him be anathema.

Can. 29. If anyone says that he who has fallen after baptism cannot by the grace of God rise again (ibid., chap. 14), or that he can indeed recover again the lost justice but by faith alone without the sacrament of penance, contrary to what the Holy Roman and Universal Church, instructed by Christ the Lord and his apostles, has hitherto professed, observed, and taught, let him be anathema.

Can. 30. If anyone says that after the reception of the grace of justification the guilt is so remitted and the debt of eternal punishment so blotted out to every repentant sinner, that no debt of temporal punishment remains to be discharged either in this world or in purgatory before the gates of heaven can be opened, let him be anathema.

Can. 31. If anyone says that the one justified sins when he performs good works with a view to an eternal reward (*supra*, chap. 11 at the end), let him be anathema.

Can. 32. If anyone says that the good works of the one justified are in such manner the gifts of God that they are not also the good merits of him justified; or that the one justified by the good works that he performs by the grace of God and the merit of Jesus Christ, whose living member he is, does not truly merit an increase of grace, eternal life, and in case he dies in grace the attainment of eternal life itself and also an increase of glory, let him be anathema.

Can. 33. If anyone says that the Catholic doctrine of justification as set forth by the holy council in the present decree, derogates in some respect from the glory of God or the merits of our Lord Jesus Christ, and does not rather illustrate the truth of our faith and no less the glory of God and of Christ Jesus, let him be anathema.

Seventh Session celebrated on the third day of March 1547

Decree Concerning the Sacraments

Foreword

For the completion of the salutary doctrine on justification, which was promulgated with the unanimous consent of the fathers in the last session, it has seemed proper to deal with the most holy sacraments of the church, through which all true justice either begins, or being begun is increased, or being lost is restored. Wherefore, in order to destroy the errors and extirpate the heresies that in our stormy times are directed against the most holy sacraments, some of which are a revival of heresies long ago condemned by our fathers, while others are of recent origin, all of which are exceedingly detrimental to the purity of the Catholic Church and the salvation of souls, the holy, ecumenical, and general Council of Trent, lawfully assembled in the Holy Ghost, the same legates of the apostolic see presiding, adhering to the teaching of the holy Scriptures, to the apostolic traditions, and to the unanimous teaching of other councils and of the fathers, has thought it proper to establish and enact these present canons; hoping, with the help of the Holy Spirit, to publish later those that are wanting for the completion of the work begun.

Canons on the Sacraments in General

Canon 1. If anyone says that the sacraments of the new law were not all instituted by our Lord Jesus Christ, or that there are more or less than seven, namely, baptism, confirmation, Eucharist, penance, extreme unction, order [i.e., ordination], and matrimony, or that any one of these seven is not truly and intrinsically a sacrament, let him be anathema.

Can. 2. If anyone says that these sacraments of the new law do not differ from the sacraments of the old law, except that the ceremonies are different and the external rites are different, let him be anathema.

Can. 3. If anyone says that these seven sacraments are so equal to each other that one is not for any reason more excellent than the other, let him be anathema.

Can. 4. If anyone says that the sacraments of the new law are not necessary for salvation but are superfluous, and that without them or without the desire of them men obtain from God through faith alone the grace of justification, although all are not necessary for each one, let him be anathema.

Can. 5. If anyone says that these sacraments have been instituted for the nourishment of faith alone, let him be anathema.

Can. 6. If anyone says that the sacraments of the new law do not contain the grace which they signify, or that they do not confer that grace on those who place no obstacles in its way, as though they are only outward signs of grace or justice received through faith and certain marks of Christian profession, whereby among men believers are distinguished from unbelievers, let him be anathema.

Can. 7. If anyone says that grace, so far as God's part is concerned, is not imparted through the sacraments always and to all men even if they receive them rightly, but only sometimes and to some persons, let him be anathema.

Can. 8. If anyone says that by the sacraments of the new law grace is not conferred *ex opere operato* [i.e., simply by what is done in the sacrament], but that faith alone in the divine promise is sufficient to obtain grace, let him be anathema.

Can. 9. If anyone says that in three sacraments, namely, baptism, confirmation, and order, there is not imprinted on the soul a character, that is, a certain spiritual and indelible mark, by reason of which they cannot be repeated, let him be anathema.

Can. 10. If anyone says that all Christians have the power to administer the Word and all the sacraments, let him be anathema.

Can. 11. If anyone says that in ministers, when they effect and confer the sacraments, there is not required at least the intention of doing what the church does, let him be anathema.

Can. 12. If anyone says that a minister who is in mortal sin, although he observes all the essentials that pertain to the effecting or conferring of a sacrament, neither effects nor confers a sacrament, let him be anathema.

Can. 13. If anyone says that the received and approved rites of the Catholic Church, accustomed to be used in the administration of the sacraments, may be despised or omitted by the ministers without sin and at their pleasure, or may be changed by any pastor of the churches to other new ones, let him be anathema.

Canons on Baptism

Canon 1. If anyone says that the baptism of John had the same effect as the baptism of Christ, let him be anathema.

Can. 2. If anyone says that true and natural water is not necessary for baptism and thus twists into some metaphor the words of our Lord Jesus Christ, *Unless a man be born again of water and the Holy Ghost* (John 3:5), let him be anathema.

Can. 3. If anyone says that in the Roman Church, which is the mother and mistress of all churches, there is not the true doctrine concerning the sacrament of baptism, let him be anathema.

Can. 4. If anyone says that the baptism which is given by heretics in the name of the Father, and of the Son, and of the Holy Ghost, with the intention of doing what the church does, is not true baptism, let him be anathema.

Can. 5. If anyone says that the baptism is optional, that is, not necessary for salvation (John 3:5), let him be anathema.

Can. 6. If anyone says that one baptized cannot, even if he wishes, lose grace, however much he may sin, unless he is unwilling to believe, let him be anathema.

Can. 7. If anyone says that those baptized are by baptism made debtors only to faith alone, but not to the observance of the whole law of Christ, let him be anathema.

Can. 8. If anyone says that those baptized are free from all the precepts of holy Church, whether written or unwritten, so that they are not bound to observe them unless they should wish to submit to them of their own accord, let him be anathema.

Can. 9. If anyone says that the remembrance of the baptism received is to be so impressed on men that they may understand that all the vows made after baptism are void in virtue of the promise already made in that baptism, as if by those vows they detracted from the faith which they professed and from the baptism itself, let him be anathema.

Can. 10. If anyone says that by the sole remembrance and the faith of the baptism received, all sins committed after baptism are either remitted or made venial, let him be anathema.

Can. 11. If anyone says that baptism, truly and rightly administered, must be repeated in the one converted to repentance after having denied the faith of Christ among the infidels, let him be anathema.

Can. 12. If anyone says that no one is to be baptized except at that age at which Christ was baptized, or when on the point of death, let him be anathema.

Can. 13. If anyone says that children, because they have not the act of believing, are not after having received baptism to be numbered among the faithful, and that for this reason are to be rebaptized when they have reached the years of discretion; or that it is better that the baptism of such be omitted than that, while not believing by their own act, they should be baptized in the faith of the church alone, let him be anathema.

Can. 14. If anyone says that those who have been thus baptized when children, are, when they have grown up, to be questioned whether they will ratify what their sponsors promised in their name when they were baptized, and in case they answer in the negative, are to be left to their own will; neither are they to be compelled in the meantime to a Christian life by any penalty other than exclusion of the reception of the Eucharist and the other sacraments, until they repent, let him be anathema.

Canons on Confirmation

Canon 1. If anyone says that the confirmation of those baptized is an empty ceremony and not a true and proper sacrament; or that of old it was nothing more than a sort of instruction, whereby those approaching adolescence gave an account of their faith to the church, let him be anathema.

Can. 2. If anyone says that those who ascribe any power to the holy chrism [i.e., anointing oil] of confirmation, offer insults to the Holy Ghost, let him be anathema.

Can. 3. If anyone says that the ordinary minister of holy confirmation is not the bishop alone, but any simple priest, let him be anathema.

Thirteenth Session which is the third under the Supreme Pontiff, Julius III, celebrated on the eleventh day of October 1551

Decree Concerning the Most Holy Sacrament of the Eucharist

The holy, ecumenical, and general Council of Trent, lawfully assembled in the Holy Ghost, the same legate and nuncios of the holy apostolic see presiding, although convened, not without the special guidance and direction of the Holy Ghost, for the purpose of setting forth the true and ancient doctrine concerning faith and the sacraments, and of applying a remedy to all the heresies and the other most grievous troubles by which the church of God is now miserably disturbed and rent into many and various parts, yet, even from the outset, has especially desired that it might pull up by the roots the cockles (Matt. 13:30) of execrable errors and schisms which the enemy has in these our troubled times disseminated regarding the doctrine, use, and worship of the sacred Eucharist, which our Savior left in his church as a symbol of that unity and charity with which he wished all Christians to be mutually bound and united. Wherefore, this holy council, stating that sound and genuine doctrine of the venerable and divine sacrament of the Eucharist, which the Catholic Church, instructed by our Lord Jesus Christ himself and by his apostles, and taught by the Holy Ghost who always brings to her mind all truth (Luke 12:12; John 14:26; 16:13), has held and will preserve even to the end of the world, forbids all the faithful of Christ to presume henceforth to believe, teach, or preach with regard to the most Holy Eucharist otherwise than is explained and defined in this present decree.

Chapter 1

The Real Presence of Our Lord Jesus Christ in the Most Holy Sacrament of the Eucharist. First of all, the holy council teaches and openly and plainly professes that after the consecration of bread and wine, our Lord Jesus Christ, true God and true man, is truly, really, and substantially contained in the august sacrament of the holy Eucharist under the appearance of those sensible things. For there is no repugnance in this that our Savior sits always at the right hand of the Father in heaven according to the natural mode of existing, and yet is in many other places sacramentally present to us in his own substance by a manner of existence which, although we can scarcely express in words, yet with our understanding illumined by faith, we can conceive and ought most firmly to believe is possible to God (Matt. 19:26; Luke 18:27). For thus all our forefathers, as many as were in the true church of Christ and who treated of this most holy sacrament, have most openly professed that our Redeemer instituted this wonderful sacrament at the last supper, when, after blessing the bread and wine, he testified in clear and definite words that he gives them his own body and his own blood. Since these words, recorded by the holy Evangelists (Matt. 26:26–28; Mark 14:22–24; Luke 22:19–20) and afterwards repeated by Saint Paul (1 Cor. 11:24–25), embody that proper and clearest meaning in which they were understood by the fathers, it is a most contemptible action on the part of some contentious and wicked men to twist them into fictitious and imaginary tropes by which the truth of the flesh and blood of Christ is denied, contrary to the universal sense of the church, which, as *the pillar and ground of truth* (1 Tim. 3:15), recognizing with a mind ever grateful and unforgetting this most excellent favor of Christ, has detested as satanical these untruths devised by impious men.

Chapter 2

The Reason for the Institution of This Most Holy Sacrament. Therefore, our Savior, when about to depart from this world to the Father, instituted this sacrament, in which he poured forth, as it were, the riches of his divine love toward men, *making a remembrance of his wonderful works* (Ps. 111:4), and commanded us in the participation of it to reverence his memory and *to show forth his death until he comes* (Luke 22:19; 1 Cor. 11:24–26) to judge the world. But he wished that this sacrament should be received as the spiritual food of souls (Matt. 26:26–28), whereby they may be nourished and strengthened, living by the faith of him who said: *He that eateth me, the same also shall live by me* (John 6:58), and as an antidote whereby we may be freed from daily faults and be preserved from mortal sins. He wished it furthermore to be a pledge of our future glory and everlasting happiness, and thus be a symbol of that one body of which he is the head (1 Cor. 11:3; Eph. 5:23) and to which he wished us to be united as members by the closest bond of faith, hope, and charity, that we might *all speak the same thing and there might be no schisms among us* (1 Cor. 1:10).

Chapter 3

The Excellence of the Most Holy Eucharist over the Other Sacraments. The most Holy Eucharist has indeed this in common with the other sacraments, that it is a symbol of a sacred thing and a visible form of an invisible grace; but there is found in it this excellent and peculiar characteristic, that the other sacraments then first have the power of sanctifying when one uses them, while in the Eucharist there is the Author himself of sanctity before it is used. For the apostles had not yet received the Eucharist from the hands of the Lord, when he himself told them that what he was giving them was his own body (Matt. 26:26; Mark 14:22). This has always been the belief of the church of God, that immediately after the consecration the true body and the true blood of our Lord, together with his soul and divinity, exist under the form of bread and wine, the body under the form of bread and the blood under the form of wine *ex vi verborum* [i.e., from the power of the words]; but the same body also under the form of wine and the same blood under the form of bread and the soul under both, in virtue of that natural connection and concomitance whereby the parts of Christ the Lord, *who hath now risen from the dead, to die no more* (Rom. 6:9), are mutually united; also the divinity on account of its admirable hypostatic [i.e., substantial] union with his body and soul. Wherefore, it is very true that as much is contained under either form as under both. For Christ is whole and entire under the form of bread and under any part of that form; likewise the whole Christ is present under the form of wine and under all its parts.

Chapter 4

Transubstantiation. But since Christ our Redeemer declared that to be truly his own body which he offered under the form of bread (Luke 22:19; John 6:48–58; 1 Cor. 11:24), it has, therefore, always been a firm belief in the church of God, and this holy council now declares it anew, that by the consecration of the bread and wine a change is brought about of the whole substance of the bread into the substance of the body of Christ our Lord, and of the whole substance of the wine into the substance of his blood. This change the holy Catholic Church properly and appropriately calls transubstantiation.

Chapter 5

The Worship and Veneration to Be Shown to This Most Holy Sacrament. There is, therefore, no room for doubt that all the faithful of Christ may, in accordance with a custom received in the Catholic Church, give to this most holy sacrament in veneration the worship of *latria* [i.e., worship in the purest sense], which is due to the true God. Neither is it to be less adored for the reason that it was instituted by Christ the Lord in order to be received (Matt. 26:26). For we believe that in it the same God is present of whom the eternal Father, when introducing him into the world, says: *and let all the angels of God adore him* (Heb. 1:6); whom the magi, falling down, adored (Matt 2:11); who, finally, as the Scriptures testify, was adored by the apostles in Galilee (Matt. 28:17; Luke 24:52).

The holy council declares, moreover, that the custom that this sublime and venerable sacrament be celebrated with special veneration and solemnity every year on a fixed festival day, and that it be borne reverently and with honor in processions through the streets and public places, was very piously and religiously introduced into the church of God. For it is most reasonable that some days be set aside as holy on which all Christians may with special and unusual demonstration testify that their minds are grateful to and mindful of their common Lord and Redeemer for so ineffable and truly divine a favor whereby the victory and triumph of his death are shown forth.

And thus indeed did it behoove the victorious truth to celebrate a triumph over falsehood and heresy, that in the sight of so much splendor and in the midst of so great joy of the universal church, her enemies may either vanish weak and broken, or, overcome with shame and confounded, may at length repent.

Chapter 6

The Reservation of the Sacrament of the Holy Eucharist and Taking It to the Sick. The custom of reserving the holy Eucharist in a sacred place is so ancient that even the period of the Nicene Council recognized that usage. Moreover, the practice of carrying the sacred Eucharist to the sick and of carefully reserving it for this purpose in churches, besides being exceedingly reasonable and appropriate, is also found enjoined in numerous councils and is a very ancient observance of the Catholic Church. Wherefore, this holy council decrees that this salutary and necessary custom be by all means retained.

Chapter 7

The Preparation to be Employed That One May Receive the Sacred Eucharist Worthily. If it is unbecoming for anyone to approach any of the sacred functions except in a spirit of piety, assuredly, the more the holiness and divinity of this heavenly sacrament are understood by a Christian, the more diligently ought he to give heed lest he receive it without great reverence and holiness, especially when we read those terrifying words of the apostle: *He that eateth and drinketh unworthily, eateth and drinketh judgment to himself, not discerning the body of the Lord* (1 Cor. 11:29). Wherefore, he who would communicate, must call to mind this precept: *Let a man prove himself* (1 Cor. 11:28). Now, ecclesiastical usage declares that such an examination is necessary in order that no one conscious to himself of mortal sin, however contrite he may feel, ought to receive the sacred Eucharist without previous sacramental confession. This the holy council has decreed to be invariably observed by all Christians, even by those priests on whom it may be incumbent by their office to celebrate, provided the opportunity of a confessor is not wanting to them. But if in an urgent necessity a priest should celebrate without previous confession, let him confess as soon as possible.

Twenty-Second Session which is the sixth under the Supreme Pontiff, Pius IV, celebrated on the seventeenth day of September 1562

Doctrine Concerning the Sacrifice of the Mass

That the ancient, complete, and in every way perfect faith and teaching regarding the great mystery of the Eucharist in the Catholic Church may be retained, and with the removal of errors and heresies may be preserved in its purity, the holy, ecumenical, and general Council of Trent, lawfully assembled in the Holy Ghost, the same legates of the apostolic see presiding, instructed by the light of the Holy Ghost, teaches, declares, and orders to be preached to the faithful the following concerning it, since it is the true and only sacrifice.

Chapter 1

The Institution of the Most Holy Sacrifice of the Mass. Since under the former Testament, according to the testimony of the apostle Paul, there was no perfection because of the weakness of the Levitical priesthood, there was need, God the Father of mercies so ordaining, *that another priest should rise according to the order of Melchisedech* (Heb. 7:11), our Lord Jesus Christ, who might perfect and lead to perfection as many as were to be sanctified. He, therefore, our God and Lord, although he was by his death about to offer himself once upon the altar of the cross to God the Father that he might there accomplish an eternal redemption, nevertheless, that his priesthood might not come to an end with his death (Heb. 7:24), at the last supper, on the night he was betrayed, that he might leave to his beloved spouse the church a visible sacrifice, such as the nature of man requires, whereby that bloody sacrifice once to be accomplished on the cross might be represented, the memory thereof remain even to the end of the world, and its salutary effects applied to the remission of those sins which we daily commit, declaring himself constituted *a priest forever according to the order of Melchisedech* (Ps. 110:4), offered up to God the Father his own body and blood under the form of bread and wine, and under the forms of those same things gave to the apostles, whom he then made priests of the New Testament, that they might partake, commanding them and their successors in the priesthood by these words to do likewise: *Do this in commemoration of me* (Luke 22:19; 1 Cor. 11:24–25), as the Catholic Church has always understood and taught. For having celebrated the ancient passover which the multitude of the children of Israel sacrificed in memory of their departure from Egypt (Exod. 13), he instituted a new passover, namely, himself, to be immolated under visible signs by the church through the priests in memory of his own passage from this world to the Father, when by the shedding of his blood he redeemed and *delivered us from the power of darkness and translated us into his kingdom* (Col. 1:13). And this is indeed that clean oblation which cannot be defiled by any unworthiness or malice on the part of those who offer it; which the Lord foretold by Malachias was to be great among the Gentiles (Mal. 1:11), and which the apostle Paul has clearly indicated when he says, that they who are defiled by partaking of the table of devils cannot be partakers of the table of the Lord (1 Cor. 10:21), understanding by table in each case the altar. It is, finally, that [sacrifice] which was prefigured by various types of sacrifices during the period of nature and of the law (Gen. 4:4; 12:8, etc.), which, namely, comprises all the good things signified by them, as being the consummation and perfection of them all.

Chapter 2

The Sacrifice of the Mass Is Propitiatory Both for the Living and the Dead. And inasmuch as this divine sacrifice which is celebrated in the Mass is contained and immolated in an unbloody manner the same Christ who once offered himself in a bloody manner on the altar of the cross, the holy council teaches that this is truly propitiatory and has this effect, that if we, contrite and penitent, with sincere heart and upright faith, with fear and reverence, draw nigh to God, *we obtain mercy and find grace in seasonable aid* (Heb. 4:16). For, appeased by this sacrifice, the Lord grants the grace and gift of penitence and pardons even the gravest crimes and sins. For the victim is one and the same, the same now offering by the ministry of priests who then offered himself on the cross, the manner alone of offering being different. The fruits of that bloody sacrifice, it is well understood, are received most abundantly through this unbloody one, so far is the latter from derogating in any way from the former. Wherefore, according to the tradition of the apostles, it is rightly offered not only for the sins, punishments, satisfactions, and other necessities of the faithful who are living, but also for those departed in Christ but not yet fully purified.

Chapter 3

Masses in Honor of the Saints. And although the church has been accustomed to celebrate at certain times masses in honor and memory of the saints, she does not teach that sacrifice is offered to them but to God alone who crowned them; whence, the priest does not say: "To thee, Peter or Paul, I offer sacrifice," but, giving thanks to God for their victories, he implores their favor that they may vouchsafe to intercede for us in heaven whose memory we celebrate on earth.

Chapter 4

The Canon of the Mass. And since it is becoming that holy things be administered in a holy manner, and of all things this sacrifice is the most holy, the Catholic Church, to the end that it might be worthily and reverently offered and received, instituted many centuries ago the holy canon [i.e., prayer of consecration], which is so free from error that it contains nothing that does not in the highest degree savor of a certain holiness and piety and raise up to God the minds of those who offer. For it consists partly of the very words of the Lord, partly of the traditions of the apostles, and also of pious regulations of holy pontiffs.

Chapter 5

The Ceremonies and Rites of the Mass. And since the nature of man is such that he cannot without external means be raised easily to meditation on divine things, holy mother Church has instituted certain rites, namely, that some things in the Mass be pronounced in a low tone and others in a louder tone. She has likewise, in accordance with apostolic discipline and tradition, made use of ceremonies, such as mystical blessings, lights, incense, vestments, and many other things of this kind, whereby both the majesty of so great a sacrifice might be emphasized and the minds of the faithful excited by those visible signs of religion and piety to the contemplation of those sublime things which are hidden in this sacrifice.

Chapter 6

The Mass in Which the Priest Alone Communicates. The holy council wishes indeed that at each mass the faithful who are present should communicate, not only in spiritual desire but also by the sacramental partaking of the Eucharist, that thereby they may derive from this most holy sacrifice a more abundant fruit; if, however, that is not always done, it does not on that account condemn as private and illicit those masses in which the priest alone communicates sacramentally, but rather approves and commends them, since these masses also ought to be considered as truly common, partly because at them the people communicate spiritually and partly also because they are celebrated by a public minister of the church, not for himself only but for all the faithful who belong to the body of Christ.

Chapter 7

The Mixture of Water with Wine in the Offering of the Chalice. The holy council in the next place calls to mind that the church has instructed priests to mix water with the wine that is to be offered in the chalice; because it is believed that Christ the Lord did this, and also because from his side there came blood and water (John 19:34); the memory of this mystery is renewed by this mixture, and since in the Apocalypse of Saint John the "people" are called "waters" (Apoc. 17:1, 15), the union of the faithful people with Christ their head is represented.

Chapter 8

The Mass May Not Be Celebrated in the Vernacular. Its Mysteries to Be Explained to the People. Although the Mass contains much instruction for the faithful, it has, nevertheless, not been deemed advisable by the fathers that it should be celebrated everywhere in the vernacular tongue. Wherefore, the ancient rite of each church, approved by the holy Roman Church, the mother and mistress of all churches, being everywhere retained, that the sheep of Christ may not suffer hunger, or *the little ones ask for bread and there is none to break it unto them* (Lam. 4:4), the holy councils command pastors and all who have the *cura animarum* [i.e., care of souls] that they, either themselves or through others, explain frequently during the celebration of the Mass some of the things read during the Mass, and that among other things they explain some mystery of this most holy sacrifice, especially on Sundays and festival days.

Chapter 9

Preliminary Remarks on the Following Canons. Since many errors are at this time disseminated and many things taught and discussed by many persons that are in opposition to this ancient faith, which is founded on the holy gospel, the traditions of the apostles, and the teaching of the holy fathers, the holy council, after many and grave deliberations concerning these matters, has resolved with the unanimous consent of all to condemn and eliminate from holy church by means of the following canons whatever is opposed to this most pure faith and sacred doctrine.

Canons on the Sacrifice of the Mass

Canon 1. If anyone says that in the Mass a true and real sacrifice is not offered to God; or that to be offered is nothing else than that Christ is given to us to eat, let him be anathema.

Can. 2. If anyone says that by those words, *Do this for a commemoration of me* (Luke 22:19; 1 Cor. 11:25), Christ did not institute the apostles priests; or did not ordain that they and other priests should offer his own body and blood, let him be anathema.

Can. 3. If anyone says that the sacrifice of the Mass is only one of praise and thanksgiving; or that it is a mere commemoration of the sacrifice consummated on the cross but not a propitiatory one; or that it profits him only who receives, and ought not to be offered for the living and the dead, for sins, punishments, satisfactions, and other necessities, let him be anathema.

Can. 4. If anyone says that by the sacrifice of the Mass a blasphemy is cast upon the most holy sacrifice of Christ consummated on the cross; or that the former derogates from the latter, let him be anathema.

Can. 5. If anyone says that it is a deception to celebrate masses in honor of the saints and in order to obtain their intercession with God, as the church intends, let him be anathema.

Can. 6. If anyone says that the canon of the Mass contains errors and is therefore to be abrogated, let him be anathema.

Can. 7. If anyone says that the ceremonies, vestments, and outward signs which the Catholic Church uses in the celebration of masses, are incentives to impiety rather than stimulants to piety, let him be anathema.

Can. 8. If anyone says that the masses in which the priest alone communicates sacramentally are illicit and therefore to be abrogated, let him be anathema.

Can. 9. If anyone says that the rite of the Roman Church, according to which a part of the canon and the words of consecration are pronounced in a low tone, is to be condemned; or that the Mass ought to be celebrated in the vernacular tongue only; or that water ought not to be mixed with the wine that is to be offered in the chalice because it is contrary to the institution of Christ, let him be anathema.

Twenty-Fifth Session which is the ninth and last under the Supreme Pontiff, Pius IV, begun on the third and closed on the fourth day of December 1563

Decree Concerning Purgatory

Since the Catholic Church, instructed by the Holy Ghost, has, following the sacred writings and ancient traditions of the fathers, taught in sacred councils and very recently in this ecumenical council that there is a purgatory, and that the souls there detained are aided by the suffrages of the faithful and chiefly by the acceptable sacrifice of the altar, the holy council commands the bishops that they strive diligently to the end that the sound doctrine of purgatory, transmitted by the fathers and sacred councils, be believed and maintained by the faithful of Christ, and be everywhere taught and preached. The more difficult and subtle questions, however, and those that do not make for edification and from which there is for the most part no increase in piety, are to be excluded from popular instructions to uneducated people (1 Tim. 1:4; 2 Tim. 2:23; Titus 3:9). Likewise, things that are uncertain or that have the appearance of falsehood they shall not permit to be made known publicly and discussed. But those things that tend to a certain kind of curiosity or superstition, or that savor of filthy lucre, they shall prohibit as scandals and stumbling blocks to the faithful. The bishops shall see to it that the suffrages of the living, that is, the sacrifice of the Mass, prayers, alms, and other works of piety which they have been accustomed to perform for the faithful departed, be piously and devoutly discharged in accordance with the laws of the church, and that ' whatever is due on their behalf from testamentary bequests or other ways, be discharged by the priests and ministers of the church and others who are bound to render this service not in a perfunctory manner, but diligently and accurately.

On the Invocation, Veneration, and Relics of Saints, and on Sacred Images

The holy council commands all bishops and others who hold the office of teaching and have charge of the *cura animarum* [i.e., care of souls], that in accordance with the usage of the Catholic and apostolic Church, received from the primitive times of the Christian religion, and with the unanimous teaching of the holy fathers and the decrees of sacred councils, they above all instruct the faithful diligently in matters relating to intercession and invocation of the saints, the veneration of relics, and the legitimate use of images, teaching them that the saints who reign together with Christ offer up their prayers to God for men, that it is good and beneficial suppliantly to invoke them and to have recourse to their prayers, assistance and support in order to obtain favors from God through his Son, Jesus Christ our Lord, who alone is our Redeemer and Savior; and that they think impiously who deny that the saints who enjoy eternal happiness in heaven are to be invoked, or who assert that they do not pray for men, or that our invocation of them to pray for each of us individually is idolatry, or that it is opposed to the Word of God and inconsistent with the honor of the *one mediator of God and men, Jesus Christ* (1 Tim. 2:5), or that it is foolish to pray vocally or mentally to those who reign in heaven. Also, that the holy bodies of the holy martyrs and of others living with Christ, which were the living members of Christ and the temple of the Holy Ghost (1 Cor. 3:16; 6:19; 2 Cor. 6:16), to be awakened by him to eternal life and to be glorified, are to be venerated by the faithful, through which many benefits are bestowed by God on men, so that those who maintain that veneration and honor are not due to the relics of the saints, or that these and other memorials are honored by the faithful without profit, and that the places dedicated to the memory of the saints for the purpose of obtaining their aid are visited in vain, are to be utterly condemned, as the church has already long since condemned and now again condemns them. Moreover, that the images of Christ, of the virgin mother of God, and of the other saints are to be placed and retained especially in the churches, and that due honor and veneration are to be given them; not, however, that any divinity or virtue is believed to be in them by reason of which they are to be venerated, or that something is to be asked of them, or that trust is to be placed in images, as was done of old by the Gentiles who placed their hope in idols (Ps. 135:15–18); but because the honor which is shown them is referred to the prototypes which they represent, so that by means of the images which we kiss and before which we uncover the head and prostrate ourselves, we adore Christ and venerate the saints whose likeness they bear. That is what was defined by the decrees of the councils, especially of the Second Council of Nicea, against the opponents of images.

Moreover, let the bishops diligently teach that by means of the stories of the mysteries of our redemption portrayed in paintings and other representations the people are instructed and confirmed in the articles of faith, which ought to be borne in mind and constantly reflected upon; also that great profit is derived from all holy images, not only because the people are thereby reminded of the benefits and gifts bestowed on them by Christ, but also because through the saints the miracles of God and salutary examples are set before the eyes of the faithful, so that they may give God thanks for those things, may fashion their own life and conduct in imitation of the saints, and be moved to adore and love God and cultivate piety. But if anyone should teach and maintain anything contrary to these decrees, let him be anathema. If any abuses shall have found their way into these holy and salutary observances, the holy council desires earnestly that they be completely removed, so that no representation of false doctrines and such as might be the occasion of grave error to the uneducated be exhibited. And if at times it happens, when this is beneficial to the illiterate, that the stories and narratives of the holy Scriptures are portrayed and exhibited, the people should be instructed that not for that reason is the divinity represented in picture as if it can be seen with bodily eyes or expressed in colors or figures.

Furthermore, in the invocation of the saints, the veneration of relics, and the sacred use of images, all superstition shall be removed, all filthy quest for gain eliminated, and all lasciviousness avoided, so that images shall not be painted and adorned with a seductive charm, or the celebration of saints and the visitation of relics be perverted by the people into boisterous festivities and drunkenness, as if the festivals in honor of the saints are to be celebrated with revelry and with no sense of decency. Finally, such zeal and care should be exhibited by the bishops with regard to these things that nothing may appear that is disorderly or unbecoming and confusedly arranged, nothing that is profane, nothing disrespectful, since holiness becometh the house of God (Ps. 93:5). That these things may be the more faithfully observed, the holy council decrees that no one is permitted to erect or cause to be erected in any place or church, howsoever exempt, any unusual image unless it has been approved by the bishop; also that no new miracles be accepted and no relics recognized unless they have been investigated and approved by the same bishop, who, as soon as he has obtained any knowledge of such matters, shall, after consulting theologians and other pious men, act thereon as he shall judge consonant with truth and piety. But if any doubtful or grave abuse is to be eradicated, or if indeed any graver question concerning these matters should arise, the bishop, before he settles the controversy, shall await the decision of the metropolitan and of the bishops of the province in a provincial synod; so, however, that nothing new or anything that has not hitherto been in use in the church, shall be decided upon without having first consulted the most holy Roman pontiff.

_9_

Profession of the Tridentine Faith (1564)

Shortly after the Council of Trent finished its work, Pope Pius IV (1559–1565) acted on a suggestion that came from the council to prepare a brief summation of Trent's most salient decisions. A group of cardinals drew up the document which was then promulgated in two papal bulls as a binding statement of faith for the teaching officers of the church. The creed provided a succinct restatement of the teaching of Trent on the most controversial questions of the age. First, however, it reaffirmed belief in the Nicene Creed, which the third session of the council in February 1546 had confirmed as the foundation of the faith. This profession also added (par. 10) a specific affirmation concerning the centrality of the Roman Catholic Church itself and the pope as apostolic successor to Saint Peter. And it closed (par. 12) with a solemn vow to believe the faith as defined by the Catholic Church as the only path to salvation.

The creed was widely influential in the Catholic Church almost to the present. Its original title in the papal bulls was _Forma professionis ortodoxae fidei catolicae_ (The Form for Professing the Orthodox Catholic Faith), and it has also been called the "Creed of Pius IV" and "The Creed of the Council of Trent." It takes its customary name from the Latin rendering of Trent (*Tridentum*). Another of its titles has been the "Profession of Converts," for it was frequently used as a vehicle for Protestants who moved to Rome to confess their faith.

Text

Schaff, Philip. *The Creeds of Christendom*, 2:58–59, 207–10. 6th ed. New York: Harper and Brothers, 1931.

Additional Reading

Schaff, Philip. *The Creeds of Christendom*, 1:96–99. 6th ed. New York: Harper and Brothers, 1931.

Profession of the Tridentine Faith

I. I,_____, with a firm faith believe and profess all and every one of the things contained in that creed which the holy Roman Church makes use of:

"I believe in one God, the Father almighty; Maker of heaven and earth, and of all things visible and invisible.

"And in one Lord Jesus Christ, the only-begotten Son of God, begotten of the Father before all worlds [God of God], Light of Light, very God of very God, begotten, not made, being of one substance [essence] with the Father; by whom all things were made; who, for us men and for our salvation, came down from heaven, and was incarnate by the Holy Ghost of the virgin Mary, and was made man; and was crucified also for us under Pontius Pilate; he suffered and was buried; and the third day he rose again, according to the Scriptures; and ascended into heaven, and sitteth on the right hand of the Father; and he shall come again, with glory, to judge both the quick and the dead; whose kingdom shall have no end.

"And [I believe] in the Holy Ghost, the Lord and Giver of life; who proceedeth from the Father [and the Son]; who with the Father and the Son together is worshiped and glorified; who spake by the Prophets. And [I believe] one holy catholic and apostolic church. I acknowledge one baptism for the remission of sins; and I look for the resurrection of the dead, and the life of the world to come. Amen."

II. I most steadfastly admit and embrace apostolic and ecclesiastic traditions, and all other observances and constitutions of the same church.

III. I also admit the holy Scriptures, according to that sense which our holy mother Church has held and does hold, to which it belongs to judge of the true sense and interpretation of the Scriptures; neither will I ever take and interpret them otherwise than according to the unanimous consent of the fathers.

IV. I also profess that there are truly and properly seven sacraments of the new law, instituted by Jesus Christ our Lord, and necessary for the salvation of mankind, although not all for every one, to wit: baptism, confirmation, the Eucharist, penance, extreme unction, holy orders, and matrimony; and that they confer grace; and that of these, baptism, confirmation, and ordination cannot be reiterated without sacrilege. I also receive and admit the received and approved ceremonies of the Catholic Church, used in the solemn administration of the aforesaid sacraments.

V. I embrace and receive all and every one of the things which have been defined and declared in the holy Council of Trent concerning original sin and justification.

VI. I profess, likewise, that in the Mass there is offered to God a true, proper, and propitiatory sacrifice for the living and the dead; and that in the most holy sacrament of the Eucharist there is truly, really, and substantially, the body and blood, together with the soul and divinity of our Lord Jesus Christ; and that there is made a change of the whole essence of the bread into the body, and of the whole essence of the wine into the blood; which change the Catholic Church calls transubstantiation.

VII. I also confess that under either kind alone Christ is received whole and entire, and a true sacrament.

VIII. I firmly hold that there is a purgatory, and that the souls therein detained are helped by the suffrages of the faithful. Likewise, that the saints reigning with Christ are to be honored and invoked, and that they offer up prayers to God for us, and that their relics are to be had in veneration.

IX. I most firmly assert that the images of Christ, and of the perpetual virgin the mother of God, and also of other saints, ought to be had and retained, and that due honor and veneration are to be given them. I also affirm that the power of indulgences was left by Christ in the church, and that the use of them is most wholesome to Christian people.

X. I acknowledge the holy Catholic Apostolic Roman Church for the mother and mistress of all churches; and I promise and swear true obedience to the bishop of Rome, successor to Saint Peter, prince of the apostles, and vicar of Jesus Christ.

XI. I likewise undoubtingly receive and profess all other things delivered, defined, and declared by the sacred canons and general councils, and particularly by the holy Council of Trent; and I condemn, reject, and anathematize all things contrary thereto, and all heresies which the church has condemned, rejected, and anathematized.

XII. I do, at this present, freely profess and truly hold this true Catholic faith, without which no one can be saved; and I promise most constantly to retain and confess the same entire and inviolate, with God's assistance, to the end of my life. And I will take care, as far as in me lies, that it shall be held, taught, and preached by my subjects, or by those the care of whom shall appertain to me in my office. This I promise, vow, and swear—so help me God, and these holy Gospels of God.

10

The Thirty-Nine Articles of the Church of England (1571)

The Thirty-Nine Articles are the historical doctrinal standard of the Church of England and the worldwide network of Episcopal churches in communion with the archbishop of Canterbury. The articles are a result of the sixteenth-century English Reformation, and more specifically of the liturgical genius of Thomas Cranmer (1489–1556), who served as archbishop of Canterbury from 1532 to 1553. Cranmer and like-minded colleagues prepared several statements of more or less Protestant faith during the reign of Henry VIII (1509–1547), whose divorce from Catherine of Aragon provided the political impetus for the English Reformation. But it was not until the reign of Edward VI that England's reformers were able to proceed with more thorough efforts. Shortly before Edward's death, Cranmer presented a doctrinal statement of forty-two topics, or articles, as the last of his major contributions to the development of Anglicanism. These articles were suppressed during the Roman Catholic reign of Edward's successor, Mary Tudor (1553–1558), but became the basis for the Thirty-Nine Articles which Elizabeth the Great (1558–1603) and her Parliament established as the doctrinal position of the Church of England. Early in Elizabeth's reign a Latin version of the Thirty-Nine Articles with some concessions to Roman Catholics was proposed by the Church of England's convocation. The concessions were mostly removed in 1571, when the definitive edition was ratified. It is this 1571 English version that is reproduced below. Elizabeth promoted the articles as an instrument of national policy (to solidify her kingdom religiously) and as a theological *via media* (to encompass as wide a spectrum of English Christians as possible). Since her day much controversy has swirled over their theological significance. In more recent years they have been defended by the evangelical and Catholic wings of the Anglican-Episcopalian community who, although they differ among themselves over the meaning of the articles, still consider them valid. By contrast more liberal (or "broad") Anglicans regard the articles as simply a valuable historical document.

The Thirty-Nine Articles repudiate teachings and practices that Protestants in general condemned in the Roman Catholic Church. They deny, for example, supererogation of merit (14), transubstantiation (28), the sacrifice of the Mass (31), and implicitly the sinlessness of Mary (15). On the other hand, they affirm with Protestants on the Continent that Scripture is the final authority on salvation (6), that Adam's fall compromised human free will (10), that justification is by faith in Christ's merit (11), that both bread and wine should be served to all in the Lord's supper (30), and that ministers may marry (32). The articles borrow some wording from Lutheran confessions, especially on the Trinity (1), the church (19), and the sacraments (25). But on baptism (27, "a sign of regeneration") and on the Lord's supper (28, "the body of Christ is given, taken, and eaten, in the supper only after a heavenly and spiritual manner"), the articles resemble Reformed and Calvinistic beliefs more than Lutheran. Article 17 on predestination and election is much debated, for it pictures election unto life in terms very similar to those used by Reformed confessions, and yet—like the Lutherans—is silent on the question of reprobation to damnation. While the Forty-Two Articles of 1553 gave considerable space to denouncing views of radical Protestants, the Thirty-Nine Articles do not. Thus, the Thirty-Nine Articles do not contain the attacks on antinomianism, soul sleep, millennialism, and universalism of the early statement. They do, however, reaffirm the propriety of creeds (8), the necessity of clerical ordination (23), the right of the sovereign to influence religion (37), the right of private property (38), and the legitimacy of official oaths (39)—all beliefs that had been challenged by some radical reformers.

The articles also reflect their English environment clearly. Articles 6 and 20 allow the monarch considerable space for regulating the external church life of England. Article 20 also sides more with Luther than with Zwingli in treating the authority of Scripture as the *final* and *last* word on religious matters rather than as the *only* word. Article 34 maintains the sovereign's right to "chief government" over the whole realm, including the church, even as it restricts the monarch from exercising strictly clerical functions of preaching or administering the sacraments. (In 1801 the American Episcopal Church exchanged this article for one more in keeping with New World views on the separation of church and state.)

The Thirty-Nine Articles remain an important statement of sixteenth-century reform. They are Protestant in affirming the final authority of Scripture. They join common Reformation convictions on justification by grace through faith in Christ. They lean toward Lutheranism in permitting beliefs and practices that do not contradict Scripture. They contain statements which, like Zwingli in Zurich, give the state authority to regulate the church. They are "Catholic" in their respect for tradition and in their belief that religious ceremonies should be everywhere the same within a realm. They have been ambiguous enough to provide controversy for many theologians, but also attractive enough to nurture the faith of countless ordinary believers. In the text below, spelling has been modernized.

Text

Hardwick, Charles. *A History of the Articles of Religion*. Cambridge: John Deighton, 1851.

Additional Reading

Bromiley, Geoffrey W. *Thomas Cranmer: Theologian*. New York: Oxford University Press, 1956.

Brooks, Peter Newman. *Cranmer in Context: Documents from the English Reformation*. Minneapolis: Fortress, 1989.

Cross, Claire, ed. *The Royal Supremacy in the Elizabethan Church*. New York: Barnes and Noble, 1969.

Dickens, A. G. *The English Reformation*. New York: Schocken, 1964.

O'Donovan, Oliver. *On the Thirty-Nine Articles: A Conversation with Tudor Christianity*. Exeter: Paternoster, 1986.

Parker, T. H. L., ed. *English Reformers*. Philadelphia: Westminster, 1966.

The Thirty-Nine Articles

1
Of faith in the holy Trinity

There is but one living and true God, everlasting, without body, parts, or passions, of infinite power, wisdom, and goodness, the Maker and Preserver of all things both visible and invisible. And in unity of this Godhead there are three Persons, of one substance, power, and eternity, the Father, the Son, and the Holy Ghost.

2
Of the Word or Son of God which was made very man

The Son, which is the Word of the Father, begotten from everlasting of the Father, the very and eternal God, of one substance with the Father, took man's nature in the womb of the blessed virgin, of her substance: so that two whole and perfect natures, that is to say the Godhead and manhood, were joined together in one person, never to be divided, whereof is one Christ, very God and very man, who truly suffered, was crucified, dead, and buried, to reconcile his Father to us, and to be a sacrifice, not only for original guilt, but also for all actual sins of men.

3
Of the going down of Christ into hell

As Christ died for us, and was buried, so also it is to be believed that he went down into hell.

4
Of the resurrection of Christ

Christ did truly rise again from death, and took again his body, with flesh, bones, and all things appertaining to the perfection of man's nature, wherewith he ascended into heaven, and there sits, until he returns to judge all men at the last day.

5
Of the Holy Ghost

The Holy Ghost, proceeding from the Father and the Son, is of one substance, majesty, and glory, with the Father and the Son, very and eternal God.

6
Of the sufficiency of the holy Scriptures for salvation

Holy Scripture contains all things necessary to salvation, so that whatsoever is not read therein nor may be proved thereby is not to be required of any man, that it should be believed as an article of the faith or be thought requisite as necessary to salvation.

In the name of holy Scripture, we do understand those canonical books of the Old and New Testament, of whose authority was never any doubt in the church. *Of the names and number of the canonical books.* Genesis, Exodus, Leviticus, Numbers, Deuteronomy, Joshua, Judges, Ruth, the first book of Samuel, the second book of Samuel, the first book of Kings, the second book of Kings, the first book of Chroni, the second book of Chroni, the first book of Esdras, the second book of Esdras, the book of Esther, the book of Job, the Psalms, the Proverbs, Ecclesia (or preacher), Cantica (or Songs of Sol), four Prophets the greater, twelve Prophets the less.

And the other books, (as Jerome says) the church does read for example of life and instruction of manners: but yet does it not apply them to establish any doctrine. Such are these following: the third book of Esdras, the fourth book of Esdras, the book of Tobias, the book of Judith, the rest of the book of Esther, the book of Wisdom, Jesus the son of Sirach, Baruch (the prophet), Song of the Three Children, the story of Susanna, of Bel and the Dragon, the prayer of Manasses, the first book of Machab, and the second book of Machab. All the books of the New Testament, as they are commonly received, we do receive and account them for canonical.

7
Of the Old Testament

The Old Testament is not contrary to the New, for both in the Old and New Testaments everlasting life is offered to mankind by Christ, who is the only Mediator between God and man, being both God and man. Wherefore they are not to be heard which feign that the old fathers did look only for transitory promises. Although the Law given from God by Moses, as touching ceremonies and rites, does not bind Christian men, nor the civil precepts thereof, ought of necessity to be received in any commonwealth, yet notwithstanding, no Christian man whatsoever is free from the obedience of the commandments, which are called moral.

8
Of the three creeds

The three creeds—the Nicene Creed, the Athanasian Creed, and that which is commonly called the Apostles' Creed—ought thoroughly to be received and believed, for they may be proved by most certain warranties of holy Scripture.

9
Of original or birth sin

Original sin stands not in the following of Adam (as the Pelagians do vainly talk) but it is the fault and corruption of the nature of every man, that naturally are engendered of the offspring of Adam, whereby man is very far gone from original righteousness and is of his own nature inclined to evil, so that the flesh lusts always contrary to the spirit, and therefore in every person born into this world, it deserves God's wrath and damnation. And this infection of nature doth remain, yea in them that are regenerated, whereby the lust of the flesh called in Greek φρόνημα σαρκὸς (which some do expound, the wisdom, some sensuality, some the desire of the flesh) is not subject to the Law of God. And although there is no condemnation for them that believe and are baptized, yet the apostle does confess that concupiscence and lust have of themselves the nature of sin.

10
Of free will

The condition of man after the fall of Adam is such that he cannot turn and prepare himself by his own natural strength and good works to faith and calling upon God. Wherefore we have no power to do good works pleasant and acceptable to God without the grace of God by Christ preventing us [i.e., enabling], that we may have a good will, and working with us, when we have that good will.

11
Of the justification of man

We are accounted righteous before God, only for the merit of our Lord and Savior Jesus Christ, by faith, and not for our own works or deservings. Wherefore, that we are justified by faith only is a most wholesome doctrine, and very full of comfort, as more largely is expressed in the homily on justification.

12
Of good works

Albeit that good works, which are the fruits of faith and follow after justification, cannot put away our sins and endure the severity of God's judgment, yet are they pleasing and acceptable to God in Christ and do spring necessarily out of a true and lively faith, in so much that by them a lively faith may be as evidently known as a tree discerned by the fruit.

13
Of works before justification

Works done before the grace of Christ and the inspiration of his Spirit are not pleasant to God, forasmuch as they spring not of faith in Jesus Christ, neither do they make men meet to receive grace, or (as the school [i.e., medieval] authors say) deserve grace of congruity; yea rather for that they are not done as God has willed and commanded them to be done, we doubt not but that they have the nature of sin.

14
Of works of supererogation

Voluntary works besides, over, and above God's commandments, which they call works of supererogation, cannot be taught without arrogance and impiety. For by them men do declare that they do not only render unto God as much as they are bound to do, but that they do more for his sake than of bound duty is required: Whereas Christ says plainly, When you have done all that are commanded you, say, We are unprofitable servants.

15
Of Christ alone without sin

Christ in the truth of our nature, was made like unto us in all things (except sin) from which he was clearly void, both in his flesh and in his spirit. He came to be the lamb without spot, who by the sacrifice of himself once made, should take away the sins of the world: and sin (as Saint John says) was not in him. But all we the rest (although baptized and born again in Christ) yet offend in many things, and if we say we have no sin, we deceive ourselves, and the truth is not in us.

16
Of sin after baptism

Not every deadly sin willingly committed after baptism is sin against the Holy Ghost and unpardonable. Wherefore, the grant of repentance is not to be denied to such as fall into sin after baptism. After we have received the Holy Ghost, we may depart from grace given, and fall into sin, and by the grace of God (we may) arise again and amend our lives. And, therefore, they are to be condemned which say they can no more sin as long as they live here, or deny the place of forgiveness to such as truly repent.

17
Of predestination and election

Predestination to life is the everlasting purpose of God whereby (before the foundations of the world were laid) he has constantly decreed by his council secret to us, to deliver from curse and damnation those whom he has chosen in Christ out of mankind, and to bring them by Christ to everlasting salvation, as vessels made to honor. Wherefore they which are indued with so excellent a benefit of God are called according to God's purpose by his Spirit working in due season; they through grace obey the calling; they are justified freely; they are made sons of God by adoption; they are made like the image of his only begotten Son Jesus Christ; they walk religiously in good works; and at length by God's mercy, they attain to everlasting felicity.

As the godly consideration of predestination and our election in Christ is full of sweet, pleasant, and unspeakable comfort to godly persons, and such as feel in themselves the working of the Spirit of Christ, mortifying the works of the flesh and their earthly members, and drawing up their mind to high and heavenly things, as well because it does greatly establish and confirm their faith of eternal salvation to be enjoyed through Christ, as because it does fervently kindle their love toward God. So, for curious and carnal persons, lacking the Spirit of Christ, to have continually before their eyes the sentence of God's predestination is a most dangerous downfall, whereby the devil does thrust them either into desperation or into recklessness of most unclean living, no less perilous than desperation.

Furthermore, we must receive God's promises in such wise, as they be generally set forth to us in holy Scripture; and in our doings, that will of God is to be followed, which we have expressly declared unto us in the Word of God.

18
Of obtaining eternal salvation,
only by the name of Christ

They also are to be had accursed that presume to say that every man shall be saved by the law or sect which he professes, so that he be diligent to frame his life according to that law and the light of nature. For holy Scripture does set out unto us only the name of Jesus Christ, whereby men must be saved.

19
Of the church

The visible church of Christ is a congregation of faithful men in which the pure Word of God is preached and the sacraments are duly ministered according to Christ's ordinance in all those things that of necessity are requisite to the same.

As the churches of Jerusalem, Alexandria, and Antioch have erred, so also the Church of Rome has erred, not only in their living and manner of ceremonies, but also in matters of faith.

20
Of the authority of the church

The church has power to decree rites or ceremonies and authority in controversies of faith. And yet it is not lawful for the church to ordain anything that is contrary to God's written Word, neither may it so expound one place of Scripture that it be repugnant to another. Wherefore, although the church is a witness and a keeper of holy Writ, yet, as it ought not to decree anything against the same, ought it not to enforce anything to be believed for necessity of salvation.

21
Of the authority of general councils

General councils may not be gathered together without the commandment and will of princes. And when they are gathered together (forasmuch as they are an assembly of men, whereof all are not governed with the Spirit and Word of God) they may err, and sometimes have erred, even in things pertaining unto God. Wherefore, things ordained by them as necessary to salvation have neither strength nor authority, unless it may be declared that they be taken out of holy Scripture.

22
Of purgatory

The Roman doctrine concerning purgatory, pardons, worshiping and adoration of images and as of relics, and also invocation of saints, is a fond [i.e., foolish] thing, vainly invented and grounded upon no warranty of Scripture, but rather repugnant to the Word of God.

23
Of ministering in the congregation

It is not lawful for any man to take upon him the office of public preaching or ministering the sacraments in the congregation before he ise lawfully called and sent to execute the same. And those we ought to judge lawfully called and sent which are chosen and called to this work by men who have public authority given unto them in the congregation, to call and send ministers into the Lord's vineyard.

24
Of speaking in the congregation, in such a tongue as the people understand

It is a thing plainly repugnant to the Word of God and the custom of the primitive church to have public prayer in the church or to minister the sacraments in a tongue not understood of the people.

25
Of the sacraments

Sacraments ordained of Christ are not only badges or tokens of Christian men's profession, but rather they are certain sure witnesses and effectual signs of grace and God's good will toward us, by the which he does work invisible in us and does not only quicken, but also strengthen and confirm our faith in him.

There are two sacraments ordained of Christ our Lord in the gospel, that is to say, baptism and the supper of the Lord.

Those five, commonly called sacraments, that is to say, confirmation, penance, orders, matrimony, and extreme unction, are not to be counted for sacraments of the gospel, being such as have grown partly of the corrupt following of the apostles, partly are states of life allowed in the Scriptures, but yet have not like nature of sacraments with baptism and the Lord's supper, for that they have not any visible sign or ceremony ordained of God.

The sacraments were not ordained of Christ to be gazed upon, or to be carried about, but that we should duly use them. And in such only, as worthily receive the same, they have a wholesome effect or operation. But they that receive them unworthily purchase to themselves damnation, as Saint Paul says.

26
Of the unworthiness of the ministers, which hinder not the effect of the sacraments

Although in the visible church the evil are ever mingled with the good and sometimes the evil have chief authority in the ministration of the Word and sacraments, yet forasmuch as they do not the same in their own name but in Christ's, and do minister by his commission and authority, we may use their ministry, both in hearing the Word of God and in the receiving of the sacraments. Neither is the effect of Christ's ordinance taken away by their wickedness, nor the grace of God's gifts diminished from such as by faith and rightly do receive the sacraments ministered unto them, which are effectual because of Christ's intention and promise, although they are ministered by evil men.

Nevertheless, it appertains to the discipline of the church that enquiry be made of evil ministers, and that they be accused by those that have knowledge of their offenses, and finally being found guilty by just judgment be deposed.

27
Of baptism

Baptism is not only a sign of profession and mark of difference whereby Christian men are discerned from others that are not christened, but it is also a sign of regeneration or new birth, whereby as by an instrument, they that receive baptism rightly are grafted into the church; the promises of the forgiveness of sin and of our adoption to be the sons of God, by the Holy Ghost, are visibly signed and sealed; and grace is increased by virtue of prayer unto God. The baptism of young children is in any wise to be retained in the church, as most agreeable with the institution of Christ.

28
Of the Lord's supper

The supper of the Lord is not only a sign of the love that Christians ought to have among themselves one to another, but rather it is a sacrament of our redemption by Christ's death. Insomuch that to such as rightly, worthily, and with faith receive the same bread which we break is a partaking of the body of Christ, and likewise the cup of blessing, is a partaking of the blood of Christ.

Transubstantiation (or the change of the substance of bread and wine) in the supper of the Lord cannot be proved by holy Writ, but is repugnant to the plain words of Scripture, overthrows the nature of a sacrament, and has given occasion to many superstitions.

The body of Christ is given, taken, and eaten in the supper only after a heavenly and spiritual manner. And the mean whereby the body of Christ is received and eaten in the supper is faith.

The sacrament of the Lord's supper was not by Christ's ordinance reserved, carried about, lifted up, or worshiped.

29
Of the wicked which do not eat the body of Christ in the use of the Lord's supper

The wicked, and such as are void of a lively faith, although they do carnally and visibly press with their teeth (as Saint Augustine says) the sacrament of the body and blood of Christ, yet in no wise are they partakers of Christ but rather to their condemnation do eat and drink the sign or sacrament of so great a thing.

30
Of both kinds

The cup of the Lord is not to be denied to the laypeople. For both the parts of the Lord's sacrament, by Christ's ordinance and commandment, ought to be ministered to all Christian men alike.

31
Of the one oblation of Christ finished upon the cross

The offering of Christ once made is the perfect redemption, propitiation, and satisfaction for sin, but that alone. Wherefore the sacrifices of masses, in the which it was commonly said that the priests did offer Christ for the quick and the dead, to have remission of pain or guilt, were blasphemous fables and dangerous deceits.

32
Of the marriage of priests

Bishops, priests, and deacons are not commanded by God's Law either to vow the estate of single life or to abstain from marriage. Therefore it is lawful also for them, as for all other Christian men, to marry at their own discretion, as they shall judge the same to serve better to godliness.

33
Of excommunicate persons, how they are to be avoided

That person which by open denunciation of the church is rightly cut off from the unity of the church and excommunicated ought to be taken of the whole multitude of the faithful as a heathen and publican [i.e., dishonest tax collector] until he is openly reconciled by penance and received into the church by a judge that has authority thereto.

34
Of the traditions of the church

It is not necessary that traditions and ceremonies be in all places one, or utterly alike, for at all times they have been diverse and may be changed according to the diversity of countries, times, and men's manners, so that nothing is ordained against God's Word. Whosoever through his private judgment, willingly and purposely does openly break the traditions and ceremonies of the church which are not repugnant to the Word of God and are ordained and approved by common authority, ought to be rebuked openly (that others may fear to do the like) as he that offends against the common order of the church, hurts the authority of the magistrate, and wounds the consciences of the weak brethren.

Every particular or national church has authority to ordain, change, and abolish ceremonies or rites of the church ordained only by man's authority, so that all things are done to edifying.

35
Of homilies

The second book of homilies, the several titles whereof we have joined under this article, do contain a godly and wholesome doctrine, and necessary for these times, as does the former book of homilies, which was set forth in the time of Edward the Sixth: and therefore we judge them to be read in churches by the ministers diligently and distinctly, that they may be understood of the people.

Of the names of the homilies

1 Of the right use of the church.
2 Against peril of idolatry.
3 Of repairing and keeping clean of churches.
4 Of good works, first of fasting.
5 Against gluttony and drunkenness.
6 Against excess of apparel.
7 Of prayer.
8 Of the place and time of prayer.
9 That common prayers and sacraments ought to be ministered in a known tongue.
10 Of the reverent estimation of God's Word.
11 Of alms doing.
12 Of the nativity of Christ.
13 Of the passion of Christ.
14 Of the resurrection of Christ.
15 Of the worthy receiving of the sacrament of the body and blood of Christ.
16 Of the gifts of the Holy Ghost.
17 For the Rogation days.
18 Of the state of matrimony.
19 Of repentance.
20 Against idleness.
21 Against rebellion.

36
Of consecration of bishops and ministers

The book of consecration of archbishops and bishops and ordering of priests and deacons, lately set forth in the time of Edward the Sixth and confirmed at the same time by authority of parliament, does contain all things necessary to such consecration and ordering [i.e., ordaining]; neither has it anything that of itself is superstitious or ungodly. And, therefore, whosoever are consecrated or ordered [i.e., ordained] according to the rites of that book, since the second year of the aforenamed King Edward unto this time, or hereafter shall be consecrated or ordered [i.e., ordained] according to the same rites, we decree all such to be rightly, orderly, and lawfully consecrated and ordered [i.e., ordained].

37
Of the civil magistrates

The Queen's Majesty has the chief power in this Realm of England and her other dominions, unto whom the chief government of all estates of this realm, whether they be ecclesiastical or civil, in all causes does appertain, and is not, nor ought to be subject to any foreign jurisdiction.

Where we attribute to the Queen's Majesty the chief government, by which titles we understand the minds of some slanderous folks to be offended, we give not to our princes the ministering either of God's Word or of sacraments, the which thing the injunctions also lately set forth by Elizabeth our Queen, do most plainly testify, but that only prerogative which we see to have been given always to all godly princes in holy Scriptures by God himself, that is, that they should rule all estates and degrees committed to their charge by God, whether they be ecclesiastical or temporal, and restrain with the civil sword the stubborn and evildoers.

The bishop of Rome has no jurisdiction in this Realm of England.

The laws of the realm may punish Christian men with death for heinous and grievous offenses.

It is lawful for Christian men, at the commandment of the magistrate, to wear weapons and serve in the wars.

38
Of Christian men's goods, which are not common

The riches and goods of Christians are not common, as touching the right, title, and possession of the same, as certain Anabaptists do falsely boast. Notwithstanding every man ought of such things as he possesses, liberally to give alms to the poor, according to his ability.

39
Of a Christian man's oath

As we confess that vain and rash swearing is forbidden Christian men by our Lord Jesus Christ and James his apostle, so we judge that Christian religion does not prohibit, but that a man may swear when a magistrate requires, in a cause of faith and charity, so it be done according to the prophets' teaching, in justice, judgment, and truth.

Index of Names

Index of Subjects

Printed in the United Kingdom
by Lightning Source UK Ltd.
102740UKS00001B/406